The Listeners

ROBERT MACDONALD
*The Project was his life, and alien contact
could be the answer to his prayers—or
it could tear his world apart.*

MARIA CHAVEZ MACDONALD
*She adored her husband.
But she would not—could not—share him.*

GEORGE THOMAS
*A muckraking reporter, a bitter poet,
a man trapped in his own Inferno.
His assignment: bury the Project.*

JEREMIAH JONES
*The charismatic evangelist preached that Man
is alone with God in the Universe.
It would take a miracle to change his mind.*

ANDREW WHITE
*America's first black president.
The aliens were a very unwelcome policy
complication—for the country and for the man.*

**—AND WHAT THEY HEARD WOULD
CHANGE THEIR LIVES FOREVER!**

THE LISTENERS

JAMES E. GUNN

A Del Rey Book

BALLANTINE BOOKS • NEW YORK

A Del Rey Book
Published by Ballantine Books

Library of Congress Catalog Card Number: 72-1219

ISBN 0-345-30036-X

Manufactured in the United States of America

First Ballantine Books Edition: May 1985

Cover art by Rick Sternbach

To Walter Sullivan, and to Carl Sagan and all the other scientists, whose books and articles and lectures and speculations provided, so clearly, the inspiration and source material for this book—may their listening be rewarded and may all their messages be answered....

Acknowledgments

The letter by Giuseppe Cocconi to Sir Bernard Lovell is reprinted by permission of Professor Cocconi.

The poem attributed to Kirby Congdon is "The Exploration," published in INSIDE OUTER SPACE, Anchor Books, copyright 1970 Robert Vas Dias, and is reprinted by permission of the author.

The epigraphs for each chapter are taken from "The Listeners" by Walter de la Mare. Permission to include the excerpts has been granted by The Literary Trustees of Walter de la Mare, and The Society of Authors as their representative.

Quotations attributed to Freeman J. Dyson dated 1964 are from a letter in the April 1964 *Scientific American* and are reprinted by permission by Professor Dyson and *Scientific American*.

Quotations attributed to Herman Kahn and Anthony J. Wiener are from their book, THE YEAR 2000, copyright © 1967 The Hudson Institute, Inc., published by The Macmillan Company, and are reprinted by permission of the publisher.

The poem attributed to Alice Meynell is "Christ in the Universe." "Christ in the Universe" is reprinted by permission of Charles Scribner's Sons from LATER POEMS by Alice Meynell.

The quotations attributed to Carl Sagan dated 1966 are taken from INTELLIGENT LIFE IN THE UNIVERSE by I. S. Shklovsky and Carl Sagan, published by Holden-Day, Inc., copyright 1966 Holden-Day, Inc., and are reprinted by permission of Dr. Sagan and the publisher.

The lines of poetry attributed to William Butler Yeats are from "The Song of Wandering Aengus" and "The Second Coming," and are reprinted by permission of The Macmillan Company from COLLECTED POEMS by William Butler Yeats. Copyright 1906 The Macmillan Company, renewal copyright 1934 William Butler Yeats; and copyright 1924 The Macmillan Company, renewal copyright 1952 Bertha Georgie Yeats.

"Robert MacDonald" was first published in *Galaxy Magazine*, September 1968, as "The Listeners."

"George Thomas" was first published in the Magazine of *Fantasy and Science Fiction*, September 1972, as "The Voices."

"William Mitchell" was first published in *Galaxy Magazine*, May-June 1971, as "The Message."

"Andrew White" was first published in *Galaxy Magazine*, January-February 1972, as "The Answer."

"The Computer" was first published in *Galaxy Magazine*, May-June 1972, as "The Reply."

Illustrations on pp. 123 and 140 by Lance Williams.

Contents

1

Robert MacDonald — 2025

"Is there anybody there?" said the Traveler,
Knocking on the moonlit door....

The voices babbled.

MacDonald heard them and knew that there was meaning in them, that they were trying to communicate and that he could understand them and respond to them if he could only concentrate on what they were saying, but he couldn't bring himself to make the effort. He tried again.

"Back behind everything, lurking like a silent shadow behind the closed door, is the question we can never answer except positively: Is there anybody there?"

That was Bob Adams, eternally the devil's advocate, looking querulously at the others around the conference table. His round face was sweating, although the mahogany-paneled room was cool.

Saunders puffed hard on his pipe. "But that's true of all science. The image of the scientist eliminating all negative possibilities is ridiculous. Can't be done. So he goes ahead on faith and statistical probability."

MacDonald watched the smoke rise above Saunders' head in clouds and wisps until it wavered in the draft from the air duct, thinned out, disappeared. He could not see it, but the odor reached his nostrils. It was an aromatic blend easily distinguishable from the flatter smell of cigarettes being smoked by Adams and some of the others.

Wasn't this their task? MacDonald wondered. To detect the thin smoke of life that drifts through the universe, to separate one trace from another, molecule by molecule, and then force them to reverse their entropic paths into their ordered and meaningful original form.

All the king's horses, and all the king's men.... Life

itself is impossible, he thought, but men exist by reversing entropy.

Down the long table cluttered with overflowing ash trays and coffee cups and doodled scratch pads Olsen said, "We always knew it would be a long search. Not years but centuries. The computers must have sufficient data, and that means bits of information approximating the number of molecules in the universe. Let's not chicken out now."

> *"If seven maids with seven mops*
> *Swept it for half a year,*
> *Do you suppose," the Walrus said,*
> *"That they could get it clear?"*

". . . Ridiculous," someone was saying, and then Adams broke in. "It's easy for you to talk about centuries when you've been here only three years. Wait until you've been at it for ten years, like I have. Or Mac here who has been on the Project for twenty years and head of it for fifteen."

"What's the use of arguing about something we can't know anything about?" Sonnenborn said reasonably. "We have to base our position on probabilities. Shklovsky and Sagan estimated that there are more than one thousand million habitable planets in our galaxy alone. Von Hoerner estimated that one in three million have advanced societies in orbit around them; Sagan said one in one hundred thousand. Either way it's good odds that there's somebody there—three hundred or ten thousand in our segment of the universe. Our job is to listen in the right place or in the right way or understand what we hear."

Adams turned to MacDonald. "What do you say, Mac?"

"I say these basic discussions are good for us," MacDonald said mildly, "and we need to keep reminding ourselves what it is we're doing, or we'll get swallowed in a quicksand of data. I also say that it's time now to get down to the business at hand—what observations do we make tonight and the rest of the week before our next staff meeting?"

Saunders began, "I think we should make a methodical

sweep of the entire galactic lens, listening on all wave-lengths—"

"We've done that a hundred times," said Sonnenborn.

"Not with my new filter—"

"Tau Ceti still is the most likely," said Olsen. "Let's really give it a hearing—"

MacDonald heard Adams grumbling, half to himself, "If there is anybody, and they are trying to communicate, some amateur is going to pick it up on his ham set, decipher it on his James Bond coderule, and leave us sitting here on one hundred million dollars of equipment with egg all over our faces—"

"And don't forget," MacDonald said, "tomorrow is Saturday night and Maria and I will be expecting you all at our place at eight for the customary beer and bull. Those who have more to say can save it for then."

MacDonald did not feel as jovial as he tried to sound. He did not know whether he could stand another Saturday-night session of drink and discussion and dissension about the Project. This was one of his low periods when everything seemed to pile up on top of him, and he could not get out from under, or tell anybody how he felt. No matter how he felt, the Saturday nights were good for the morale of the others.

Pues no es posible que esté continuo el arco armado ni la condición y flaqueza humana se pueda sus-tenar sin alguna lícita recreación

Within the Project, morale was always a problem. Besides, it was good for Maria. She did not get out enough. She needed to see people. And then . . .

And then maybe Adams was right. Maybe nobody was there. Maybe nobody was sending signals because there was nobody to send signals. Maybe man was alone in the universe. Alone with God. Or alone with himself, whichever was worse.

Maybe all the money was being wasted, and the effort, and the preparation—all the intelligence and education and ideas being drained away into an endlessly empty cavern.

Habe nun, ach! Philosophie,
Juristerei und Medizin,
Und leider auch Theologie
Durchaus studiert, mit heissem Bemühn.
Da steh' ich nun, ich armer Tor!
Und bin so klug als wie zuvor;
Heisse Magister, heisse Doktor gar,
Und ziehe schon an die zehen Jahr
Herauf, herab und quer und krumm
Meine Schüler an der Nase herum—
Und sehe, dass wir nichts wissen können!

Poor fool. Why me? MacDonald thought. Could not some other lead them better, not by the nose but by his real wisdom? Perhaps all he was good for was the Saturday-night parties. Perhaps it was time for a change.

He shook himself. It was the endless waiting that wore him down, the waiting for something that did not happen, and the Congressional hearings were coming up again. What could he say that he had not said before? How could he justify a project that already had gone on for nearly fifty years without results and might go on for centuries more?

"Gentlemen," he said briskly, "to our listening posts."

By the time he had settled himself at his disordered desk, Lily was standing beside him.

"Here's last night's computer analysis," she said, putting down in front of him a thin folder. "Reynolds says there's nothing there, but you always want to see it anyway. Here's the transcription of last year's Congressional hearings." A thick binder went on top of the folder. "The correspondence and the actual appropriation measure are in another file if you want them."

MacDonald shook his head.

"There's a form letter from NASA establishing the ground rules for this year's budget and a personal letter from Ted Wartinian saying that conditions are really tight and some cuts look inevitable. In fact, he says there's a possibility the Project might be scrubbed."

Lily glanced at him. "Not a chance," MacDonald said confidently.

"There's a few applications for employment. Not as many as we used to get. The letters from school children I answered myself. And there's the usual nut letters from people who've been receiving messages from outer space, and from one who's had a ride in a UFO. That's what he called it—not a saucer or anything. A feature writer wants to interview you and some others for an article on the Project. I think he's with us. And another one who sounds as if he wants to do an exposé."

MacDonald listened patiently. Lily was a wonder. She could handle everything in the office as well as he could. In fact, things might run smoother if he were not around to take up her time.

"They've both sent some questions for you to answer. And Joe wants to talk to you."

"Joe?"

"One of the janitors."

"What does he want?" They couldn't afford to lose a janitor. Good janitors were harder to find than astronomers, harder even than electronicians.

"He says he has to talk to you, but I've heard from some of the lunchroom staff that he's been complaining about getting messages on his—on his—"

"Yes?"

"On his false teeth."

MacDonald sighed. "Pacify him somehow, will you, Lily? If I talk to him we might lose a janitor."

"I'll do my best. And Mrs. MacDonald called. Said it wasn't important and you needn't call back."

"Call her," MacDonald said. "And, Lily—you're coming to the party tomorrow night, aren't you?"

"What would I be doing at a party with all the brains?"

"We want you to come. Maria asked particularly. It isn't all shop talk, you know. And there are never enough women. You might strike it off with one of the young bachelors."

"At my age, Mr. MacDonald? You're just trying to get rid of me."

"Never."

"I'll get Mrs. MacDonald." Lily turned at the door. "I'll think about the party."

MacDonald shuffled through the papers. Down at the

bottom was the only one he was interested in—the computer analysis of last night's listening. But he kept it there, on the bottom, as a reward for going through the others. Ted was really worried. *Move over, Ted.* And then the writers. He supposed he would have to work them in somehow. At least it was part of the fallout to locating the Project in Puerto Rico. Nobody just dropped in. And the questions. Two of them caught his attention.

How did you come to be named Project Director? That was the friendly one. *What are your qualifications to be Director?* That was the other. How would he answer them? Could he answer them at all?

Finally he reached the computer analysis, and it was just like those for the rest of the week, and the week before that, and the months and the years before that. No significant correlations. Noise. There were a few peaks of reception—at the twenty-one-centimeter line, for instance—but these were merely concentrated noise. Radiating clouds of hydrogen, as the Little Ear functioned like an ordinary radio telescope.

At least the Project showed some results. It was feeding star survey data tapes into the international pool. Fallout. Of a process that had no other product except negatives.

Maybe the equipment wasn't sensitive enough. Maybe. They could beef it up some more. At least it might be a successful ploy with the Committee, some progress to present, if only in the hardware. You don't stand still. You spend more money or they cut you back—or off.

Note: Saunders—plans to increase sensitivity.

Maybe the equipment wasn't discriminating enough. But they had used up a generation of ingenuity canceling out background noise, and in its occasional checks the Big Ear indicated that they were doing adequately on terrestrial noise, at least.

Note: Adams—new discrimination gimmick.

Maybe the computer wasn't recognizing a signal when it had one fed into it. Perhaps it wasn't sophisticated enough to perceive certain subtle relationships. . . . And yet sophisticated codes had been broken in seconds. And the Project was asking it to distinguish only where a signal existed, whether the reception was random noise or had some element of the unrandom. At this level it wasn't even being asked to note the influence of consciousness.

Note: ask computer—is it missing something? Ridiculous? Ask Olsen.

Maybe they shouldn't be searching the radio spectrum at all. Maybe radio was a peculiarity of man's civilization. Maybe others had never had it or had passed it by and now had more sophisticated means of communication. Lasers, for instance. Telepathy, or what might pass for it with man. Maybe gamma rays, as Morrison suggested years before Ozma.

Well, maybe. But if it were so, somebody else would have to listen for those. He had neither the equipment nor the background nor the working lifetime left to tackle something new.

And maybe Adams was right.

He buzzed Lily. "Have you reached Mrs. MacDonald?"

"The telephone hasn't answered—"

Unreasoned panic...

"—Oh, here she is now, Mr. MacDonald, Mrs. MacDonald."

"Hello, darling, I was alarmed when you didn't answer." That had been foolish, he thought, and even more foolish to mention it.

Her voice was sleepy. "I must have been dozing." Even drowsy, it was an exciting voice, gentle, a little husky, that speeded MacDonald's pulse. "What did you want?"

"You called me," MacDonald said.

"Did I? I've forgotten."

"Glad you're resting. You didn't sleep well last night."

"I took some pills."

"How many?"

"Just the two you left out."

"Good girl. I'll see you in a couple of hours. Go back to sleep. Sorry I woke you."

But her voice wasn't sleepy anymore. "You won't have to go back tonight, will you? We'll have the evening together?"

"We'll see," he promised.

But he knew he would have to return.

* * *

MacDonald paused outside the long, low concrete building which housed the offices and laboratories and computers. It was twilight. The sun had descended below the green hills, but orange and purpling wisps of cirrus trailed down the western sky.

Between MacDonald and the sky was a giant dish held aloft by skeleton metal fingers—held high as if to catch the stardust that drifted down at night from the Milky Way.

> Go and catch a falling star,
>   Get with child a mandrake root,
> Tell me where all past years are,
>   Or who cleft the Devil's foot;
> Teach me to hear mermaids singing,
>
>   Or to keep off envy's stinging,
>   And find
>   What wind
> Serves to advance an honest mind.

Then the dish began to turn, noiselessly, incredibly, and to tip. And it was not a dish anymore but an ear, a listening ear cupped by the surrounding hills to overhear the whispering universe.

Perhaps this was what kept them at their jobs, MacDonald thought. In spite of all disappointments, in spite of all vain efforts, perhaps it was this massive machinery, as sensitive as their fingertips, which kept them struggling with the unfathomable. When they grew weary at their electronic listening posts, when their eyes grew dim with looking at unrevealing dials and studying uneventful graphs, they could step outside their concrete cells and renew their dull spirits in communion with the giant mechanism they commanded, the silent, sensing instrument in which the smallest packets of energy, the smallest waves of matter, were detected in their headlong, eternal flight across the universe. It was the stethoscope with which they took the pulse of the all and noted the birth and death of stars, the probe with which, here on an insignificant planet of an undistinguished star on the edge of its galaxy, they explored the infinite.

Or perhaps it was not just the reality but the imagery, like poetry, which soothed their doubting souls, the bowl held up to catch Donne's falling star, the ear cocked to hear the suspected shout that faded to an indistinguishable murmur by the time it reached them. And one thousand miles above them was the giant, five-mile-in-diameter network, the largest radio telescope ever built, which men had cast into the heavens to catch the stars.

If they had the Big Ear for more than an occasional reference check, MacDonald thought practically, then they might get some results. But he knew the radio astronomers would never relinquish time to the frivolity of listening for signals that never came. It was only because of the Big Ear that the Project had inherited the Little Ear. There had been talk recently about a larger net, twenty miles in diameter. Perhaps when it was done, if it were done, the Project might inherit time on the Big Ear.

If they could endure until then, MacDonald thought, if they could steer their fragile vessel of faith between the Scylla of self-doubt and the Charybdis of Congressional appropriations.

The images were not all favorable. There were others that went boomp in the night. There was the image, for instance, of man listening, listening, listening to the silent stars, listening for an eternity, listening for signals that would never come, because—the ultimate horror—man was alone in the universe, a cosmic accident of self-awareness which needed and would never receive the comfort of companionship. To be alone, to be all alone, would be like being all alone on earth, with no one to talk to, ever— like being alone inside a bone prison, with no way to get out, no way to communicate with anyone outside, no way to know if anyone was outside. . . .

Perhaps that, in the end, was what kept them going— to stave off the terrors of the night. While they listened there was hope; to give up now would be to admit final defeat. Some said they should never have started; then they never would have the problem of surrender. Some of the new religions said that. The Solitarians, for one. There is nobody there; we are the one, the only created intelligence in the universe. Let us glory in our uniqueness. But the older religions encouraged the Project to continue. Why would God have created the myriads of other stars and other planets if He had not intended them for living creatures; why should man only be created in His image? Let us find out, they said. Let us communicate with them. What revelations have they had? What saviors have redeemed them?

These are the words which I spake unto you, while I was yet with you, that all things must be fulfilled, which were written in the law of Moses, and in the prophets, and in the psalms, concerning me.... Thus it is written, and thus it behoved Christ to suffer, and to rise from the dead the third day: and that repentance and remission of sins should be preached in his name among all nations, beginning at Jerusalem. And we are witnesses of these things.

And, behold, I send the promise of my Father upon you: but tarry ye in the city of Jerusalem, until ye be endued with power from on high.

Dusk had turned to night. The sky had turned to black. The stars had been born again. The listening had begun. MacDonald made his way to his car in the parking lot behind the building, coasted until he was behind the hill, and turned on the motor for the long drive home.

The hacienda was dark. It had that empty feeling about it that MacDonald knew so well, the feeling it had for him when Maria went to visit friends in Mexico City. But it was not empty now. Maria was here.

He opened the door and flicked on the hall light. "Maria?" He walked down the tiled hall, not too fast, not too slow. *"¿Querida?"* He turned on the living room light as he passed. He continued down the hall, past the dining room, the guest room, the study, the kitchen. He reached the dark doorway to the bedroom. "Maria Chavez?"

He turned on the bedroom light, low. She was asleep, her face peaceful, her dark hair scattered across the pillow. She lay on her side, her legs drawn up under the covers.

*Men che dramma
Di sangue m'e rimaso, che no tremi;
Conosco i segni dell' antica fiamma.*

MacDonald looked down at her, comparing her features one by one with those he had fixed in his memory. Even now, with those dark, expressive eyes closed, she was the most beautiful woman he had ever seen. What glories they had known! He renewed his spirit in the warmth of his remembrances, recalling moments with loving details.

C'est de quoy j'ay le plus de peur que la peur.

He sat down upon the edge of the bed and leaned over to kiss her upon the cheek and then upon her upthrust shoulder where the gown had slipped down. She did not waken. He shook her shoulder gently. "Maria!" She turned upon her back, straightening. She sighed, and her eyes came open, staring blankly. "It is Robby," MacDonald said, dropping unconsciously into a faint brogue.

Her eyes came alive and her lips smiled sleepily. "Robby. You're home."

"Yo te amo," he murmured, and kissed her. As he pulled himself away, he said, "I'll start dinner. Wake up and get dressed. I'll see you in half an hour. Or sooner."

"Sooner," she said.

He turned and went to the kitchen. There was romaine lettuce in the refrigerator, and as he rummaged further, some thin slices of veal. He prepared Caesar salad and veal scaloppine, doing it all quickly, expertly. He liked to cook. The salad was ready, and the lemon juice, tarragon, white wine, and a minute later, the beef bouillon had been added to the browned veal when Maria appeared.

She stood in the doorway, slim, lithe, lovely, and sniffed the air. "I smell something delicious."

It was a joke. When Maria cooked, she cooked Mexican, something peppery that burned all the way into the stomach and lay there like a banked furnace. When MacDonald cooked, it was something exotic—French, perhaps, or Italian, or Chinese. But whoever cooked, the other had to appreciate it or take over all the cooking for a week.

MacDonald filled their wine glasses. *"A la très-bonne, à la très-belle,"* he said, *"qui fait ma joie et ma santé."*

"To the Project," Maria said. "May there be a signal received tonight."

MacDonald shook his head. One should not mention what one desires too much. "Tonight there is only us."

Afterward there were only the two of them, as there had been now for twenty years. And she was as alive and as urgent, as filled with love and laughter, as when they first had been together.

At last the urgency was replaced by a vast ease and contentment in which for a time the thought of the Project faded into something remote which one day he would return to and finish. "Maria," he said.

"Robby?"

"Yo te amo, corazón."

"Yo te amo, Robby."

Gradually then, as he waited beside her for her breathing to slow, the Project returned. When he thought she was asleep, he got up and began to dress in the dark.

"Robby?" Her voice was awake and frightened.

"¿Querida?"

"You are going again?"

"I didn't want to wake you."

"Do you have to go?"

"It's my job."

"Just this once. Stay with me tonight."

He turned on the light. In the dimness he could see that her face was concerned but not hysterical. *"Rast ich, so rost ich.* Besides, I would feel ashamed."

"I understand. Go, then. Come home soon."

He put out two pills on the little shelf in the bathroom and put the others away again.

The headquarters building was busiest at night when the radio noise of the sun was least and listening to the stars was best. Girls bustled down the halls with coffee pots, and men stood near the water fountain, talking earnestly.

MacDonald went into the control room. Adams was at the control panel; Montaleone was the technician. Adams looked up, pointed to his earphones with a gesture of futility, and shrugged. MacDonald nodded at him, nodded at Montaleone, and glanced at the graph. It looked random to him.

Adams leaned past him to point out a couple of peaks. "These might be something." He had removed the earphones.

"Odds," MacDonald said.

"Suppose you're right. The computer hasn't sounded any alarms."

"After a few years of looking at these things, you get the feel of them. You begin to think like a computer."

"Or you get oppressed by failure."

"There's that."

The room was shiny and efficient, glass and metal and plastic, all smooth and sterile; and it smelled like electricity. MacDonald knew that electricity had no smell, but that was the way he thought of it. Perhaps it was the ozone that smelled or warm insulation or oil. Whatever it was, it wasn't worth the time to find out, and MacDonald didn't really want to know. He would rather think of it as the smell of electricity. Perhaps that was why he was a failure as a scientist. "A scientist is a man who wants to know why," his teachers always had told him.

MacDonald leaned over the control panel and flicked a switch. A thin, hissing noise filled the room. It was something like air escaping from an inner tube—a susurration of surreptitious sibilants from subterranean sessions of seething serpents.

He turned a knob and the sound became what someone—Tennyson—had called "the murmuring of innumerable bees." Again, and it became Matthew Arnold's

> ...*melancholy, long withdrawing roar*
> *Retreating, to the breath*
> *Of the night wind, down the vast edges drear*
> *And naked shingles of the world.*

He turned the knob once more, and the sound was a babble of distant voices, some shouting, some screaming, some conversing calmly, some whispering—all of them trying beyond desperation to communicate, and everything just below the level of intelligibility. If he closed his eyes, MacDonald could almost see their faces, pressed against a distant screen, distorted with the awful effort to make themselves heard and understood.

But they all insisted on speaking at once. MacDonald wanted to shout at them. "Silence, everybody! All but you—there, with the purple antenna. One at a time and we'll listen to all of you if it takes a hundred years or a hundred lifetimes."

"Sometimes," Adams said, "I think it was a mistake to put in the speaker system. You begin to anthropomorphize. After a while you begin to hear things. Sometimes you even get messages. I don't listen to the voices anymore. I used to wake up in the night with someone whispering to me. I was just on the verge of getting the message that would solve everything, and I would wake up." He flicked off the switch.

"Maybe somebody will get the message," MacDonald said. "That's what the audio frequency translation is intended to do. To keep the attention focused. It can mesmerize and it can torment, but these are the conditions out of which spring inspiration."

"Also madness," Adams said. "You've got to be able to continue."

"Yes." MacDonald picked up the earphones Adams had put down and held one of them to his ear.

"Tico-tico, tico-tico," it sang. "They're listening in Puerto Rico. Listening for words that never come. Tico-tico, tico-tico. They're listening in Puerto Rico. Can it be the stars are stricken dumb?"

MacDonald put the earphones down and smiled. "Maybe there's inspiration in that, too."

"At least it takes my mind off the futility."

"Maybe off the job, too? Do you really want to find anyone out there?"

"Why else would I be here? But there are times when I wonder if we would be better off not knowing."

"We all think that sometimes," MacDonald said.

In his office he attacked the stack of papers and letters again. When he had worked his way to the bottom, he sighed and got up, stretching. He wondered if he would feel better, less frustrated, less uncertain, if he were working on the Problem instead of just working so somebody else could work on the Problem. But somebody had to do it. Somebody had to keep the Project going, personnel coming in, funds in the bank, bills paid, feathers smoothed.

Maybe it was more important that he do all the dirty little work in the office. Of course it was routine. Of course Lily could do it as well as he. But it was important that he do it, that there be somebody in charge who believed in the Project—or who never let his doubts be known.

Like the Little Ear, he was a symbol—and it is by symbols men live—or refuse to let their despair overwhelm them.

The janitor was waiting for him in the outer office.

"Can I see you, Mr. MacDonald?" the janitor said.

"Of course, Joe," MacDonald said, locking the door of his office carefully behind him. "What is it?"

"It's my teeth, sir." The old man got to his feet and with a deft movement of his tongue and mouth dropped his teeth into his hand.

MacDonald stared at them with a twinge of revulsion. There was nothing wrong with them. They were a carefully constructed pair of false teeth, but they looked too real. MacDonald always had shuddered away from those things which seemed to be what they were not, as if there were some treachery in them.

"They talk to me, Mr. MacDonald," the janitor mumbled, staring at the teeth in his hand with what seemed like suspicion. "In the glass beside my bed at night, they whisper to me. About things far off, like. Messages like."

MacDonald stared at the janitor. It was a strange word for the old man to use, and hard to say without teeth. Still, the word had been "messages." But why should it be strange? He could have picked it up around the offices or the laboratories. It would be odd, indeed, if he had not picked up something about what was going on. Of course: messages.

"I've heard of that sort of thing happening," MacDonald said. "False teeth accidentally constructed into a kind of crystal set, that pick up radio waves. Particularly near a powerful station. And we have a lot of stray frequencies floating around, what with the antennas and all. Tell you what, Joe. We'll make an appointment with the

Project dentist to fix your teeth so that they don't bother you. Any small alteration should do it."

"Thank you, Mr. MacDonald," the old man said. He fitted his teeth back into his mouth. "You're a great man, Mr. MacDonald."

MacDonald drove the ten dark miles to the hacienda with a vague feeling of unease, as if he had done something during the day or left something undone that should have been otherwise.

But the house was dark when he drove up in front, not empty-dark as it had seemed to him a few hours before, but friendly-dark. Maria was asleep, breathing peacefully.

The house was brilliant with lighted windows that cast long fingers into the night, probing the dark hills, and the sound of many voices stirred echoes until the countryside itself seemed alive.

"Come in, Lily," MacDonald said at the door, and was reminded of a winter scene when a Lily had met the gentlemen at the door and helped them off with their overcoats. But that was another Lily and another occasion and another place and somebody else's imagination. "I'm glad you decided to come." He had a can of beer in his hand, and he waved it in the general direction of the major center of noisemaking. "There's beer in the living room and something more potent in the study—190 proof grain alcohol, to be precise. Be careful with that. It will sneak up on you. But—*nunc est bibendum!*"

"Where's Mrs. MacDonald?" Lily asked.

"Back there, somewhere." MacDonald waved again. "The men, and a few brave women, are in the study. The women, and a few brave men, are in the living room. The kitchen is common territory. Take your choice."

"I really shouldn't have come," Lily said. "I offered to spell Mr. Saunders in the control room, but he said I hadn't been checked out. It isn't as if the computer couldn't handle it all alone, and I know enough to call somebody if anything unexpected should happen."

"Shall I tell you something, Lily?" MacDonald said. "The computer could do it alone. And you and the computer could do it better than any of us, including me. But if the men ever feel that they are unnecessary, they would feel more useless than ever. They would give up. And they mustn't do that."

"Oh, Mac!" Lily said.

"They mustn't do that. Because one of them is going to come up with the inspiration that solves it all. Not me. One of them. We'll send somebody to relieve Charley before the evening is over."

> *Wer immer strebens sich bemüht,*
> *Den können wir erlösen.*

Lily sighed. "Okay, boss."

"And enjoy yourself!"

"Okay, boss, okay."

"Find a man, Lily," MacDonald muttered. And then he, too, turned toward the living room, for Lily had been the last who might come.

He listened for a moment at the doorway, sipping slowly from the warming can.

"—work more on gamma rays—"

"Who's got the money to build a generator? Since nobody's built one yet, we don't even know what it might cost."

"—gamma-ray sources should be a million times more rare than radio sources at twenty-one centimeters—"

"That's what Cocconi said nearly fifty years ago. The same arguments. Always the same arguments."

"If they're right, they're right."

"But the hydrogen-emission line is so uniquely logical. As Morrison said to Cocconi—and Cocconi, if you remember, agreed—it represents a logical, prearranged rendezvous point. 'A unique, objective standard of frequency, which must be known to every observer of the universe,' was the way they put it."

"—but the noise level—"

MacDonald smiled and moved on to the kitchen for a cold can of beer.

"—Bracewell's 'automated messengers'?" a voice asked querulously.

"What about them?"

"Why aren't we looking for them?"

"The point of Bracewell's messengers is that they make themselves known to us!"

"Maybe there's something wrong with ours. After a few million years in orbit—"

"—laser beams make more sense."

"And get lost in all that star shine?"

"As Schwartz and Townes pointed out, all you have to do is select a wavelength of light that is absorbed by stellar atmospheres. Put a narrow laser beam in the center of one of the calcium absorption lines—"

In the study they were talking about quantum noise.

"Quantum noise favors low frequencies."

"But the noise itself sets a lower limit on those frequencies."

"Drake calculated the most favorable frequencies, considering the noise level, lie between 3.2 and 8.1 centimeters."

"Drake! Drake! What did he know? We've had nearly fifty years experience on him. Fifty years of technological advance. Fifty years ago we could send radio messages one thousand light-years and laser signals ten light-years. Today those figures are ten thousand and five hundred at least."

"What if nobody's there?" Adams said gloomily.

Ich bin der Geist der stets vernient.

"Short-pulse it, like Oliver suggested. One hundred million billion watts in a ten billionth of a second would smear across the entire radio spectrum. Here, Mac, fill this, will you?"

And MacDonald wandered away through the clustering guests toward the bar.

"And I told Charley," said a woman to two other women in the corner, "if I had a dime for every dirty diaper I've changed, I sure wouldn't be sitting here in Puerto Rico—"

"—neutrinos," said somebody.

"Nuts," said somebody else, as MacDonald poured grain alcohol carefully into the glass and filled it with orange juice, "the only really logical medium is Q waves."

"I know—the waves we haven't discovered yet but are going to discover about ten years from now. Only here it is nearly fifty years after Morrison suggested it, and we still haven't discovered them."

MacDonald wended his way back across the room.

"It's the night work that gets me," said someone's wife. "The kids up all day, and then he wants me there to greet him when he gets home at dawn. Brother!"

"Or what if everybody's listening?" Adams said gloomily. "Maybe everybody's sitting there, listening, just the way we are, because it's so much cheaper than sending."

"Here you are," MacDonald said.

"But don't you suppose somebody would have thought of that by this time and begun to send?"

"Double-think it all the way through and figure what just occurred to you would have occurred to everybody else, so you might as well listen. Think about it—everybody sitting around, listening. If there is anybody. Either way it makes the skin creep."

"All right, then, we ought to send something."

"What would you send?"

"I'd have to think about it. Prime numbers, maybe."

"Think some more. What if a civilization weren't mathematical?"

"Idiot! How would they build an antenna?"

"Maybe they'd rule-of-thumb it, like a ham. Or maybe they have built-in antennae."

"And maybe you have built-in antennae and don't know it."

MacDonald's can of beer was empty. He wandered back toward the kitchen again.

"—insist on equal time with the Big Ear. Even if nobody's sending we could pick up the normal electronic commerce of a civilization tens of light-years away. The problem would be deciphering, not hearing."

"They're picking it up now, when they're studying the relatively close systems. Ask for a tape and work out your program."

"All right, I will. Just give me a chance to work up a request—"

MacDonald found himself beside Maria. He put his arm around her waist and pulled her close. "All right?" he said.

"All right."

Her face was tired, though, MacDonald thought. He dreaded the notion that she might be growing older, that she was entering middle age. He could face it for himself. He could feel the years piling up inside his bones. He still thought of himself, inside, as twenty, but he knew that he was forty-seven, and mostly he was glad that he had found happiness and love and peace and serenity. He even was willing to pay the price in youthful exuberance and belief in his personal immortality. But not Maria!

> *Nel mezzo del cammin di nostra vita*
> *Mi ritrovai per una selva oscura,*
> *Che la diritta via era smarrita.*

"Sure?"

She nodded.

He leaned close to her ear. "I wish it was just the two of us, as usual."

"I, too."

"I'm going to leave in a little while—"

"Must you?"

"I must relieve Saunders. He's on duty. Give him an opportunity to celebrate a little with the others."

"Can't you send somebody else?"

"Who?" MacDonald gestured with good-humored futility at all the clusters of people held together by bonds of ordered sounds shared consecutively. "It's a good party. No one will miss me."

"I will."

"Of course, *querida.*"

"You are their mother, father, priest, all in one," Maria said. "You worry about them too much."

"I must keep them together. What else am I good for?"

"For much more."

MacDonald hugged her with one arm.

"Look at Mac and Maria, will you?" said someone who was having trouble with his consonants. "What goddamned devotion!"

MacDonald smiled and suffered himself to be pounded on the back while he protected Maria in front of him. "I'll see you later," he said.

As he passed the living room someone was saying,

"Like Edie said, we ought to look at the long-chain molecules in carbonaceous chondrites. No telling how far they've traveled—or been sent—or what messages might be coded in the molecules."

As he closed the front door behind him, the noise dropped to a roar and then a mutter. He stopped for a moment at the door of the car and looked up at the sky.

E quindi uscimmo a riveder le stelle.

The noise from the hacienda reminded him of something—the speakers in the control room. All those voices talking, talking, talking, and from here he could not understand a thing.

Somewhere there was an idea if he could only concentrate on it hard enough. But he had drunk one beer too many—or perhaps one too few.

After the long hours of listening to the voices, MacDonald always felt a little crazy, but tonight it was worse than usual. Perhaps it was all the conversation before, or the beers, or something else—some deeper concern that would not surface.

Tico-tico, tico-tico . . .

Even if they could pick up a message, they still would likely be dead and gone before any exchange could take place even with the nearest likely star. What kind of mad dedication could sustain such perseverance?

They're listening in Puerto Rico. . . .

Religion could. At least once it did, during the era of cathedral building in Europe, the cathedrals that took centuries to build.

"What are you doing, fellow?"

"I'm working for ten francs a day."

"And what are you doing?"

"I'm laying stone."

"And you—what are you doing?"

"I am building a cathedral."

They were building cathedrals, most of them. Most of them had that religious mania about their mission that would sustain them through a lifetime of labors in which no progress could be seen.

Listening for words that never come . . .

The mere layers of stone and those who worked for

pay alone eliminated themselves in time and left only those who kept alive in themselves the concept, the dream.

But they had to be a little mad to begin with.

Can it be the stars are stricken dumb?

Tonight he had heard the voices nearly all night long. They kept trying to tell him something, something urgent, something he should do, but he could not quite make out the words. There was only the babble of distant voices, urgent and unintelligible.

Tico-tico, tico-tic...

He had wanted to shout "Shut up!" to the universe. "One at a time!" "You first!" But of course there was no way to do that. Or had he tried? Had he shouted?

They're listening with ears this big!

Had he dozed at the console with the voices mumbling in his ears, or had he only thought he dozed? Or had he only dreamed he waked. Or dreamed he dreamed?

Listening for thoughts just like their own.

There was madness to it all, but perhaps it was a divine madness, a creative madness. And is not that madness that which sustains man in his terrible self-knowledge, the driving madness which demands reason of a casual universe, the awful aloneness which seeks among the stars for companionship?

Can it be that we are all alone?

The ringing of the telephone half penetrated through the mists of mesmerization. He picked up the handset, half expecting it would be the universe calling, perhaps with a clipped British accent, "Hello there, Man. Hello. Hello. I say, we seem to have a bad connection, what? Just wanted you to know that we're here. Are you there? Are you listening? Message on the way. May not get there for a couple of centuries. Do be around to answer, will you? That's a good being. Righto...."

Only it wasn't. It was the familiar American voice of Charley Saunders saying, "Mac, there's been an accident. Olsen is on his way to relieve you, but I think you'd better leave now. It's Maria."

Leave it. Leave it all. What does it matter? But leave the controls on automatic; the computer can take care of it all. Maria! Get in the car. Start it. Don't fumble! That's it. Go. Go. Car passing. Must be Olsen. No matter.

What kind of accident? Why didn't I ask? What does it matter what kind of accident? Maria. Nothing could have happened. Nothing serious. Not with all those people around. *Nil desperandum*. And yet—why did Charley call if it was not serious? Must be serious. I must be prepared for something bad, something that will shake the world, that will tear my insides.

I must not break up in front of them. Why not? Why must I appear infallible? Why must I always be cheerful, imperturbable, my faith unshaken? Why me? If there is something bad, if something impossibly bad has happened to Maria, what will matter? Ever? Why didn't I ask Charley what it was? Why? The bad can wait; it will get no worse for being unknown.

What does the universe care for my agony? I am nothing. My feelings are nothing to anyone but me. My only possible meaning to the universe is the Project. Only this slim potential links me with eternity. My love and my agony are me, but the significance of my life or death are the Project.

By the time he reached the hacienda, MacDonald was breathing evenly. His emotions were under control. Dawn had grayed the eastern sky. It was a customary hour for Project personnel to be returning home.

Saunders met him at the door. "Dr. Lessenden is here. He's with Maria."

The odor of stale smoke and the memory of babble still lingered in the air, but someone had been busy. The party remains had been cleaned up. No doubt they all had pitched in. They were good people.

"Betty found her in the bathroom off your bedroom. She wouldn't have been there except the others were occupied. I blame myself. I shouldn't have let you relieve me. Maybe if you had been here— But I knew you wanted it that way."

"No one's to blame. She was alone a great deal," MacDonald said. "What happened?"

"Didn't I tell you? Her wrists. Slashed with a razor. Both of them. Betty found her in the bathtub. Like pink lemonade, she said."

A fist tightened inside MacDonald's gut and then slowly relaxed. Yes, it had been that. He had known it, hadn't he? He had known it would happen ever since the sleeping pills, even though he had kept telling himself, as she had told him, that the overdose had been an accident.

Or had he known? He knew only that Saunders' news had been no surprise.

Then they were at the bedroom door, and Maria was lying under a blanket on the bed, scarcely making it mound over her body, and her arms were on top of the blankets, palms up, bandages like white paint across the olive perfection of her arms, now, MacDonald reminded himself, no longer perfection but marred with ugly red lips that spoke to him of hidden misery and untold sorrow and a life that was a lie. . . .

Dr. Lessenden looked up, sweat trickling down from his hairline. "The bleeding is stopped, but she's lost a good deal of blood. I've got to take her to the hospital for a transfusion. The ambulance should be here any minute." MacDonald looked at Maria's face. It was paler than he had ever seen it. It looked almost waxen, as if it were already arranged for all time on a satin pillow. "Her chances are fifty-fifty," Lessenden said in answer to his unspoken question.

And then the attendants brushed their way past him with their litter.

"Betty found this on her dressing table," Saunders said. He handed MacDonald a slip of paper folded once.

MacDonald unfolded it: *Je m'en vay chercher un grand Peut-être*.

Everyone was surprised to see MacDonald at the office. They did not say anything, and he did not volunteer the information that he could not bear to sit at home, among the remembrances, and wait for word to come. But they asked him about Maria, and he said, "Dr. Lessenden is hopeful. She's still unconscious. Apparently will be for some time. The doctor said I might as well wait here as at the hospital. I think I made them nervous. They're hopeful. Maria's still unconscious. . . ."

O lente, lente currite, noctis equi!
The stars move still, time runs, the clock will strike. . . .
Finally MacDonald was alone. He pulled out paper and

pencil and worked for a long time on the statement, and then he balled it up and threw it into the wastebasket, scribbled a single sentence on another sheet of paper, and called Lily.

"Send this!"

She glanced at it. "No, Mac."

"Send it!"

"But—"

"It's not an impulse. I've thought it over carefully. Send it."

Slowly she left, holding the piece of paper gingerly in her fingertips. MacDonald pushed the papers around on his desk, waiting for the telephone to ring. But without knocking, unannounced, Saunders came through the door first.

"You can't do this, Mac," Saunders said.

MacDonald sighed. "Lily told you. I would fire that girl if she weren't so loyal."

"Of course she told me. This isn't just you. It affects the whole Project."

"That's what I'm thinking about."

"I think I know what you're going through, Mac—" Saunders stopped. "No, of course I don't know what you're going through. It must be hell. But don't desert us. Think of the Project!"

"That's what I'm thinking about. I'm a failure, Charley. Everything I touch—ashes."

"You're the best of us."

"A poor linguist? An indifferent engineer? I have no qualifications for this job, Charley. You need someone with ideas to head the Project, someone dynamic, someone who can lead, someone with—charisma."

A few minutes later he went over it all again with Olsen. When he came to the qualifications part, all Olsen could say was, "You give a good party, Mac."

It was Adams, the skeptic, who affected him most. "Mac, you're what I believe in instead of God."

Sonnenborn said, "You are the Project. If you go, it all falls apart. It's over."

"It seems like it, always, but it never happens to those things that have life in them. The Project was here before

I came. It will be here after I leave. It must be longer lived than any of us, because we are for the years and it is for the centuries."

After Sonnenborn, MacDonald told Lily wearily, "No more, Lily."

None of them had had the courage to mention Maria, but MacDonald considered that failure, too. She had tried to communicate with him a month ago when she took the pills, and he had been unable to understand. How could he riddle the stars when he couldn't even understand those closest to him? Now he had to pay.

What would Marie want? He knew what she wanted, but if she lived, he could not let her pay that price. Too long she had been there when he wanted her, waiting like a doll put away on a shelf for him to return and take her down, so that he could have the strength to continue.

And somehow the agony had built up inside her, the dreadful progress of the years, most dread of all to a beautiful woman growing old, alone, too much alone. He had been selfish. He had kept her to himself. He had not wanted children to mar the perfection of their being together.

Perfection for him; less than that for her.

Perhaps it was not too late for them if she lived. And if she died—he would not have the heart to go on with work to which, he knew now, he could contribute nothing.

And finally the call came. "She's going to be all right, Mac," Lessenden said. And after a moment, "Mac, I said—"

"I heard."

"She wants to see you."

"I'll be there."

"She said to give you a message. 'Tell Robby I've been a little crazy in the head. I'll be better now. That "great perhaps" looks too certain from here. And tell him not to be crazy in the head too.'"

MacDonald put down the telephone and walked through the doorway and through the outer office, a feeling in his chest as if it were going to burst. "She's going to be all right," he threw over his shoulder at Lily.

"Oh, Mac—"

In the hall, Joe the janitor stopped him. "Mr. Mac-Donald—"

MacDonald stopped. "Been to the dentist yet, Joe?"

"No, sir, not yet, but it's not—"

"Don't go. I'd like to put a tape recorder beside your bed for a while, Joe. Who knows?"

"Thank you, sir. But it's— They say you're leaving, Mr. MacDonald."

"Somebody else will do it."

"You don't understand. Don't go, Mr. MacDonald!"

"Why not, Joe?"

"You're the one who cares."

MacDonald had been about to move on, but that stopped him.

Ful wys is he that can himselven knowe!

He turned and went back to the office. "Have you got that sheet of paper, Lily?"

"Yes, sir."

"Have you sent it?"

"No, sir."

"Bad girl. Give it to me."

He read the sentence on the paper once more: "I have great confidence in the goals and ultimate success of the Project, but for personal reasons I must submit my resignation."

He studied it for a moment.

A dwarf standing on the shoulder of a giant may see further than the giant himself.

And he tore it up.

COMPUTER RUN

IN THE BEGINNING WAS THE WORD, AND THE WORD WAS HYDROGEN ....HARLOW SHAPLEY, 1958...

NO ONE WOULD HAVE BELIEVED IN THE LAST YEARS OF THE NINE-TEENTH CENTURY THAT THIS WORLD WAS BEING WATCHED KEENLY AND CLOSELY BY INTELLIGENCES GREATER THAN MAN'S AND YET AS MORTAL AS HIS OWN....YET ACROSS THE GULF OF SPACE, MINDS THAT ARE TO OUR MINDS AS OURS ARE TO THOSE OF THE BEASTS THAT PERISH, INTELLECTS VAST AND COOL AND UNSYMPATHETIC, RE-GARDED THIS EARTH WITH ENVIOUS EYES, AND SLOWLY AND SURELY DREW THEIR PLANS AGAINST US....H. G. WELLS, 1898...

INDIVIDUALS DIE. HOWEVER, THE TOTAL AMOUNT OF LIVING MAT-TER PERSEVERES, AND EVEN INCREASES. WE CAN IMAGINE A SPHER-ICAL ORGANISM WITH THE CYCLES OF PHYSIOLOGICAL PROCESSES CLOSED COMPLETELY IN THEMSELVES. SUCH AN ORGANISM WILL BE IMMORTAL AND PHOTOSYNTHETIC, AND IT CAN DEVELOP EVEN A HIGHER CONSCIOUSNESS....THE MAIN ACTIVITY OF THE HIGHEST LIVING ORGANISMS IN THE UNIVERSE CAN BE ALSO THE COLONIZA-TION OF OTHER WORLDS. SUCH BEINGS, PROBABLY, COULD NOT BE OF SPHERICAL FORM, AND THEY WILL NOT BE IMMORTAL.

ON AT LEAST ONE PLANET, SOMEWHERE, BEINGS HAVE ACHIEVED A TECHNOLOGY PERMITTING THEM TO OVERCOME THE FORCE OF GRAVITY AND TO COLONIZE THE UNIVERSE....COLONIZATION NOW IS THE NORMAL MANNER IN WHICH LIFE SPREADS. EVOLUTION, WITH ALL ITS SUFFERINGS, IS RARE....

IN THE NEAR FUTURE SHORT RADIO WAVES WILL PENETRATE OUR ATMOSPHERE AND THEY WILL BE THE MAIN MEANS OF STELLAR COM-MUNICATION....KONSTANTIN EDUARDOVICH TSIOLKOVSKY, 1934...

THE CHANGES I NOTED WERE TAKING PLACE PERIODICALLY, AND WITH SUCH A CLEAR SUGGESTION OF NUMBERS AND ORDER THAT THEY WERE NOT TRACEABLE TO ANY CAUSE THEN KNOWN TO ME. I

WAS FAMILIAR, OF COURSE, WITH SUCH ELECTRICAL DISTURBANCES AS ARE PRODUCED BY THE SUN, AURORA BOREALIS, AND EARTH CURRENTS, AND I WAS AS SURE AS I COULD BE OF ANY FACT THAT THESE VARIATIONS WERE DUE TO NONE OF THESE CAUSES.... IT WAS SOME TIME AFTERWARD WHEN THE THOUGHT FLASHED UPON MY MIND THAT THE DISTURBANCES I HAD OBSERVED MIGHT BE DUE TO INTELLIGENT CONTROL.... THE FEELING IS CONSTANTLY GROWING ON ME THAT I HAD BEEN THE FIRST TO HEAR THE GREETING OF ONE PLANET TO ANOTHER....

FAINT AND UNCERTAIN THOUGH THEY WERE, THEY HAVE GIVEN ME A DEEP CONVICTION AND FOREKNOWLEDGE, THAT ERE LONG ALL HUMAN BEINGS ON THIS GLOBE, AS ONE, WILL TURN THE EYES TO THE FIRMAMENT ABOVE, WITH FEELINGS OF LOVE AND REVERENCE, THRILLED BY THE GLAD NEWS: "BRETHREN! WE HAVE A MESSAGE FROM ANOTHER WORLD, UNKNOWN AND REMOTE. IT READS: ONE ... TWO ... THREE...." NIKOLA TESLA, 1900...

WHO KNOWS FOR CERTAIN? WHO SHALL HERE DECLARE IT?
WHENCE WAS IT BORN, WHENCE CAME CREATION?
THE GODS ARE LATER THAN THIS WORLD'S FORMATION;
WHO THEN CAN KNOW THE ORIGINS OF THE WORLD?

NONE KNOWS WHENCE CREATION AROSE;
AND WHETHER HE HAS OR HAS NOT MADE IT;
HE WHO SURVEYS IT FROM THE LOFTY SKIES,
ONLY HE KNOWS—OR PERHAPS HE KNOWS NOT.
                                        RIG-VEDA, C. 1000 B.C....

ONE DAY, WHILE CONSIDERING THE QUESTION OF GAMMA RAY PRODUCTION FROM THE CRAB NEBULA (WHICH APPARENTLY IS THE RESULT OF SYNCHROTRON RADIATION PRODUCED BY THE SUPERNOVA EXPLOSION OF 1054 A.D.), GIUSEPPE COCCONI BEGAN TO WONDER IF INTERSTELLAR MESSAGES COULD BE SENT BY MEANS OF GAMMA RAYS: THEY ARE RARE, AND THEY STAND OUT IN THE SKY. WHY WOULDN'T ANOTHER CIVILIZATION SEE GAMMA RAYS AS A VEHICLE FOR INTERSTELLAR SIGNALING?

HIS FRIEND AND COLLEAGUE, PHILIP MORRISON, POINTED OUT THAT GAMMA RAYS ARE DIFFICULT TO GENERATE AND DIFFICULT TO RECEIVE. RADIO FREQUENCIES, ON THE OTHER HAND, WERE PLENTIFUL AND CHEAP TO RECEIVE.

PERHAPS ONE OF THE BIG RADIO TELESCOPES MIGHT BE PERSUADED TO SEARCH SOME LIKELY STARS....

IN A UNIVERSE WHOSE SIZE IS BEYOND HUMAN IMAGINING, WHERE OUR WORLD FLOATS LIKE A DUST MOTE IN THE VOID OF NIGHT, MEN HAVE GROWN INCONCEIVABLY LONELY. WE SCAN THE TIME SCALE AND THE MECHANISMS OF LIFE ITSELF FOR PORTENTS AND SIGNS OF THE INVISIBLE. AS THE ONLY THINKING MAMMALS ON THE PLANET—PERHAPS THE ONLY THINKING ANIMALS IN THE ENTIRE SIDEREAL UNIVERSE—THE BURDEN OF CONSCIOUSNESS HAS GROWN HEAVY UPON US. WE WATCH THE STARS, BUT THE SIGNS ARE UNCERTAIN. WE UNCOVER THE BONES OF THE PAST AND SEEK FOR OUR ORIGINS. THERE IS A PATH THERE, BUT IT APPEARS TO WANDER. THE VAGARIES OF THE ROAD MAY HAVE A MEANING, HOWEVER; IT IS THUS WE TORTURE OURSELVES....LOREN EISELEY, 1946...

THE MID-ATLANTIC FISH FARM HAS JUST HARVESTED A BUMPER CROP OF THE NEW, IMPROVED NORTH ATLANTIC COD. THE SO-CALLED SUPERCOD WEIGHS TWENTY-FIVE POUNDS, HAS A FLAVOR THAT FISH-FANCIERS CLAIM IS SUPERIOR TO ANYTHING YET TO COME OUT OF THE GENETIC LABORATORIES, AND CAN BE ORDERED TOMORROW FROM YOUR LOCAL MARKET....

WOULD ANY CIVILIZATION WITH A SUPERIOR TECHNOLOGY WISH TO DO HARM TO ONE THAT HAS JUST ENTERED THE COMMUNITY OF INTELLIGENCE? I DOUBT IT. IF I WERE LOOKING THROUGH A MICROSCOPE AND SAW A GROUP OF BACTERIA SPELL OUT, LIKE A COLLEGE BAND, "PLEASE DO NOT PUT IODINE ON THIS PLATE. WE WANT TO TALK TO YOU," MY FIRST INCLINATION WOULD CERTAINLY NOT BE TO RUSH THE BACTERIA INTO A STERILIZER. I DOUBT THAT ADVANCED SOCIETIES CRUSH OUT ANY COMPETITIVE FORM OF INTELLIGENCE, ESPECIALLY WHEN THERE IS CLEARLY NO DANGER....PHILIP MORRISON, 1961...

AFTER DEBATE LASTING NEARLY THREE WEEKS, THE APPROPRIATION BILL FOR SUCH SCIENTIFIC PROGRAMS AS THE MOON COLONY AND THE LISTENING PROJECT IN PUERTO RICO IS EXPECTED TO PASS THE HOUSE OF REPRESENTATIVES TODAY, WITH SOME SMALL CHANCE THAT A LAST-MINUTE AMENDMENT MAY ELIMINATE ONE PROJECT OR ANOTHER. CONSIDERED IN MOST DANGER IS THE PUERTO RICAN PROGRAM TO LISTEN FOR COMMUNICATIONS FROM OTHER WORLDS WHICH HAS REGISTERED NOTHING BUT NEGATIVE RESULTS SINCE IT WAS BEGUN NEARLY FIFTY YEARS AGO.

ANOTHER BILL, WHICH WOULD RAISE THE MINIMUM ANNUAL INCOME FROM ITS PRESENT $10,000 TO $12,000 OVER THE NEXT TWO

YEARS, IS EXPECTED, ON THE OTHER HAND, TO RECEIVE ONLY TOKEN OPPOSITION FROM CONGRESSMEN WHO FEEL THAT IT SHOULD BE HIGHER.

PRESIDENT WHITE HAS ANNOUNCED THAT HE WILL SIGN BOTH MEASURES....

DEAR DR. LOVELL,

...SOME WEEK AGO, WHILE DISCUSSING WITH COLLEAGUES AT CORNELL THE EMISSION OF SYNCHROTRON RADIATION BY ASTRONOMICAL OBJECTS, I REALIZED THAT THE JODRELL BANK RADIO TELESCOPE COULD BE USED FOR A PROGRAM THAT COULD BE SERIOUS ENOUGH TO DESERVE YOUR CONSIDERATION, THOUGH AT FIRST SIGHT IT LOOKS LIKE SCIENCE FICTION.

IT WILL BE BETTER IF I ITEMIZE THE ARGUMENTS.

(1) LIFE ON PLANETS SEEMS NOT TO BE A VERY RARE PHENOMENON. OUT OF TEN SOLAR PLANETS ONE IS FULL OF LIFE AND MARS COULD HAVE SOME. THE SOLAR SYSTEM IS NOT PECULIAR; OTHER STARS WITH SIMILAR CHARACTERISTICS ARE EXPECTED TO HAVE AN EQUIVALENT NUMBER OF PLANETS. THERE IS A GOOD CHANCE THAT, AMONG THE, SAY, 100 STARS CLOSEST TO THE SUN, SOME HAVE PLANETS BEARING LIFE WELL ADVANCED IN EVOLUTION.

(2) THE CHANCES ARE THEN GOOD THAT IN SOME OF THESE PLANETS ANIMALS EXIST EVOLVED MUCH FARTHER THAN MEN. A CIVILIZATION ONLY A FEW HUNDRED YEARS MORE ADVANCED THAN OURS WOULD HAVE TECHNICAL POSSIBILITIES BY FAR GREATER THAN THOSE AVAILABLE NOW TO US.

(3) ASSUME THAT AN ADVANCED CIVILIZATION EXISTS IN SOME OF THESE PLANETS, I.E., WITHIN SOME 10 LIGHT YEARS FROM US. THE PROBLEM IS: HOW TO ESTABLISH A COMMUNICATION?

AS FAR AS WE KNOW THE ONLY POSSIBILITY SEEMS TO BE THE USE OF ELECTROMAGNETIC WAVES, WHICH CAN CROSS THE MAGNETIZED PLASMAS FILLING THE INTERSTELLAR SPACES WITHOUT BEING DISTORTED.

SO I WILL ASSUME THAT "BEINGS" ON THESE PLANETS ARE ALREADY SENDING TOWARD THE STARS CLOSEST TO THEM BEAMS OF ELECTROMAGNETIC WAVES MODULATED IN A RATIONAL WAY, E.G., IN TRAINS CORRESPONDING TO THE PRIME NUMBERS, HOPING IN A SIGN OF LIFE....

SIGNED/GIUSEPPE COCCONI

IT IS A PROJECT WHICH HAS TO BE FUNDED BY THE *CENTURY*, NOT BY THE FISCAL YEAR. FURTHERMORE, IT IS A PROJECT WHICH IS VERY

LIKELY TO FAIL *COMPLETELY.* IF YOU SPEND A LOT OF MONEY AND GO AROUND EVERY TEN YEARS AND SAY, "WE HAVEN'T HEARD ANYTHING YET," YOU CAN IMAGINE HOW YOU MAKE OUT BEFORE A CONGRESSIONAL COMMITTEE. BUT I THINK IT IS NOT TOO SOON TO HAVE THE FUN OF THINKING ABOUT IT, AND I THINK IT IS A MUCH LESS CHILDISH SUBJECT TO THINK ABOUT THAN ASTRONOMICAL SPACE TRAVEL.... EDWARD M. PURCELL, 1960...

FREDERICK PLAYER, DISTINGUISHED SOUTH AFRICAN COMPOSER AND CONDUCTOR, EMERGED FROM TWO MONTHS OF LOW-TEMPERATURE HIBERNATION AND SAID, "I NEVER FELT BETTER." DURING HIS LONG SLEEP, WHICH HE ENTERED AT HIS PHYSICIAN'S ORDERS WHEN HE COLLAPSED DURING A RECENT CONCERT, HE COMPLETED, HE SAID, THE "SLOW MOVEMENT" OF HIS NEW SYMPHONY WHICH HE HAS TITLED "NEW WORLDS."

ONE IN ONE HUNDRED THOUSAND STARS HAVE ADVANCED SOCIETIES IN ORBIT AROUND THEM.... CARL SAGAN, 1961...

ONE IN THREE MILLION.... SEBASTIAN VON HOERNER, 1961...

THE NUMBER OF EXTANT CIVILIZATIONS SUBSTANTIALLY IN ADVANCE OF OUR OWN IN THE GALAXY TODAY APPEARS TO BE PERHAPS BETWEEN FIFTY THOUSAND AND ONE MILLION. THE AVERAGE DISTANCE BETWEEN TECHNICAL CIVILIZATIONS IS BETWEEN A FEW HUNDRED LIGHT YEARS AND ABOUT ONE THOUSAND LIGHT YEARS. THE AVERAGE AGE OF COMMUNICATING TECHNICAL CIVILIZATION IS TEN THOUSAND YEARS.... CARL SAGAN, 1966...

WE SHALL ASSUME THAT LONG AGO THEY ESTABLISHED A CHANNEL OF COMMUNICATION THAT WOULD ONE DAY BECOME KNOWN TO US, AND THAT THEY LOOK FORWARD PATIENTLY TO THE ANSWERING SIGNALS FROM THE SUN WHICH WOULD MAKE KNOWN TO THEM THAT A NEW SOCIETY HAS ENTERED THE COMMUNITY OF INTELLIGENCE. ... PHILIP MORRISON AND GIUSEPPE COCCONI, 1959...

> *COPERNICUS, BRAHE, TESLA, MARCONI,*
> *MORRISON, DRAKE, STRUVE, DYSON, COCCONI,*
> *GALILEO, BURKE, BROWN, TSIOLKOVSKY,*
> *PURCELL, MASCALL, SAGAN, HOYLE, SHKLOVSKY,*
> *VON HOERNER, STORMER, SPITZER, UREY,*
> *BLACKETT, BUSSARD, BERKNER, LILLY,*

*LOWELL, LOVELL, WHIPPLE, FRANKLIN,
GREENSTEIN, HASKINS, LEDERBERG, EWEN,
FREUDENTHAL, MICHAEL, RAIBLE, PEARMAN,
GOLAY, BOEHM, MEAD, SMITH, HANDLESMAN,
SCHACHTER, VAN DE HULST, TOWNES, KILLIAN,
OPPENHEIMER, OLIVER, SCHWARZ, CAMERON,
FROMAN, SIMPSON, CALVIN, SACCHI,
JANSKY, ATCHLEY, WEBB, HUANG, MACQUARRIE...*

WE SUBMIT THE FOREGOING LINE OF ARGUMENT DEMONSTRATES THAT THE PRESENCE OF INTERSTELLAR SIGNALS IS ENTIRELY CONSISTENT WITH ALL WE KNOW, AND THAT IF SIGNALS ARE PRESENT THE MEANS OF DETECTING THEM IS NOW AT HAND. FEW WILL DENY THE PROFOUND IMPORTANCE, PRACTICAL AND PHILOSOPHICAL, WHICH THE DETECTION OF INTERSTELLAR COMMUNICATION WOULD HAVE. WE THEREFORE FEEL THAT A DISCRIMINATING SEARCH FOR SIGNALS DESERVES A CONSIDERABLE EFFORT. THE PROBABILITY OF SUCCESS IS DIFFICULT TO ESTIMATE; BUT IF WE NEVER SEARCH, THE CHANCE OF SUCCESS IS ZERO.... MORRISON AND COCCONI, 1959...

THE UNITED STATES BUREAU OF ENVIRONMENT TODAY PROPOSED THAT WEATHER CONTROL BE CENTRALIZED UNDER THE GENERAL DIRECTION OF THE UNITED NATIONS. "WE HAVE HAD CONSIDERABLE SUCCESS IN MODIFYING WEATHER IN THIS COUNTRY," A BUREAU SPOKESMAN SAID, "BUT WEATHER IS A WORLDWIDE, INTERDEPENDENT PHENOMENON, AND WEATHER CONTROL WILL NEVER BE COMPLETELY SUCCESSFUL UNTIL IT CAN BE APPROACHED ON A GLOBAL BASIS."

WITHIN FIFTY YEARS WE WILL HAVE DEVELOPED RADIO TECHNOLOGY TO THE POINT WHERE FURTHER IMPROVEMENTS WILL NO LONGER INFLUENCE OUR ABILITY TO COMMUNICATE WITH OTHER WORLDS. THE LIMITATIONS, HENCEFORTH, WILL BE BACKGROUND NOISE IN SPACE AND OTHER NATURAL FACTORS. SINCE OUR RADIO TECHNOLOGY IS NOW FIFTY YEARS OLD, THIS MEANS THAT CIVILIZATIONS CHARACTERISTICALLY JUMP, IN THE BRIEF SPAN OF ONE CENTURY, FROM HAVING NO CAPACITY FOR INTERSTELLAR COMMUNICATION TO HAVING THE MAXIMUM CAPABILITY. ON AN ASTRONOMICAL TIME SCALE, A CIVILIZATION PASSES ABRUPTLY FROM A STATE OF NO RADIO ABILITY TO ONE OF PERFECT RADIO ABILITY. IF WE COULD EXAMINE A LARGE NUMBER OF LIFE-BEARING PLANETS, WE MIGHT EXPECT TO FIND IN VIRTUALLY EVERY CASE EITHER COM-

PLETE IGNORANCE OF RADIO TECHNIQUES, OR COMPLETE MASTERY. ...FRANK D. DRAKE, 1960...

DO WE REALLY EXPECT A SUPERIOR COMMUNITY TO BE ON THE NEAREST OF THOSE STARS WHICH WE CANNOT AT THE MOMENT POS-ITIVELY RULE OUT? UNLESS SUPERIOR COMMUNITIES ARE EX-TREMELY ABUNDANT, IS IT NOT MORE LIKELY THAT THE NEAREST IS SITUATED AT LEAST TEN TIMES FARTHER OFF, SAY, BEYOND ONE HUNDRED LIGHT YEARS?...

EVEN RULING OUT UNLIKELY CANDIDATES, WE MUST STILL SCAN ONE THOUSAND STARS TO FIND THE HIGHLY ADVANCED CIVILIZATION THAT WE ARE LOOKING FOR AND THAT CIVILIZATION, IN TURN, MUST DIRECT ITS CALLING SIGNAL AT ONE THOUSAND STARS IN THE HOPE, ULTI-MATELY, OF FINDING SOMEONE ELSE. REMEMBER THAT THROUGHOUT MOST OF THE THOUSANDS OF MILLIONS OF YEARS OF THE EARTH'S EXISTENCE SUCH ATTENTION WOULD HAVE BEEN FRUITLESS. ... RONALD N. BRACEWELL, 1960...

WE MUST EXPECT MOST SOCIETIES THAT HAVE CROSSED THE THRESHOLD OF CIVILIZATION TO BE MORE ADVANCED THAN OUR OWN. ... FRANK D. DRAKE, 1960...

A NEW STRAIN OF CORN DEVELOPED BY GENETIC SCI-ENTISTS IS PRODUCING RECORD YIELDS OF A HIGH PROTEIN SUPERCORN WHICH PROMISES TO ELIMINATE REMAINING POCKETS OF STARVATION AND PROTEIN DEFICIENCY AS SOON AS SUFFICIENT QUANTITIES OF SEED CAN BE DISTRIBUTED AND THE PUBLIC IN VARIOUS PARTS OF THE WORLD EDU-CATED TO ITS MINOR DIFFERENCES IN TASTE AND TEXTURE.

IT WOULD BE MORE LOGICAL TO ASSUME THAT SUPERIOR CIVILIZATIONS WOULD SEND AUTOMATED MESSENGERS TO ORBIT EACH CANDIDATE STAR AND AWAIT THE POSSIBLE AWAKENING OF A CIVILIZATION ON ONE OF THAT STAR'S PLANETS. ... RONALD N. BRACEWELL, 1960...

WE ARE NOT FAR FROM THE DEVELOPMENT OF LASERS ABLE TO COMMUNICATE ON WAVELENGTHS OF VISIBLE LIGHT, OR IN ADJACENT PORTIONS OF THE SPECTRUM BE-

TWEEN PLANETS OF TWO STARS SEPARATED BY A NUMBER OF LIGHT YEARS. THE RAPID PROGRESS OF SCIENCE IMPLIES THAT ANOTHER CIVILIZATION MORE ADVANCED THAN OURSELVES BY ONLY A FEW THOUSAND YEARS, MIGHT POSSESS CAPABILITIES WE NOW RULE OUT. THEY MAY HAVE ALREADY BEEN ABLE TO SEND US AN EXPLORATORY INSTRUMENTED PROBE. SINCE NONE HAS YET BEEN SEEN, PERHAPS IT WOULD BE APPROPRIATE TO EXAMINE HIGH-RESOLUTION STELLAR SPECTRA FOR LINES WHICH ARE UNUSUALLY NARROW, AT PECULIAR FREQUENCIES, OR VARYING IN INTENSITY.... CHARLES H. TOWNES AND ROBERT N. SCHWARTZ, 1961...

THE LONG-CHAIN MOLECULES NOW BEING EXTRACTED FROM CERTAIN METEORITES MIGHT HAVE BEEN PUT THERE BY SOME REMOTE CIVILIZATION AND HURLED TOWARD US IN GREAT NUMBERS. MIGHT THESE LONG MOLECULES CONTAIN CODED INFORMATION? SHOULD WE, PERHAPS, INTERCEPT COMETS IN FLIGHT TO SEE IF THEY HAVE ANY MESSAGES FROM AFAR?...LESLIE C. EDIE, 1962...

ONE'S OWN SUN COULD BE USED AS A SIGNALING LIGHT BY PLACING A CLOUD OF PARTICLES IN ORBIT AROUND IT. THE CLOUD WOULD CUT OFF ENOUGH LIGHT TO MAKE THE SUN APPEAR TO BE FLASHING WHEN SEEN FROM A DISTANCE.... PHILIP MORRISON, 1963...

CANST THOU BIND THE CHAINS OF THE PLEIADES, OR LOOSE THE BANDS OF ORION?... JOB, BEFORE THIRD CENTURY B.C....

ARAB AND ISRAELI OFFICIALS TODAY COMMEMORATED THE TENTH ANNIVERSARY OF THE COMPLETION OF THE BIG DAM ON THE JORDAN RIVER WHICH HAS MADE THE NEGEV DESERT THE BREADBASKET OF THE MIDDLE EAST.

MEANWHILE UNREST IN SIBERIA HAS BROUGHT THE SOVIET PREMIER FLYING BACK TO MOSCOW FROM FRIENDSHIP PACT TALKS WITH CHINESE SPOKESMEN IN PEKING....

LIGHTS COME AND GO IN THE NIGHT SKY. MEN, TROUBLED AT LAST BY THE THINGS THEY BUILD, MAY TOSS IN

THEIR SLEEP AND DREAM BAD DREAMS, OR LIE AWAKE WHILE THE METEORS WHISPER GREENLY OVERHEAD. BUT NOWHERE IN ALL SPACE OR ON A THOUSAND WORLDS WILL THERE BE MEN TO SHARE OUR LONELINESS. THERE MAY BE WISDOM; THERE MAY BE POWER; SOMEWHERE ACROSS SPACE GREAT INSTRUMENTS, HANDLED BY STRANGE, MANIPULA- TIVE ORGANS, MAY STARE VAINLY AT OUR FLOATING CLOUD WRACK, THEIR OWNERS YEARNING AS WE YEARN. NEVER- THELESS, IN THE NATURE OF LIFE AND IN THE PRINCIPLES OF EVOLUTION WE HAVE HAD OUR ANSWER. OF MEN ELSE- WHERE, AND BEYOND, THERE WILL BE NONE FOREVER.... LOREN EISELEY, 1946...

AS THE FIRST ASTRONAUT TO SET FOOT ON THE PLANET MARS AND RETURN, TELL US—IS THERE ANY LIFE ON MARS? WELL, THERE'S A LITTLE BIT ON SATURDAY NIGHT, BUT THE REST OF THE WEEK IT'S PRETTY DULL.

LOOK AT THE STARS! LOOK, LOOK UP AT THE SKIES!
 O LOOK AT ALL THE FIRE-FOLK SITTING IN THE AIR!
 THE BRIGHT BOROUGHS, THE CIRCLE CITADELS THERE!
DOWN IN DIM WOODS THE DIAMOND DELVES! THE ELVES'- EYES!
THE GRAY LAWNS COLD WHERE GOLD, WHERE QUICKGOLD LIES!...

GERARD MANLEY HOPKINS, 1877...

"SOMETHING LIKE THIS HAS BEEN TALKED ABOUT AND SPEC- ULATED ABOUT FOR YEARS.... MATHEMATICALLY, IT'S BEEN AN ODDS-ON BET THAT SOMEWHERE IN OUR GALAXY THERE'D BE ANOTHER RACE WITH A CIVILIZATION EQUAL TO OR FURTHER ADVANCED THAN OURS. NOBODY COULD EVER GUESS WHERE OR WHEN WE'D MEET THEM. BUT IT LOOKS LIKE WE'VE DONE IT NOW!"

"D'YOU SUPPOSE THEY'LL BE FRIENDLY, SIR?"

"IT'S MOVING.... HEADING FOR US. JUST WHAT WE'D DO IF A STRANGE SPACESHIP APPEARED IN OUR HUNTING GROUNDS! FRIENDLY? MAYBE! WE'RE GOING TO TRY TO CONTACT THEM. WE HAVE TO. BUT I SUSPECT THIS IS THE END OF THIS EXPEDITION. THANK GOD FOR THE BLASTERS!"... MURRAY LEINSTER, 1945...

THOSE WHO FEEL THAT THE GOOD JUSTIFIES THE GREAT AMOUNT OF EFFORT REQUIRED WILL CONTINUE TO CARRY ON THIS RESEARCH, SUSTAINED BY THE POSSIBILITY THAT SOMETIME IN THE FUTURE, PERHAPS A HUNDRED YEARS FROM NOW, OR PERHAPS NEXT WEEK, THE SEARCH WILL BE SUCCESSFUL. ...FRANK D. DRAKE, 1960...

2

George Thomas — 2027

...a host of phantom listeners
That dwelt in the lone house then
Stood listening in the quiet of the moonlight
To that voice from the world of men...

He came past the saucer-shaped valley lined with metal plates, past the big metal dish fixed against the sky, past the parking lot surfaced with packed white sea shells.

A crater shaped to hold the silence of the stars;
an empty cup waiting patiently to be filled...

He came out of the vertical sunlight into the dark, through the glass doors into the one-story concrete building, down its cool, brightening corridors to the office marked "Director," and past the middle-aged secretary to the office she guarded, where a man stood up behind a desk piled with papers.

They came into the corridor to watch the intruder,
the pallid scientists and their own brown clerks,
their faces furrowed with facts, their eyes empty of
meaning like blind oscilloscopes...

"My name is George Thomas," the newcomer said.

"I'm Robert MacDonald," said the man behind the desk.

They shook hands. MacDonald had a good handshake, Thomas thought, almost gentle but not feeble, as if he didn't have to prove anything.

"I know," Thomas said. "You're director of this Project." A sensitive man could draw inferences from the way he said it; Thomas didn't care.

The room was cool and pleasant and spare, a little like the man who worked in it. The air in the corridor had smelled of machine oil and ozone, but here was a smell that Thomas knew better, a smell that made him feel comfortable, of paper and old books. Behind the simple desk were tall book shelves built into the wall and on the shelves were books with real leather bindings in brown and dark red and dark green. From where he sat Thomas could not quite make out the titles, but from a word or two he could tell that some of them, at least, were in foreign languages.

His fingers twitched to take one in his hands, to feel the grainy, slightly slick texture of its binding, to turn the brittle pages. . . .

"*Era* magazine has commissioned me to do a profile in depth of the Project," Thomas said.

"And kill it."

Thomas was past showing surprise, almost past feeling it, he thought. "To prepare it for burial. It's already dead."

"Do you have reasons for saying so or merely prejudice?"

Thomas shifted in his chair. "The Project has continued for more than fifty years without a positive result. In fifty years even hope dies."

"'There's life in the old girl yet.'"

Thomas recognized the quotation. "Literature survives," he conceded, "but little else." He looked at MacDonald again.

The Director of the Project is forty-nine. He looks it. But his eyes are blue and unfaded, and his long face holds within it the musculature that often accompanies strength of will and sometimes even strength of character.

"Why do you think I intend to kill the Project?"

MacDonald smiled; it illuminated his face. Thomas wondered what it would be like to smile like that.

"*Era* is the magazine of the upper class, many of whom are mandarins, others are technocrats, and some of both are Solitarians; *Era* reinforces their prejudices, bolsters their self-esteem, and supports their interests. The Project threatens all three, in particular the effortless working of our technological society."

"You give our upper classes too much credit; they don't think that deeply."

"*Era* does that for them. And even if this all were not true, the Project still represents for *Era* a tempting target for its arrows of wit, and today's game is to see what you can kill with laughter."

"You do *Era* and me an injustice," Thomas protested casually. "The magazine's motto is 'Truth and Wit.' Note that truth comes first."

"'*Fiat justitia, et pereat mundus,*'" MacDonald murmured.

"'Let justice be done, though the world perish,'" Thomas translated automatically. "Who said that?"

"Emperor Ferdinand I. Do you know of him?"

"There were so many Ferdinands."

"Of course," MacDonald said. "Of course! George Thomas. You did that magnificent translation of the *Commedia*, what, ten-fifteen years ago?"

"Seventeen," Thomas said. He did not like the way the word came out, but it was too late to call it back. He pretended to be trying to read the papers on MacDonald's desk.

"You're a poet, not a reporter. You wrote a novel a few years later, *The Inferno*. About today's damned, with a vision and sensitivity virtually equal to that of its immortal predecessor. It was meant to be the first book of a trilogy, surely. Did I miss the later books?"

"No."

MacDonald had a way of stabbing him with kindliness, Thomas thought. "What a man must be is wise enough to recognize failure and turn to something in which he has some chance of success."

"And a man must believe sufficiently in himself—or in his cause—that he persists in spite of disappointments and the inexorable metronome of the years."

They looked at each other, the older man who was not yet old and the younger man who was no longer young, and they understood each other, Thomas thought.

First a talented linguist, then an indifferent electrical engineer—as if he were deliberately preparing himself for the Project—MacDonald joined the

*Project twenty-one years ago. Five years later he
was named Director. He is said to have a beautiful
wife and a marriage in which there is some hint of
scandal. He has grown old listening for voices he
has yet to hear. And what of George Thomas, poet
and novelist, who found success too soon and fame
too young and discovered that success can be just
another face of failure and fame can be a kind of
death that draws the jackals of both sexes who eat
up time and talent. . . .*

"I'm recording this, you know," Thomas said.

"I thought you were," MacDonald said. "Is this how
you achieve the sound of reality?"

"Partly. But it's not for that. I have a good memory,
and reality doesn't sound as real as you might think. Mostly
I record to placate *Era*'s libel lawyers."

"You are in the right business."

"Reporter?"

"Undertaker."

"I see death all around me."

"I see life."

"Despair."

"Hope. *L'amor che muove il sole e l'altro stelle.*"

He thinks I am still in hell, Thomas thought, that I
have not finished my *Inferno*, and that he is in paradise.
He is a subtle man and knows me better than he lets on.

"Lasciate ogni speranza voi ch'entrate! We understand
each other," Thomas said. "Hope and faith keep this Project going—"

"And scientific probability."

Thomas felt the gentle humming against his belly of
the recorder clipped to his waistband. "That's another
name for faith. And after more than fifty years even scientific probability becomes more than a little improbable.
Perhaps that is what my profile will demonstrate."

"Fifty years is but the flicker of an eyelash on God's
face."

"Fifty years is a man's working life. It has been most
of your life. I don't expect you to give it up without a
struggle, but it won't do you any good. Are you going to
cooperate with me or fight me?"

"Is there anything we can tell you or show you that will change your mind?"

"I'll be as honest with you as I hope you will be with me: I doubt it, not because my mind is closed but because I doubt that there is anything to show. Like any good reporter, I start from a point of basic skepticism; to me this Project looks like the biggest and longest boondoggle of all time, and the only thing that can change my mind is a message."

"From the publisher or from God?"

"From another world. That's what this project is all about, isn't it?"

MacDonald sighed. "Yes, that's what it's all about. Suppose we strike a bargain."

"You know what happens to those who strike bargains with the devil."

"I'll take the chance that you are not the devil but his advocate, a man like the rest of us, lost in hell, with human fears, hopes, and desires—including the desire to seek the truth and, finding it, to communicate it to his fellow beings wherever they are."

"'What is truth?' said jesting Pilate . . ."

"'And would not stay for an answer.' We will stay. The bargain concerns your willingness to do as much. We will cooperate with your investigation if you will listen to what we have to say, and hear, and look at what we have to show, and see."

"Of course. That's what I'm here to do."

"I should tell you that we would have cooperated without your promise."

Thomas smiled. It may have been his first real smile since he entered the room, he thought. "I should tell you that I would have listened and looked without your cooperation."

The sparring was over, and Thomas was not sure who had gained an advantage. He was not used to feeling uncertain at this point, and it bothered him. MacDonald was a formidable opponent—all the more because he truly did not think of himself as an opponent but a colleague in the search for truth—and Thomas knew that he could never relax. He had no doubt that he could destroy MacDonald and the Project, but the game was more complex than that: it had to be played in such a way that the destruction did not include *Era* and Thomas. It was not that Thomas cared about *Era* or Thomas, but he could not lose the game.

Thomas asked MacDonald's permission to photograph him and his papers at his desk and to leaf through the papers on it. MacDonald shrugged.

Upon MacDonald's desk there are books and papers intermingled. The books are Intelligent Life in the Universe *and* The Voices of the Thirties. *The papers are of three kinds: all kinds of letters from many parts of the world, some scientific, some fan mail, some news inquiries, some crackpot notes; inter-Project memorandums, technical and formal; official reports and graphs describing the continuing work of the Project. The last are at the bottom of the neat stack on the left-hand side of the desk, like a reward for plowing through the rest, and the rest are scattered on the right-hand side with brief notes on them about the nature of the response, if any, or routing.*

When Thomas had completed his inspection, MacDonald guided his tour of the building. It was efficient but spartan: painted concrete walls, tiled floors, radiant ceiling fixtures. The offices were standard cubicles, each with its blackboard scribbled with equations or circuit diagrams, individualized only by choice of books, an occasional drape on a window or rug on a floor, and a collection of personal items like clocks, radios, recorders, TVs, pipes, pictures, paintings. . . .

MacDonald introduced Thomas to the professional staff. Olsen, the computer expert, who seemed young for his peppered hair; Sonnenborn, the intense mathematician and historian of intersteller communication, verbal, curious, incisive; Saunders, the slow-talking, pipe-smoking philosopher, the lean,

*sandy designer of proposals and attacks; Adams,
the red-faced, round-faced, sweating electronics
engineer, whose responses tolled his inner doubts . . .*

Thomas picked Adams to guide him through the technical aspects of the Project. The choice was natural; MacDonald could have raised no objections if he had wanted to. He smiled—it was, perhaps, a knowing smile—and said, "You will come home to dinner with me. I want you to meet Maria, and Maria will want to meet you. Bob, tell him anything he wants to know."

With MacDonald's instruction or without, Thomas thought, Adams would be the source of the inside information he needed, not just about techniques and goals but about people, and that was the most important of all. In every group there is an Adams.

The offices were places of quiet, sustained effort. In spite of its continuous history of failure, the Project maintained its morale. The personnel worked as if it were the first year, not the fifty-first.

The technical areas were different; they were lifeless. The computers and the hulking electronic consoles crouched silently, their lights extinguished, their relays stilled. Some of them had their insides spread out in front of them while men in white suits searched through them like diviners seeking oracles in the entrails of chickens. The green windows of their eyes were blank. The hum of their electronic pulse was gone. They were dead, and the sterile white walls of the rooms in which they were laid out was the operating pit in which they had died from lack of meaning.

To Adams it was different. "Here in the daytime it looks normal enough. Everything quiet. Everything in its proper shape. But at night, when the listening begins—Do you believe in ghosts, Mr. Thomas?"

"Every civilization has its ghosts. Usually they are the gods of the last one."

"The ghosts of this civilization are in its machines," Adams said. "Year after year the machines will do your bidding, mechanically, without complaint, and then suddenly they will become possessed and do things for which they were never created, give answers for which they were never questioned, ask questions for which there are no answers. At night these machines come alive. They nod, they wink, they whisper to each other, they chuckle."

Thomas ran his hand along the front of a console. It was slick and dead. "And they tell you nothing."

Adams looked at Thomas. "They tell us a great deal. It just isn't what we asked them for. We don't know the right questions, maybe. Or we don't know how to ask them properly. The machines know. I'm sure of it. They keep telling us, over and over. We just don't understand them. Maybe we don't want to understand them."

Thomas turned toward Adams. "Why not?"

"Maybe they're trying to tell us that there's nobody out there. Think of that! That there's nobody there, nobody but us in the whole wide universe. All of it is just for us, a vast show we can look at but never touch, spread out to impress the only creature capable of understanding it—and capable of feeling lonely."

"Then this whole Project would be folly, wouldn't it?"

Adams shook his head. "Call it man's attempt to stay sane. Because we can't ever know for sure; we can't eliminate all possibilities. So we keep searching because it is too terrifying to give up and admit we are alone."

"Wouldn't it be more terrifying to learn that we are not alone?"

"Do you think so?" Adams asked politely. "Everyone has his own great fear. Mine is that there is no one there, even though my mind tells me that this is what is. I have talked to others who dreaded to hear something, and I couldn't understand them, even though I could understand how they might have feelings I feel stirred by other terrors."

"Tell me how it works," Thomas said politely. There would be time later to exploit Adams' fears.

The listening continues as it began more than fifty years ago, largely by radio waves picked up by radio telescopes; by giant arrays of antennae built into valleys, by smaller steerable dishes, by spiderwebs of metal cast into space. The listening is mostly at the twenty-one-centimeter frequency of neutral hydrogen. Other wavelengths are sampled, but the

*listeners keep returning to nature's standard cali-
brating frequency or its whole multiples. A lifetime
of engineering ingenuity has gone into multiplying
the sensitivity of the receivers and canceling out the
natural noise of the universe and of earth. And after
it all is canceled, what is left—now as then—is
nothing. Zero. And still they listen. And still they
strain their ears to hear.*

"Why don't you quit?" Thomas asked.

"It's been only fifty years or so. That's only a second
of galactic time."

"If somebody or something were signaling, those signals surely would have been heard by now. That must be
clear."

"Perhaps there's nobody there," Adams mused and
then his eyes became aware of Thomas again. "Or maybe
everybody's listening."

Thomas raised his eyebrows.

"It's much cheaper to listen, you know. Much cheaper.
Everybody might be sitting there glued to their receivers,
and nobody's sending. Only we *are* sending."

"We're sending?" Thomas asked quickly. "Who autho-
rized that?"

"This place is pretty uncomfortable if you're not working," Adams said. "Let's get a cup of coffee, and I'll tell
you about it."

The lunchroom was a converted office filled by two
small tables, each with four chairs, and lined on three
sides with coin-operated machines that hummed very softly
as they went about their business of keeping food and
drink hot or cold.

Adams sipped his coffee and went over the entire history of the Project, beginning with Project Ozma and the
inspired speculations of Cocconi, Morrison, and Drake,
and the subsequent contributions of Bracewell, Townes,
and Schwartz, Oliver, Golay, Dyson, von Hoerner,
Shklovsky, Sagan, Struve, Atchley, Calvin, Huang, and
Lilly whose efforts to communicate with the dolphin gave
to the infant group the name "order of the dolphin."

From the first it was clear that there *ought* to be other
intelligent creatures in the universe. The process of planet

formation, once thought to be the chance (and unlikely) near-collision of two stars, was recognized as a natural occurrence when stars were forming out of gaseous clouds and rock and metal fragments. One or two percent of the stars in our galaxy probably had planets which could support life. Since there were 150 billion stars in our galaxy, at least a billion, perhaps two or three, had habitable planets.

"One billion solar systems where life can develop!" Adams said. "And it seems reasonable to assume that where life can develop it will develop."

"Life, yes, but man is unique," Thomas said.

"Are you a Solitarian?" Adams asked.

"No, but that is not to say that I do not consider some of their beliefs well founded."

"Perhaps man is unique," Adams said, "although there are many galaxies. But is intelligence unique? It has high survival value. Once it has occurred, even by accident, it is likely to prevail."

"But technology is another thing," Thomas said, sipping his hot black coffee.

"Quite another thing," Adams agreed. "It happened to us only very recently, you know, about midway during the main sequence time of our sun during which life can be expected to exist. Hominids have lived on Earth only for one-tenth of one percent of Earth's existence, civilization has existed for about one-millionth of Earth's lifespan, and technical civilization, only one-billionth. Considering the late emergence of all three and the fact that there must be older planets, if there is intelligent life on other worlds some of it must be farther advanced than we, and some, much farther advanced. But—"

"But—"

"But why don't we hear from them?" Adams cried out.

"Have you tried everything?"

"Not only the radio frequencies—we've explored gamma rays, lasers, neutrinos, even long-chain molecules in carbonaceous meteorites and absorption lines in the spectrum of stars. The only thing we haven't tried is 'Q' waves."

"What are those?"

Adams was absently sketching diagrams on the gray

surface of the table. Thomas noticed that the table was covered with fainter, washed-away marks where others had sketched. "What Morrison many years ago called 'the method we haven't discovered yet but are going to discover ten years from now,'" Adams said. "Only we haven't discovered it. The only other thing we haven't tried is sending messages. That's more expensive. We could never find the funds—not now, not without some hope of success. Even then we would have to decide whether we wish to broadcast to the universe or even to one solar system the presence here of intelligent, civilized life."

"But we are sending, you said."

"We've been sending since the earliest days of radio," Adams said. "Low power, most of it, unbeamed, loaded with static and other interfering transmissions, but intelligent life has made Earth the second most powerful radio source in the solar system, and in a few more decades we may equal the sun itself. If there's anybody out there to notice, that should make Earth visible."

"But you haven't heard anything?"

"What would we hear on this little apparatus?" Adams asked, nodding toward the valley beyond the walls. "What we need is some time on the Big Ear upstairs, the five-mile-in-diameter net, or the new net being built, but the astronomers won't give us the time of day."

"Why don't you quit?"

"He won't let us!"

"He?"

"Mac. No, that's not right. Yes, it is. He keeps us together, he and Maria. There was a time, not so long ago, when it looked as if it would all come apart...."

Thomas took another sip of coffee. It was cool enough to drink now, and he swallowed it all.

The drive to MacDonald's house in the Puerto Rican hills was pleasant as the day closed. The shadows draped themselves across the green slopes like the legs of purple giants. The evening breeze blew the sharp scent of salt in from the ocean. The elderly steam turbine under the hood hummed along with only an occasional vibration to betray its age.

This place must be the cleanest, quietest spot in the

whole dirty, noisy world, Thomas thought, like paradise, innocent, before the knowledge of good and evil. Like a carrier I bring the dirt and noise with me. He felt a moment of irritation that this place should exist in a world of misery and boredom and a flash of satisfaction that he had the power to destroy it.

"Did you learn all you wanted from Adams?"

"What?" Thomas said. "Oh, yes. That and more."

"I thought you would. He's a good man, Bob, a man you can count on when you need a friend, a man you can call at home in the middle of the night to say that a tire has gone flat in a rainstorm, and you know he'll come. He talks a lot and complains a lot. Don't let that keep you from seeing the person underneath."

"What of the things he told me am I not to believe?" Thomas asked.

"Believe it all," MacDonald said. "Bob wouldn't tell you anything but the truth. But there is something misleading in too much truth, even more, perhaps, than too little."

"Like your wife's attempted suicide?"

"Like that."

"And the resignation you tore up?"

"That, too."

Thomas could not tell whether there was sorrow in MacDonald's voice or fear of exposure or merely recognition of the irrepressible evils of the world.

As we drive toward his home in the hills near Arecibo, hills as silent as the voices for which he listens in the concrete building we had left, he does not deny that his wife attempted suicide a year ago or that he wrote a letter of resignation and later tore it up.

The house was a Spanish-style hacienda looking friendly and warm in the gathering darkness, beams of yellow light pouring from door and window. Stepping into the house, Thomas felt it even more, the lived-in, loved-in feeling that he had known only once or twice before in the homes of friends. To those homes he had returned more than to others, to warm himself in their relationship, until he realized what was happening to him. He would stop writing. He would look for someone to ease the ache he had inside, and he would end with a casual affair which would turn to revulsion. He would flee back to his solitary life, back to his writing, to work out on his typewriter keys the agony that pulsed through his veins. And the writing would be twisted and angry like the infernal regions he described. Why hadn't he written his purgatory? He knew why: under his fingers it kept turning back into hell.

Maria MacDonald was a mature, olive-skinned woman whose beauty went deep. She was dressed in a simple peasant blouse and skirt, and she held his hand in hers and bade him welcome to her home. He felt himself warming to her gentle smile and Latin American courtesy, and fought it. He wanted to kiss her hand. He wanted to turn it over and see the scar upon her wrist. He wanted to take her in his arms and protect her against the terrors of the night.

He did none of these. He said, "I'm here, you know, to do a piece about the Project, and I'm afraid it will not be favorable."

She turned her head a little to one side to study him. "You are not an unfriendly man, I think. You are a disappointed man, perhaps. Perhaps bitter. But you are honest. You wonder how I know these things. I have a sense about people, Mr. Thomas. Robby brings them home to me before he hires them, and I tell him about them and not once have I been wrong. Have I, Robby?"

MacDonald smiled. "Only once."

"That is a joke," Maria said. "He means I was wrong about him, but that is another story that I will tell you some time if I come to know you better, as I hope. I have this sense, Mr. Thomas, and more—I have read your translation and I have read your novel, too, which Robby tells me you have not continued. You must, Mr. Thomas. It is not good to live in the inferno. One must know it, yes, so that one can comprehend the purging of the sins that one must go through to achieve paradise."

"It was easy to write about hell," Thomas said, "but I found it impossible to imagine anything else."

"You have not yet burned away your deadly sins," Maria said. "You have not yet found anything to believe in, anything to love. Some people never find that, and it is very sad. I feel so sad for them. Do not be one of them. But I am too personal—"

"No, no—"

"You are here to enjoy our hospitality, not to endure my missionary zeal for love and marriage. But I cannot help it, you see." And she put one arm through her husband's and offered the other to Thomas as they went from the entryway down the hall tiled with terra cotta to the living room. A bright Mexican rug covered part of the polished oak floor. There, in big leather chairs, they had salty margaritas and casual conversation about New York and San Francisco and friends they might have in common, the literary life, and the political scene, and where *Era* fitted into both, and how Thomas had started writing for the magazine.

Then Maria ushered them into dinner. They sat down to what she called a "traditional Mexican *comida*." The first course was soup swarming with dumplinglike tortilla balls, vegetables, noodles, and pieces of chicken. The second course was *sopa seca*, a highly seasoned dish of rice, noodles, and cut-up tortillas in an elaborate sauce; then a fish course was followed by a salad and a main course of *cabrito*, roasted young goat, and several vegetables, and this was followed by refried beans smothered with grated cheese. With it all came feathery hot tortillas in napkin-lined baskets. The dinner ended, none too soon for Thomas, with a caramelized milk pudding Maria called "natillas piuranas," with strong black coffee, and with fresh fruit.

Protesting feebly, as the meal progressed, that he could eat no more, Thomas surrendered to Maria's insistence and ate something of each dish as it appeared, until MacDonald laughed and said, "You have fed him too much, Maria. He will be good for nothing for the rest of the evening, and we still have work to do. The Latin Americans, Mr. Thomas, have this kind of meal only upon special occasions, and then in the middle of the day after which they retire for a well-deserved siesta."

MacDonald filled their glasses with a brandy he called "pisco." "May I propose a toast," he said. "To beauty and good food!"

"To good listening!" said Maria.

"To truth!" Thomas said, to prove that he had not been charmed nor fed into complete subjugation, but his eyes were on the white line that cut across Maria's olive wrist.

"You have noticed my scar," Maria said. "That is a reminder of my folly that I will bear with me always."

"Not your folly," MacDonald said, "my deafness."

"It was a little more than a year ago," Maria said, "and I was feeling a little crazy. I could see that it was not going well with the Project and Robby was wearing down between the demands of keeping the Project going and his worry over me. It was madness, I know now, but I thought I could remove one of Robby's concerns by removing myself. I tried suicide with a razor blade, and I almost died. But I lived, and I found my sanity again, and Robby and I found each other again."

"We were never lost," MacDonald said. "We had just, temporarily, out of human inattention, stopped listening to each other."

"But you knew all this, didn't you, Mr. Thomas?" Maria said. "Are you married?"

"I was once," Thomas said.

"And it was wrong," Maria said. "That is sad. You must be married. You must have someone to love, someone to love you. Then you can write your *Purgatory*, your *Paradise*."

An infant cried somewhere in the house. Maria looked up happily. "And Robby and I found something else."

She moved gracefully from the room and returned in a moment with a baby in her arms. It was two or three months old, Thomas thought, and it had dark hair and bright dark eyes in an olive face, like its mother, and the eyes seemed to see Thomas where he stood by the dinner table.

"This is Bobby, our son," Maria said. If she had been alive before, she was doubly alive now, Thomas thought. This was the magnetism that turned painters toward madonnas for their subjects.

"We were lucky," MacDonald said. "We waited a long time to have a child, but Bobby came easily and he is normal, not handicapped as are some children of older parents. I think he will grow up to be an ordinary boy burdened with the love of parents old enough to be his grandparents, and I only hope we can understand him."

"I hope he can understand you," Thomas said, and then, "Mrs. MacDonald, why don't you make your husband give up this hopeless Project?"

"I don't make Robby do anything," Maria said. "The Project is his life, just as he and Bobby are my life. You think there is something bad about it, a treachery, a deception, but you do not know my husband or the men he has gathered to work with him if you honestly think that. They believe in what they are doing."

"Then they are fools."

"No, the fools are those who do not believe, who cannot believe. It may be that there is no one out there or if there is someone out there he will never speak to us or we to him, but our listening is an act of faith akin to living itself. If we should stop listening, we would begin dying and we would soon be gone, the world and its people, our technical civilization and even the farmers and peasants, because life is faith, life is commitment. Death is giving up."

"You have not seen the world the way I have seen it," Thomas said. "It is dying."

"Not while men like these still strive," Maria said.

"You give us too much credit," MacDonald said.

"No, I do not," Maria said to Thomas. "My husband is a great man. He listens with his heart. Before you leave this island, you will know that, and you will believe. I have seen others come like you, doubting, eager to destroy, and Robby has taken them in, has given them faith and hope, and they have left, believing."

"I do not intend to be taken in," Thomas said.

"You know what I meant."

"I know that I wish I had someone who believed in me the way you believe in your husband."

"We'd better go back," MacDonald said. "I have something to show you."

Thomas said good-bye to Maria MacDonald and thanked her for her hospitality and for her personal concern for him, and he turned and left the hacienda. When he was outside in the darkness he turned once and looked back at the house with the light pouring from it and the woman standing in the doorway of the house with a baby in her arms.

The difference between day and night is of another order than the difference between light and dark. After the sun has set, the familiar assumes different proportions: distances are elongated and objects shift their places.

As MacDonald and Thomas made their way past the valley into whose arms had been built the semisteerable radio telescope, it was not the same sterile saucer. It was a pit of mystery and shadows gathering strange echoes from the sky within its sheltered bowl, catching the stardust that drifted gently, gently through the night air.

The steerable dish that had been frozen in deathlike rigor against the sky now was alive and questing. Thomas thought he could see it quivering as it strained toward the silent dark.

The Little Ear, they called it, this giant piece of precision machinery, the largest steerable radio telescope on Earth, to distinguish it from the Big Ear, the five-mile-in-diameter network of cables in orbit. At night the visitor can sense the magic it works upon the men who think they work their will upon it. For these obsessed men, it is an ear, their ear, cocked responsively toward the silent stars, with supernal power and ingenious filters and bypasses, listening to the infinite and hearing only the slow heartbeat of the eternal.

"We inherited it from the astronomers," MacDonald was saying, "when they put up the first radio telescopes on the far side of the moon and then the first of the networks in space. The earthbound equipment no longer was worth anything, rather like an old crystal set when vacuum tubes were perfected. Instead of junking these instruments, however, they give them to us with a small budget for operation."

"Over the decades, the total must mount toward the astronomical," Thomas said, trying to shake away the effects of the evening's hospitality and the night's spells.

"It adds up," MacDonald agreed, "and we fight for our

lives every year. But there are returns. One might compare the Project to a hothouse for intellects, a giant continuing, unsolvable puzzle against which the most promising minds pit themselves and grow strong. We get the young scientists and engineers and train them and send them on to solve problems which have solutions: The Project has a surprising number of alumni, many of them overachieving."

"Is that how you justify the Project, as a kind of graduate school?"

"Oh, no. That is what our predecessors used to call fall-out or spin-off. Our ultimate goal and our most valuable goal is communication with other beings on other worlds. I offer you reasons that you may use to justify us if you cannot bring yourself to accept us as we are."

"Why would I want to justify you?"

"That you will have to find out for yourself."

Then they were inside the building, and it was different, too. The corridors that had seemed brisk and businesslike in the daytime now were charged with energy and purpose. The control room had been touched by the forefinger of God; where death had been there was life: lights came on and turned off, oscilloscopic eyes were alive with green linear motion, the relays of the consoles clicked gently, the computers chuckled to themselves, electricity whispered along wires.

Adams was seated at the control panel. He had earphones on his head, and his eyes studied the gauges and oscilloscopes spread before him. As they entered, he looked up and waved. MacDonald's eyebrows lifted; Adams shrugged. He pulled the earphones down around his neck. "The usual nothing."

"Here," MacDonald said, removing the earphones and handing them to Thomas. "You listen."

Thomas put one of the receivers to his ear.

First comes babble, like a multitude of voices heard afar or a stream rippling over a bed of rocks, squirting through crevices, and dashing itself over small waterfalls. Then the sounds grow louder, and they are voices talking earnestly but all together so that none can be heard individually but confused and one. The listener strains to hear, and all his effort only makes the voices more eager to be heard, and they talk louder still and even more indistinguishably. Like Dante, the listener "stood on the edge of the descent where the hollow of the gulf out of despair amasses thunder of infinite lament." And the voices change from eager pleadings to angry shouts, as if, like damned souls, they demand salvation from the flames in which they burn. They turn upon the listener as if to destroy him for temerity in thrusting himself among fallen angels, in all their arrogance and sinful pride. "Above I saw a thousand spirits in air rained down from heaven, who angry as if betrayed cried: 'Who is this who without death doth dare the kingdom of the dead folk to invade?'" And the listener thinks that he is one of those who shouts to be heard, damned like them in hell, able only to scream at the torment and the frustration of having no one to listen to him and to care what happens to him and to understand. "Even then I heard on all sides wailing sound, but of those making it saw no one nigh, wherefore I stood still, in amazement bound." And the listener thinks he is among giants "whose rebellious pride Jove's thunderings out of heaven still appall." All of them, like him, struggle to be heard in their mighty voices and cannot be understood. "Raphael may amech zabi almi, throat brutish mouth incontinently cried; and they were fitted for no sweeter note." And the listener felt as if consciousness were about to leave him.

And the voices were gone. MacDonald was lifting the earphones from his ears where, Thomas vaguely recalled, he had placed them himself. And he was shaken by the overpowering influence of those sounds, those voices, all kinds of voices struggling to be heard, blending together into an alien chorus, each participant singing a different song. . . .

Thomas had a moment of self-revelation in which he knew that he was lost, like the voices, and he would have to find his way out or be damned to live forever within his fleshy prison, as alone in his torment as if he were in hell itself.

"What was that?" he asked, and his voice was shaky.

"The sound of the infinite," MacDonald said. "We translate the radio signals into audio frequencies. It doesn't help us pick up anything. If anything is there it would show up on the tapes, the dials would flash, the computer would sound an alarm; it wouldn't come out as voice communication. But there is inspiration in hearing something when you're listening, and we need inspiration."

"I call it hypnosis," Thomas said. "It can help convince the doubtful that there really is something there, that they someday may be able to hear clearly what now they imagine, that there really are aliens out there trying to communicate—and it's only a trick to fool yourselves and perpetrate a fraud upon the world."

"Some are more susceptible than others," MacDonald said. "I'm sorry you took it as a personal attack. We aren't playing tricks. You knew there was no communication there."

"Yes," Thomas said, and it angered him that his voice still was shaky.

"But this is not what I wanted you to hear. This is background. Let's go to my office. You, too, Bob. Leave the watch to the technician. It doesn't matter."

They went to the office, the three of them, and settled into chairs. MacDonald's desk was clear now, waiting for the next day's deposit. But the scent of old books remained. Thomas rubbed his hands over the slick wooden arms of his chair and watched MacDonald.

"It isn't going to work," Thomas said. "Not all the hypnotic sounds in the world or the pleasant company or delightful meals or beautiful women or touching family scenes can ever compensate for the fact that this Project has been going on for more than fifty years and you haven't yet received a message."

"That's what I brought you here to say," MacDonald said. "We have."

"You haven't!" Adams said. "Why didn't I know?"

"We haven't been sure. We weren't sure until last night. We have had false alarms before, and they have been our most difficult moments. Saunders knew. It was his baby."

"The tapes from the Big Ear," Adams said.

"Yes. Saunders has been working with them, trying to clean them up. Now we're sure. Tomorrow morning I'm calling together the whole crew. We'll announce it." He turned to Thomas. "But I want your advice."

"You aren't going to try to trick me with something like this, are you, MacDonald?" Thomas asked. "The coincidence is too much."

"Coincidences happen," MacDonald said. "History is full of them. The projects that succeed, the concepts that prevail, somehow are rescued from destruction by the coincidence that arrives just before the moment of final success."

"And then to ask for help," Thomas continued. "That is the oldest ploy of all."

"Don't forget, Mr. Thomas," MacDonald said, "we are scientists. We have been searching for fifty years and more without success; we have stopped thinking, if we ever did, about what we would do if we succeeded. We need help. You know people and how to move them, what they will accept and reject, how they will react to the unknown. It is all quite logical and natural."

"It's too pat. I don't believe it."

"Believe him, George," Adams said. "He never lies."

"Everyone lies," Thomas said.

"He's right, Bob," MacDonald said. "But you will believe it, Mr. Thomas, because it's true and because it's verifiable and reproducible, and when it is released, if that is what we do with it, all the scientists will say, 'Why, yes. It's right. That's the way it would be.' Why would I fabricate something that could be so easily disproved and wreck this Project more thoroughly than anything you might write?"

"I've heard that someone who wants out of service should complain of pains in the back or voices in the head, neither of which can be disproved," Thomas said.

"The physical sciences are not subjective. And anything this big will be checked and checked again by every astronomer everywhere."

"Perhaps you hope to con me into killing the whole thing in the name of public morale."

"Can I con you, Mr. Thomas?"

"No," Thomas said, and remembered the voices and said, "I don't know. Why now? Why at this moment when I came to do this profile?"

"I don't want to minimize the significance of your assignment," MacDonald said, "but you are not the first writer to come here to do a story. We have a reporter here every week or so. It would be strange if we did not have a reporter here within a day or two of the time we received our first message. It just happened to be you."

"Well," Thomas said, "what is it? How did you stumble across it?"

"We began getting tapes from the Big Ear about a year ago—tapes of their routine radio telescopy—and began to analyze them. Saunders ran them through the computer, earphones and all, and one day he thought he heard music and voices.

"His first thought was 'delusion,' but the computer said no. Saunders did what he could to clarify them, reinforce them, subtract the noise and interference. We've developed a lot of tricks in the past fifty years. The music came through recognizably and the voices, in snatches, even better. And the voices were speaking English.

"His second thought was that the Big Ear had picked up some stray transmissions from Earth or maybe something bounced off one of the other planets. But the net wasn't pointed toward Earth or another planet. It was pointed off into space. There were other tapes going back several years, and when the Big Ear was pointed in a certain direction it got the same signals."

"What were they?" Thomas asked.

"For God's sake, Mac, let's hear it!" Adams said.

MacDonald pushed one of the buttons on his desk.

"Understand," MacDonald said, "that there was much more interference, but for this purpose Saunders cut out almost all the nonintelligible parts. The ratio of noise to sound was about fifty to one, so you're hearing only about one-fiftieth of what we have."

The sound was monophonic, although it came from two speakers built into the walls to the right and left. The impact was nothing like that of the headphones in the

control room, but the sounds had a fascination akin, perhaps, to that of the early days of radio when people sat
around a crystal set straining at faint sounds, trying to
pick up Schenectady or Pittsburgh or Fort Worth. The
sounds were radiant, Thomas thought, with the possibility
that they came from another world—or with the improb-
ability that they could have come from anywhere but Earth.

*The sounds are earthly. That is certain. There is
music, all based on the chromatic scale, and some
of it familiar, the William Tell Overture, for instance. And there are the voices, speaking English
most of them but also Russian, French, Italian, German, Spanish, English. Music. From another world?
It doesn't make sense. And yet we listen.*

*The transmission is bad. Static and other random
interruptions at times obscure whatever is being
transmitted, and what comes through is broken into
fragments, occasionally understandable, mostly
cryptic, none complete, each in a different voice.
Here, indeed, is Babel, but Babel in which enough
is clear that the listeners feel that all should make
sense.*

*For a few moments the music or the voices come
through clearly, fading in and fading back out as
the noise level rises. The listeners waver between
the impression that the voices are the dominant element occasionally interrupted by noise and the
impression that the transmission of noise is occasionally interrupted by voices.*

*Like a Greek chorus, the voices chant their lines
and imbue them with a Delphic obscurity. The listeners lean forward as if it will help them hear a
little better....*

*POPCRACKLE ice regusted CRACKLEPOP mu-
sic: that little chatterbox the one with the pretty
POPPOPCRACKLE wanna buy a duck POP-
CRACKLEPOP masked champion of justice*

CRACKLEPOPPOP music POPPOPPOPCRACK-
LE ter eleven book one hundred and POPCRACK-
LEPOP here they come jack POPPOP music
CRACKLE yoo hoo is anybody POPCRACKLE is
raymond your POPCRACKLEPOPPOP music
POPPOPCRACKLE music: wave the flag for hud-
son CRACKLEPOP um a bad boy POPPOPPOP
lux presents holly CRACKLECRACKLE music
POPPOPCRACKLE rogers in the twenty POP-
CRACKLEPOP music: cola hits the spot twelve
CRACKLE say goodnight grace POPPOP music
CRACKLEPOP could have knocked me over with
a fender POPCRACKLECRACKLE knee this is ro-
chest CRACKLEPOP music CRACKLEPOPPOP-
POP matinee idol larry POPPOP music: au revoir
pleasant CRACKLECRACKLE the little theater off
POPPOPCRACKLE eye doodit CRACKLEPOP
music POPPOPPOP who knows what evil POP-
CRAKLEPOP voss you dare shar CRACKLEPOP
you have a friend and adviser in CRACKLECRACK-
LE music POPCRACKLEPOP another trip down
allens POPPOPCRACKLE stay tuned for POP-
CRACKLE music: bar ba sol bar POP you termites
flophouse CRACKLEPOPPOPPOP at the chime
it will be ex CRACKLECRACKLEPOP people
defender of POPPOP music POPCRACKLE the
only thing we have to fear CRACKLE and now vic
and POPPOPPOP duffy ain't here CRACKLEPOP
music POPCRACKLEPOP information plea
CRACKLECRACKLE music: boo boo boo boo
POPPOPCRACKLE can a woman over thirty-five
CRACKLEPOPPOPPOP adventures of sher
POPCRACKLECRACKLE music POPPOP it's a
bird CRACKLE only genuine wrigley's POPCRACK-
LE born edits the news CRACKLECRACKLEPOP
hello everybody POPCRACKLEPOP music POP-
POPCRACKLE that's my boy CRACKLE check and
double POP

After the voices and the static had stopped, Thomas
turned to look at MacDonald. He had more than half an
hour of it on his own recorder, but he wasn't sure what

he was going to do with it or even what he thought about it. "What does it mean?"

"It's from Earth," Adams said.

"We start with that," MacDonald said. He turned and selected a book from the shelf behind him. "Take a look at this," he said to Thomas, "and maybe you'll understand it better."

The book was *The Voices of the Thirties*. Thomas leafed through it. He looked up. "This is about the early days of radio, more than ninety years ago."

"What we heard," MacDonald said, "as you would discover from this book and others if you made a careful study, was broadcast during that period; music, news, comedy, drama, adventure, what they called soap operas, mysteries, fireside chats, agony shows. . . . There was a great deal of foreign language fragments, too, but we screened them out."

"You think I'm going to believe that you received this nonsense from the stars?"

"Yes," MacDonald said. "This is what the Big Ear picked up when the astronomers listened in a direction about five-hours' right ascension, about fifty-six degrees declension, in the general direction of Capella—"

"How could Capella be sending us this Earth garbage?"

"I didn't say it was Capella," MacDonald said, "just that it was in that general direction."

"Of course," Adams said.

"It's too ridiculous," Thomas said.

"I agree," MacDonald said. "So ridiculous that it must be true. Why would I try to deceive you with something so transparently foolish when it would be simple to plant some signals almost indistinguishable from noise. Even these could be proven false in time, but we could brazen it out and maybe pick up some real signals before our deception was discovered. But this! Easily checked—and too ridiculous not to be true."

"But it's—how could Capella—or whatever—be sending—?"

"We've been listening for fifty years," MacDonald said, "but we've been transmitting for more than ninety years."

"We've been transmitting?"

"I told you, remember?" Adams said. "Ever since radio transmission began, these relatively feeble radio waves have been spreading through the universe at a speed of 186,000 miles per second."

"Capella is about forty-five light-years from Earth," MacDonald said.

"Forty-five years for the radio waves to get there," Adams said.

"Forty-five years to get back," MacDonald added.

"It's bouncing off Capella?" Thomas said.

"The signals are being sent back. They're being picked up near Capella and beamed directly back to us in a powerful, directional transmission," MacDonald said.

"Is this possible?"

"We couldn't do it," Adams said. "Not with the equipment we have now. A really big antenna in space—perhaps deep in space, far from the sun—would be able to pick up stray radio transmissions, even feeble ones like those in our early transmission history, from a hundred light-years away or more. Perhaps we would find that the galaxy is humming with radio traffic."

"Even so, it is surprising that we can discern anything at all across forty-five light-years and back. The stray signals arriving at Capella must be incredibly faint, scarcely distinguishable from noise," MacDonald said. "Of course they may be using other devices—perhaps a receiver relatively close to Earth, in the asteroid belt, for instance, which could pick up our radio broadcasts and beam them directly at Capella. This would imply, of course, that this solar system has been visited by aliens—or at least by their automated pick-up and transmission devices. It doesn't matter. The fact is that we are receiving a delayed rebroadcast, ninety years out of our past."

"But why would they do that, even if they could?" Thomas protested.

"Can you think of a better way to catch our attention?" MacDonald asked. "To tell us they know we're here and that they are there? A signal we can't miss?"

"Just a big hello?"

"That wouldn't be all," Adams said.

MacDonald nodded. "Some of the static may not be static. There seems to be some kind of order to some of it, a series of pulses, groups of on-off signals, a series of numbers, or a message in linear form or something that might make a picture if we knew how to put them together. Maybe it's nothing; maybe it's some early telegraphy. We don't know yet, but Saunders and the computers are working on it."

"It's the beginning," Thomas said. He could feel his pulse beating faster and his palms beginning to perspire. He had not felt like this since he was working on *The Inferno*.

"We are not alone," Adams said.

"What could they have said to us?" Thomas asked.

"We'll find out," MacDonald said.

"And then—?" Thomas asked.

"There's that," MacDonald agreed. "Just as there is the question before us now of how we announce what we have discovered or if we announce it at all. How will people react to the demonstrated fact of other intelligent beings in the galaxy? Will they be terrified, angry, curious, pleased, excited, exultant? Will they feel proud or suddenly inferior?"

"You've got to announce it," Thomas said. He had a deep conviction that he was right. This too was something he had not felt for a long time.

"Will they understand?"

"We must make them understand. There's a race of intelligent beings out there on a world something like ours, and they must have a great deal to say to us. What great news for humanity! It demands not fear but celebration. We must get people to see that, to feel it."

"I don't know how."

"You're joking," Thomas said. He was smiling. "You've handled me like a master psychologist, steering me the way you wanted me to go each step of the way. No matter. I'll help. I can get others. We'll communicate every way we can think of: articles, television, books, fact and fiction, interviews, polls, games, toys.... We'll make the Project the doorway to a new world and this Earth needs one right now. It's bored with what it has, and boredom is an enduring danger to the human spirit—"

"We mustn't forget," Adams said, "that there's a world of intelligent creatures near Capella who have sent us a message, who are waiting for a response. That's the main thing."

"They aren't human, you know," MacDonald said. "In fact, their environment is markedly different. Capella is a red giant—or rather twin red giants—somewhat cooler than our sun but much larger and brighter."

"And probably older, if our theories of stellar evolution are correct," Adams said.

"Capella's suns are what our sun may become in a galactic decade or two," MacDonald said. "Think what it must have meant to have evolved with two red giant suns in the sky, with the irregularities in light and dark and in orbit itself, in the nature of the world one lives on, its growing conditions, its extremes of heat and cold! What kind of creatures will have survived such conditions—and thrived?"

"What strange viewpoints they must have!" Thomas said. "Dante descended into hell to find out how other creatures lived and what they thought. Our creatures are much more alien, and all we have to do is listen."

"We, too, have our descents into hell," MacDonald said.

"I know. Are you going to tell your staff tomorrow?"

"If you think it's wise."

"It's necessary, wise or not. Urge everyone, for now, to treat the information as confidential. I'll write my profile for *Era*, with your permission, but it will be a little different from the one they expected."

"*Era* would be ideal, but would they print it?"

"For an exclusive like this, they would come out in favor of communicating with Satan and all his fallen angels. They'll toss the Solitarians into the inferno and lead the mandarins and the technocrats into the promised land. Meanwhile, I'll recruit some colleagues and we'll have a series of stories and interviews ready for all the media when *Era* hits the mail."

"It sounds good," MacDonald said.

"Meanwhile," Thomas said, "here's a thought for you: do the Capellans understand the radio transmissions they receive from Earth? And are they judging our civilization by our soap operas?"

Thomas stood up and turned off his recorder. "It's been a good day," he said. "I'll see you in the morning." And he started for the door, and, although he didn't know it until later, approached his purgatory.

COMPUTER RUN

NO FIELD OF INQUIRY IS MORE FASCINATING THAN A SEARCH FOR HUMANITY, OR SOMETHING LIKE HUMANITY, IN THE MYSTERY-FILLED HAPPY LANDS BEYOND THE BARRIERS OF INTERSTELLAR SPACE. …HARLOW SHAPLEY, 1958…

THE STRAY SIGNALS LIKELY TO REACH US FROM A SOPHISTICATED SOCIETY TEN LIGHT-YEARS AWAY ARE LIKELY TO BE TOO WEAK FOR DETECTION BY PRESENT ANTENNAS, BUT IT IS POSSIBLE TO PUT ANTENNAS IN ORBIT OR ON THE MOON WHICH WOULD HAVE MANY LISTENING ADVANTAGES. ANTENNAS AS LARGE AS 10,000 FEET IN DIAMETER MIGHT BE FEASIBLE IN SPACE, AND THEY COULD PROBABLY DETECT EMISSIONS GENERATED BY THE NORMAL ACTIVITY OF A CIVILIZATION TENS OF LIGHT-YEARS AWAY. ANALYSIS OF THE TAPE-RECORDED RECEPTIONS OF SEARCH ANTENNAS IN SUCH A PROJECT WOULD BE TEDIOUS, BUT THE JOB COULD PROBABLY BE HANDLED BY COMPUTERS.….J. A. WEBB, 1961…

THE CODED-PULSE METHOD OF "PILING UP SIGNALS" TO BRING THEM UP ABOVE THE BACKGROUND NOISE SUGGESTS THAT OUR CIVILIZATION MAY ITSELF BE EASILY DETECTABLE, DESPITE OUR FAILURE TO SEND SIGNALS FOR THE PURPOSE.….FRANK D. DRAKE, 1964…

> THOUGH I AM OLD WITH WANDERING
> THROUGH HOLLOW LANDS AND HILLY
>   LANDS,
> I WILL FIND OUT WHERE SHE HAS GONE,
> AND KISS HER LIPS AND TAKE HER HANDS;
> AND WALK AMONG LONG DAPPLED GRASS,
> AND PLUCK TILL TIME AND TIMES ARE DONE
> THE SILVER APPLES OF THE MOON,
> THE GOLDEN APPLES OF THE SUN.
>   WILLIAM BUTLER YEATS, 1899…

SCIENTISTS TODAY MADE THE MILK-COW OBSOLETE.

THEY CREATED THE FIRST MILK-MAKING MACHINE. THROUGH A PROCESS WHICH DUPLICATES THE BIOLOGICAL AND CHEMICAL RE-ACTIONS WITHIN THE ANIMAL, WITH CERTAIN TECHNICAL IMPROVE-MENTS TO ELIMINATE UNNECESSARY BY-PRODUCTS. SCIENTISTS PUT GRASS INTO ONE END OF THE MECHANICAL COW AND DREW FRESH MILK OUT OF THE OTHER. THE PROCESS IS CAPABLE OF OPERATING AT NINETY PERCENT EFFICIENCY AND CAN OPERATE ON WOOD PULP, STRAW, OR EVEN OLD PAPERS AND BOXES, THUS PROVIDING AN-OTHER METHOD FOR ELIMINATING OR RECYCLING THE WASTES OF CIVILIZATION....

HE STOPPED SHORT. TENSENESS FLAMED ALONG HIS NERVES. HIS MUSCLES PRESSED WITH SUDDEN, UNRELENTING STRENGTH AGAINST HIS BONES. HIS GREAT FORELEGS—TWICE AS LONG AS HIS HINDLEGS—TWITCHED WITH A SHUDDERING MOVEMENT THAT ARCHED EVERY RAZOR-SHARP CLAW. THE THICK TENTACLES THAT SPROUTED FROM HIS SHOULDERS CEASED THEIR WEAVING UNDULATION, AND GREW TAUT WITH ANXIOUS ALERTNESS.

UTTERLY APPALLED, HE TWISTED HIS GREAT CAT HEAD FROM SIDE TO SIDE, WHILE THE LITTLE HAIRLIKE TENDRILS THAT FORMED EACH EAR VIBRATED FRANTICALLY, TESTING EVERY VAGRANT BREEZE, EVERY THROB IN THE ETHER.

BUT THERE WAS NO RESPONSE, NO SWIFT TINGLING ALONG HIS INTRICATE NERVOUS SYSTEM, NOT THE FAINTEST SUGGESTION ANY-WHERE OF THE PRESENCE OF THE ALL-NECESSARY ID. HOPELESSLY, COEURL CROUCHED, AN ENORMOUS CATLIKE FIGURE SILHOUETTED AGAINST THE DIM REDDISH SKYLINE, LIKE A DISTORTED ETCHING OF A BLACK TIGER RESTING ON A BLACK ROCK IN A SHADOW WORLD.... A. E. VAN VOGT, 1939...

> BELLATRIX, POLLUX, MIZAR, SPICA,
> ANTARES, CASTOR, ALGOL, MIRA,
> > ACHERNAR
> > BARNARD'S STAR
> PROCYON, REGULUS, RIGEL, SIRIUS,
> ALDEBARAN, DENEBOLA, ARCTURUS,
> > BOLIDE
> > CEPHEID
> ALGIEBA, GEMMA, CANOPUS,
> ALPHA CENTAURI, TAU CETI, POLARIS,
> > QUASAR

WOLF-RAYET STAR
BETELGEUSE, ALTAIR, MIRACH, VEGA,
FOMALHAUT, DENEB, AND CAPELLA,
PULSAR
NEUTRON STAR...

BRAZIL HAS ACHIEVED ZERO POPULATION GROWTH, THE UNITED NATIONS BUREAU OF POPULATION STATISTICS AND CONTROL ANNOUNCED TODAY. JUBILATION RACED THROUGH THE HALLS AND CHAMBERS OF THE UNITED NATIONS BUILDING AT THE NEWS, AND DELEGATES WERE SEEN DANCING WITH EACH OTHER AS THEY CELEBRATED THE ACCOMPLISHMENT OF THE ELUSIVE INTERNATIONAL GOAL ESTABLISHED NEARLY FIFTY YEARS BEFORE. BRAZIL HAD BEEN THE LAST NATION WITH A GROWING POPULATION; IN EXCUSE, THE BPSC EXPLAINED THAT BRAZIL HAD MUCH MORE UNOCCUPIED SPACE AND MORE UNEXPLOITED NATURAL RESOURCES THAN ANY OTHER NATION....

I KNOW PERFECTLY WELL THAT AT THIS MOMENT THE WHOLE UNIVERSE IS LISTENING TO US—THAT EVERY WORD WE SAY ECHOES TO THE REMOTEST STAR.... JEAN GIRAUDOUX, 1945...

CAPELLA IS LATIN FOR "LITTLE SHE GOAT." IT IS FOUND IN THE CONSTELLATION OF AURIGA, THE CHARIOTEER, WHO WAS, IN GREEK MYTHOLOGY, THE INVENTOR OF THE CHARIOT. HIS FIRST CHARIOT, ACCORDING TO THE MYTH, WAS DRAWN BY GOATS....

STAR	TYPE	APP. MAG.	R/A	DECL.	DIST.	LUM.	MASS
CAPELLA A	GO	0.2	0514	+4558	45	120	4.2
CAPELLA B	GO						3.3

AFTER NEARLY FIFTY YEARS, PROJECT PICKS UP SIGNALS.... EXPERTS SAY MESSAGE UNDENIABLE BUT CANNOT BE TRANSLATED AT THIS TIME.... ALIENS, POSSIBLY ON WORLD CIRCLING ONE OF THE TWIN RED GIANT SUNS CALLED CAPELLA, FORTY-FIVE LIGHT-YEARS FROM EARTH, HAVE RECEIVED AND REBROADCAST EARTH'S OWN EARLY RADIO TRANSMISSIONS.... "THESE VOICES," PROJECT DIRECTOR ROBERT MACDONALD SAID, "ARE A SIGNAL THAT WE ARE NOT ALONE AS INTELLIGENT BEINGS IN THE UNIVERSE. I HOPE THAT EVERYONE WILL REJOICE WITH ME IN THIS NEWS AND HELP US SEEK AN ANSWER TO THE MESSAGE THAT LIES HIDDEN SOMEWHERE WITHIN

THIS COMMUNICATION...." A TRANSCRIPTION OF THE RECEPTION AT THE LISTENING PROJECT IN ARECIBO, PUERTO RICO, FOLLOWS....

A NEW RESPONSIVE ENVIRONMENT NIGHT SPOT OPENED IN MANHATTAN TODAY FEATURING WHAT HAS BEEN WIDELY ADVERTISED AS THE MOST TOTALLY RESPONSIVE ENVIRONMENT EVER OFFERED TO THE PUBLIC. THE PUBLIC HAS WELCOMED IT WITH A LINE WAITING TO ENTER THE NEW RESPEN AND EXPERIENCE WHAT HAS BEEN CALLED THE GREATEST RELAXATION THIS SIDE OF HIBERNATION. THE LINE STRETCHED TWICE AROUND THE BLOCK....

IT WAS FACE UP THERE ON THE PLAIN, GREASY PLANKS OF THE TABLE. THE BROKEN HALF OF THE BRONZE ICE-AX WAS STILL BURIED IN THE QUEER SKULL. THREE MAD, HATE-FILLED EYES BLAZED UP WITH A LIVING FIRE, BRIGHT AS FRESH-SPILLED BLOOD, FROM A FACE RINGED WITH A WRITHING, LOATHSOME NEST OF WORMS, BLUE, MOBILE WORMS THAT CRAWLED WHERE HAIR SHOULD GROW....DON A. STUART, 1938...

MIZ! I'M FROM THE BUREAU OF PUBLIC OPINION. WE ARE AMPLIFYING OUR AUTOMATIC OPINION SAMPLING WITH INDIVIDUAL INTERVIEWS....

GET OFF MY SET, WILL YOU? I WAS JUST GETTING READY TO WATCH MY FAVORITE PROGRAM.

YOU HAVE A PUBLIC RESPONSIBILITY TO ANSWER THE LEGITIMATE QUESTIONS OF THE BPO. HOW ELSE IS THE GOVERNMENT GOING TO RESPOND TO PUBLIC OPINION?

OKAY, OKAY, GET ON WITH IT.

HOW DO YOU FEEL ABOUT THE MESSAGE FROM ANOTHER WORLD PICKED UP BY THE LISTENING PROJECT DOWN IN PUERTO RICO?

WHAT MESSAGE?

THE MESSAGE FROM CAPELLA. THE RADIO VOICES. IT'S BEEN ON ALL THE NEWS BROADCASTS, IN ALL THE NEWSPAPERS....

I NEVER PAY ANY ATTENTION TO THAT STUFF.

YOU HAVEN'T HEARD OF IT?

NEVER HEARD OF IT. NOW CAN I WATCH MY PROGRAM?

WHAT PROGRAM IS IT?

"STATION IN SPACE...."

AND WORLDS WITHOUT NUMBER HAVE I CREATED....BUT ONLY AN ACCOUNT OF THIS EARTH, AND THE INHABITANTS THEREOF, GIVE I

UNTO YOU. FOR BEHOLD, THERE ARE MANY WORLDS THAT HAVE PASSED AWAY BY THE WORD OF MY POWER. AND THERE ARE MANY THAT NOW STAND, AND INNUMERABLE ARE THEY UNTO MAN; BUT ALL THINGS ARE NUMBERED UNTO ME, FOR THEY ARE MINE AND I KNOW THEM....AND AS ONE EARTH SHALL PASS AWAY, AND THE HEAVENS THEREOF EVEN SO SHALL ANOTHER COME; AND THERE IS NO END TO MY WORKS, NEITHER TO MY WORDS...." VISIONS OF MOSES, AS REVEALED TO JOSEPH SMITH, THE PROPHET, IN JUNE, 1830...

A SHOWING TODAY OF ONE-OF-A-KIND ART OBJECTS DESIGNED AND MANUFACTURED ENTIRELY BY A COMPUTER-AUTOMATED FAC-TORY PARTNERSHIP WAS PRAISED TODAY BY CRITICS FOR ALMOST EVERY MAJOR MEDIUM. THE EXHIBITION WILL BE ON DISPLAY FOR A MONTH AT THE MUSEUM OF MODERN ART BEFORE GOING ON TOUR OF THE NATION'S MUSEUMS.

WHEN PROGRAMMER PHYLLISS MCCLANAHAN WAS ASKED WHETHER SHE DIDN'T FIND IT NECESSARY TO DISCARD A GREAT MANY POORLY CONCEIVED OR POORLY FASHIONED ITEMS, SHE REPLIED, "NO MORE THAN THE AVERAGE ARTIST."

THE HIT OF THE SHOW WAS AN EIGHT-FOOT-TALL LUCITE FIGURE CALLED—WHETHER BY THE COMPUTER OR MS. MCCLANAHAN WAS NOT SPECIFIED—"SELF-PORTRAIT OF AN ALIEN."...

SO DEEP IS THE CONVICTION THAT THERE MUST BE LIFE OUT THERE BEYOND THE DARK, ONE THINKS THAT IF THEY ARE MORE ADVANCED THAN OURSELVES THEY MAY COME ACROSS SPACE AT ANY MOMENT, PERHAPS IN OUR GENERATION. LATER, CONTEMPLATING THE INFINITY OF TIME, ONE WONDERS IF PERCHANCE THEIR MESSAGES CAME LONG AGO, HURTLING INTO THE SWAMP MUCK OF THE STEAM-ING COAL FORESTS, THE BRIGHT PROJECTILE CLAMBERED OVER BY HISSING REPTILES, AND THE DELICATE INSTRUMENTS RUNNING MIND-LESSLY DOWN WITH NO REPORT....LOREN EISELEY, 1957...

WITH THIS AMBIGUOUS EARTH
HIS DEALINGS HAVE BEEN TOLD US. THESE ABIDE:
THE SIGNAL TO A MAID, THE HUMAN BIRTH,
THE LESSON, AND THE YOUNG MAN CRUCIFIED.

BUT NOT A STAR OF ALL
THE INNUMERABLE HOSTS OF STARS HAS HEARD
HOW HE ADMINISTERED THIS TERRESTRIAL BALL.
OUR RACE HAVE KEPT THEIR LORD'S ENTRUSTED WORD.

OF HIS EARTH-VISITING FEET
NONE KNOWS THE SECRET, CHERISHED, PERILOUS,
THE TERRIBLE, SHAMEFAST, FRIGHTENED, WHISPERED, SWEET,
HEART-SHATTERING SECRET OF HIS WAY WITH US.

NO PLANET KNOWS OF THIS.
OUR WAYSIDE PLANET, CARRYING LAND AND WAVE,
LOVE AND LIFE MULTIPLIED, AND PAIN AND BLISS,
BEARS, AS CHIEF TREASURE, ONE FORSAKEN GRAVE.

NOR, IN OUR LITTLE DAY,
MAY HIS DEVICES WITH THE HEAVENS BE GUESSED
HIS PILGRIMAGE TO THREAD THE MILKY WAY,
OR HIS BESTOWALS THERE, BE MANIFEST.

BUT, IN THE ETERNITIES,
DOUBTLESS WE SHALL COMPARE TOGETHER, HEAR
A MILLION ALIEN GOSPELS, IN WHAT GUISE
HE TROD THE PLEIADES, THE LYRE, THE BEAR.

O BE PREPARED, MY SOUL!
TO READ THE INCONCEIVABLE, TO SCAN
THE MILLION FORMS OF GOD THOSE STARS UNROLL
WHEN, IN OUR TURN, WE SHOW TO THEM A MAN.

ALICE MEYNELL, 1913...

BUT IF WE ALLOW THESE PLANETARY INHABITANTS SOME SORT
OF REASON, MUST IT NEEDS, MAY SOME SAY, BE THE SAME WITH
OURS? CERTAINLY IT MUST; WHETHER WE CONSIDER IT AS APPLIED
TO JUSTICE AND MORALITY, OR EXERCISED IN THE PRINCIPLES AND
FOUNDATIONS OF SCIENCE. FOR REASON WITH US IS THAT WHICH
GIVES US A TRUE SENSE OF JUSTICE AND HONESTY, PRAISE, KIND-
NESS, AND GRATITUDE: 'TIS THAT THAT TEACHES US TO DISTINGUISH
UNIVERSALLY BETWEEN GOOD AND BAD; AND RENDERS US CAPABLE
OF KNOWLEDGE AND EXPERIENCE IN IT. AND CAN THERE BE ANY
WHERE ANY OTHER SORT OF REASON THAN THIS? OR CAN WHAT WE
CALL JUST AND GENEROUS, IN JUPITER OR MARS BE THOUGHT UN-
JUST VILLAINY?...CHRISTIANUS HUYGENS, C. 1670...

WHAT IS NEEDED IS A NEW SPECIALTY, ANTI-CRYPTOGRAPHY, OR
THE DESIGNING OF CODES AS EASY AS POSSIBLE TO DECIPHER....
PHILIP MORRISON, 1963...

THE VAST DISTANCES BETWEEN SOLAR SYSTEMS MAY BE A FORM
OF DIVINE QUARANTINE: THEY PREVENT THE SPIRITUAL INFECTION

OF A FALLEN SPECIES FROM SPREADING; THEY BLOCK IT FROM PLAY-
ING THE ROLE OF THE SERPENT IN THE GARDEN OF EDEN....
C. S. LEWIS, MID-TWENTIETH CENTURY...

AS GOD COULD CREATE BILLIONS OF GALAXIES, SO HE COULD
CREATE BILLIONS OF HUMAN RACES EACH UNIQUE IN ITSELF. TO RE-
DEEM SUCH RACES, GOD COULD TAKE ON ANY BODILY FORM. THERE
IS NOTHING AT ALL REPUGNANT IN THE IDEA OF THE SAME DIVINE
PERSON TAKING ON THE NATURE OF MANY HUMAN RACES. CONCEIV-
ABLY, WE MAY LEARN IN HEAVEN THAT THERE HAS BEEN NOT ONE
INCARNATION OF GOD'S SON BUT MANY.... FATHER DANIEL C. RAIBLE,
1960...

THERE CAN HAVE BEEN ONLY ONE INCARNATION, ONE MOTHER OF
GOD, ONE RACE INTO WHICH GOD HAS POURED HIS IMAGE AND LIKE-
NESS....JOSEPH A BREIG, 1960...

DOES IT NOT SEEM STRANGE TO SAY THAT HIS POWER, IMMEN-
SITY, BEAUTY AND ETERNITY ARE DISPLAYED WITH LAVISH GENER-
OSITY THROUGH UNIMAGINABLE REACHES OF SPACE AND TIME, BUT
THAT THE KNOWLEDGE AND LOVE WHICH ALONE GIVE MEANING TO
ALL THIS SPLENDOR ARE CONFINED TO THIS TINY GLOBE WHERE
SELF-CONSCIOUS LIFE BEGAN TO FLOURISH A FEW MILLENNIA AGO?
...FATHER L. C. MCHUGH, 1960...

SOLITARIAN HEADQUARTERS IN HOUSTON TODAY ANNOUNCED A
SERIES OF REVIVAL MEETINGS TO BE HELD IN ITS GIANT DOMED HOUS-
TON TEMPLE. THE NEWS CAME AFTER A WEEK OF ARTICLES, INTER-
VIEWS, AND COMMENTS ABOUT THE RECENT SURPRISING DISCOVERY
AT THE LISTENING PROJECT IN ARECIBO, PUERTO RICO. "THE ONLY
MESSAGE THAT CONCERNS US," SAID JEREMIAH, LEADING EVANGEL-
IST AND FIRST-AMONG-EQUALS IN THE SOLITARIAN RELIGIOUS
ORGANIZATION, "IS THE MESSAGE FROM GOD."...

3

William Mitchell—2028

*Hearkening in an air stirred and shaken
by the lonely Traveler's call.*

The audience waited.

Every seat in the domed stadium was filled, and the aisles were clogged with people sitting and standing. The people were of all kinds: old, middle-aged, young, children, infants; men and women; rich and poor; black, brown, red, yellow, and pink; clothed for work, street, or party. They all waited for the message to begin.

Missing from the audience were the criers, the coughers, the whisperers, the talkers, the catcallers and whistlers, and the feet stompers, and the minimal noises of more than one hundred thousand persons, the shuffling and shifting, were muffled by the distant thunder of air-conditioning units trying to cope with body heat and exhalations and a Texas summer.

The bodies were packed together, shoulder to shoulder, knee to back. The sensation was not unpleasant. It was, in fact, a kind of sensual communication, as if the fleshy contact formed a kind of circuit linking each member of the audience to the rest like batteries in series, waiting for something to happen, waiting for some switch to be thrown that would put all the latent power to work digging rivers, moving mountains, destroying evil....

At least one person did not share the general mood. Mitchell pulled away from the shoulder pressing him on the left and said, "Are you sure you want to go through with this?"

Thomas looked at MacDonald. MacDonald raised one hand in deprecation and shook his head.

The three men were sitting in the top row of the stadium. The floor was far below. It was packed with ranks of portable chairs; all of them were filled. The only empty space in the vast arena was the square in the middle. Over the intervening heads stretching from the foreground almost to infinity the distant square looked very small.

Mitchell pulled away again with a barely controlled twitch of aversion, and persisted, "I've seen these things get out of control."

In front of them people turned and frowned; others, farther away, looked around to locate the source of the voices.

MacDonald shook his head quickly.

"It's not too late to go back to the booth," Mitchell said. "With the closed-circuit television and all, we'd have a much better view and a much better idea of what's going on." He turned to Thomas. "Tell him, George."

Thomas raised his shoulders and hands helplessly.

MacDonald raised his finger to his lips. "It'll be all right, Bill," he said softly. "It's not enough just to see it and hear it. You've got to feel it."

"I feel it," Mitchell muttered.

More faces were turning in their direction. Mitchell made an obscene gesture at them with his finger.

Thomas leaned toward Mitchell's ear. "The difference between you and Mac," he said softly, "is that you dislike people, and you hate situations you can't control. There's a lot like that in our business."

"People!" Mitchell muttered.

■■.■■.■ ■■ ■   ■   ■
■■■■■   ■■   ■

The lights in the stadium went out as if the hand of God had opened and let night fall over them instead of trickling through His fingers. In the darkness the roof seemed about to fall in upon them and the sense of others nearby seemed to grow as if the audience were swelling to fill the entire space.

Mitchell controlled a rush of panic. He breathed deeply. "Damn him!" he said. "He can't do this!"

But there were no screams, no scuffling, only a hushed

expectancy as if everyone were waiting for a miracle to be performed.

And a single, powerful shaft of light descended from the top of the dome, split the darkness, created a white circle in the center of the stadium floor.

In the center of the circle, almost as if it had descended with the light, stood a single figure. In the entire stadium only the figure was visible. Everyone looked at it; they could not help but look at it.

Only the part of the audience that sat in the portable chairs close to the circle could be sure what the figure was. From where Mitchell sat it seemed almost like the kind of stick drawing of a person a child might make.

Only an impression came to him—of white and flesh-pink and black, of thin, of tall, of arms held up, out-stretched to encompass the audience as the figure turned, if one could imagine an audience in the darkness. There was no other way to reconstruct the audience; it could not be seen or heard.

Slowly, however, the impression of an audience returned, only this time it was one entity, one living thing, the fleshy circuit that had connected the individual members now grown solid. The audience waited for the message.

It stared down at the figure. It stood alone in the circle of light embracing the audience. That was all. No microphone, no platform, no table or chairs, only the lonely figure in the midst of a silent audience of tens on tens of thousands.

"Speak, damn it, speak!" Mitchell muttered, but he knew the man in the circle would wait, draw out the moment into a fine, glittering wire of expectation just about to break. . . . The old bastard knew what he was doing.

The audience seemed to hold its breath.

And then the figure spoke and the voice, magically, filled the domed stadium like the voice of God, coming from nowhere, coming from everywhere. The voice moved the audience, shook it, united it. The voice reinforced the linkages, stepped up the power.

The voice spoke and there was wisdom, there was truth.

"We are alone."

The audience moaned an antiphonal response.

"That is the message," the voice said. "The message is from God.

"They say to you that the message is from another world like ours, from people like us. But they do not know. They have heard the voice of God, and they do not understand. They try to read it with their minds; they cannot do it. They must read it with their hearts. They must have faith.

"The message is from God, and it is carried by the angels who are the messengers of God. How can a message come from someone else?"

The audience waited for an answer it knew would come.

"There is no one else but man and God. We are alone with God in the universe. That is the way it is. That is the way it was meant to be."

The words rippled the audience like a wind blowing across a valley of wheat.

"Why should we be afraid?" the voice said. "Why should we refuse to recognize the truth when it is laid before us? God created the universe for his glory. God created man to wonder at the magnificence of the universe and to glorify God."

The audience took a deep breath.

"This is the meaning of the message—of man's words returned to him, of his frivolity shown him as if in a mirror—there are no others; we are alone. . . ."

The words continued to come, unbidden, uncompelled, like a great natural phenomenon, like revelation. The force built up within the audience like magnets being aligned until each field reinforced the next and the total field exerted by more than one hundred thousand persons thinking and feeling as one entity was great enough to pervade the entire city, to encompass the world, and even, perhaps, to shift the stars themselves. . . .

They walked down the empty corridor underneath the stadium, their footsteps echoing from concrete walls and floor and ceiling, little puffs of dust and powdered concrete rising as their shoes fell. Dimly lighted by occasional ceiling bulbs, the corridor seemed to go on forever.

"Well?" Thomas said and cringed from the reverberations. "Speak of 'man's words returned to him,'" he said.

"Bastard!" Mitchell said.

"'On doit se regarder soi-même un fort long temps,'" MacDonald said. "'Avant que de songer à condamner les gens.'"

"What did he say?" Mitchell asked Thomas.

"That's a quotation from Molière's 'Misanthrope' about not judging others until you've taken a good long look at yourself," Thomas said.

Mitchell shrugged. "I've taken a good, long look at him," he said.

"Are you sure this is the way?" MacDonald asked.

"This is what Judith told me," Mitchell said.

The corridor broadened into a room. Giant pistons supported the ceiling like so many hydraulic lifts. In the middle was a metal cage. Inside the cage were control panels with levers and vernier rheostats and large buttons painted red and green. The cage was locked and so were each of the controls.

The room was deserted; only their footsteps, pausing now, disturbed its silence.

"The magic," MacDonald said appreciatively.

"The son of a bitch," Mitchell said. "I think it's this way."

He led them past the control room and down another corridor to a door painted gray. He knocked lightly. When there was no response he knocked harder.

The door opened a crack. "Judith?" he said.

"Bill?" The door opened wider. A girl slipped into the corridor and gave Mitchell her hand. "Bill."

She was small and slender with dark hair and large dark eyes that seemed as if they were all pupil. She was not exceptionally pretty, Mitchell thought in his more rational moments; perhaps it was the impact on him of the large pupils. He could be objective about the matter and yet feel an attraction to her that made her seem unique in all the world and therefore beautiful.

He squeezed her hand in place of a kiss. She disliked a public display of affection. Her Puritan upbringing, he had called it when they were first going together as undergraduates. "Is the old bastard in there?" he asked.

"Bill!" she protested but without heat. "He is my father! And he's inside, resting. He's not well, you know. These sermons take a great deal of strength."

"This is Mr. MacDonald," Mitchell said. "He's in charge of the Project."

"Golly!" Judith said. "I'm honored." She really seemed impressed.

"And this is Mr. Thomas," Mitchell continued. "He's my boss."

"It's a collaboration," Thomas said.

"Judith Jones," Mitchell said. "My fiancée."

"Now, Bill," she said, "that's not strictly true."

They were talking in hushed voices like conspirators, and the reverberations in the corridor made the voices even stranger. Mitchell had an eerie sense of playing a part in a play in which the characters tried to communicate through endless, echoing caverns.

"Does your father know we're coming to see him?" MacDonald asked.

Judith shook her head. "He wouldn't still be here, if he knew. He doesn't like to meet people. He doesn't like people who want things, who want him to do things, who want to argue with him. He doesn't have time, he says, but mainly he doesn't like it."

"Are we just going to break in on him?" MacDonald asked.

Judith frowned as if she were bracing herself for something unpleasant. "I'll introduce you. Try not to disturb him—too much." She turned toward the door and then turned back. "And try not to mind that he seems rude. He really isn't. He protects himself."

She opened the door and slid back into the room, leaving the door ajar behind her. "Father," Mitchell heard her say, "some men are here to see you."

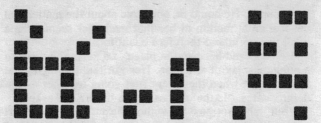

Judith opened the door quickly before her father could speak. "This is Mr. MacDonald," she said. "He's in charge of the Project. And Mr. Thomas. He works with Bill Mitchell. And you know Bill."

The man was sitting in an old metal chair beside an old makeup table and mirror, and he seemed as old as they were, old enough to be MacDonald's father instead of Judith's. His hair was pure white, and his face was lined. His eyes, as dark as Judith's, blazed up as the men entered, and then the fire was gone, as if a door had been shut in front of it, and the man looked down.

"I know Mitchell," the voice said. It was a tired voice, an old voice, a ghost of the voice that had filled the stadium above them. "I know him as a foul-mouthed blasphemer, an atheist who scoffs at the beliefs of others, a lecher with the morals of a monkey. I know, too, that I told you not to see him again. Nor do I wish to see these others...."

"Mr. Jones—" MacDonald began.

"Get out!" the old man said.

"We are both older men, Mr. Jones," MacDonald began.

"Jeremiah," the old man said.

"Mr. Jeremiah—"

"Just Jeremiah, and Jeremiah does not talk to atheists."

"I am a scientist—"

"An atheist."

"I want to talk to you about the Message."

"I have heard the Message."

"Directly?"

Jeremiah placed one long, translucent hand on each bony knee and leaned toward MacDonald, looking up. "I have heard it from God," he said harshly. "Have you heard it more directly than that?"

"Did you hear it before the Project picked it up or afterward?" MacDonald asked.

Jeremiah sat back and sighed. "Good-bye, Mr. MacDonald. You wish to trap me—"

"To talk with you—"

"The Message I speak of is not your message which comes in riddles over waves. The Message—my message—is from God, and it tells me about your message. Is your message from God?"

"It may be," MacDonald said.

Jeremiah was about to turn his back upon them, but he stopped and looked at MacDonald. So did Mitchell.

"I do not know who it is from," MacDonald said, "so it may be from God."

"But you do not think so," Jeremiah said.

"I do not think so," MacDonald said. "But I do not know. I have not had a revelation like yours. My mind is not closed; is yours?"

"A mind is not closed which is open to truth but not to falsehood," Jeremiah said. "You have not read your message, then?"

"No," MacDonald admitted. "But we will."

"When you do," Jeremiah said, dismissing them, "then come talk to me if you must."

"If—when—we do, if I send for you, will you come?"

Jeremiah's dark eyes looked into MacDonald's. "Before it is announced to the rest of the world?"

"Yes."

"I will come." A pale hand came up to support a head that drooped to meet it. When the others did not move, Jeremiah looked up. "What do you want of me?" he asked wearily.

"Your public meetings are stirring people up against the Project," MacDonald said.

The banked fires flickered. "I am speaking the truth."

"Your truth is creating an atmosphere in which people may shut down the Project, keep us from deciphering the Message, prevent us from listening for more messages."

"I speak truth," Jeremiah said. "We are alone. Nothing

can change that. What happens when people know the truth is as God wills."

"But if the Message is from God—a message to all of us, not just to you alone—should we not read it? And hear more?"

Jeremiah's long face grew longer. "The Message may be from Satan."

"In your sermon you said it was from God."

"That is true," Jeremiah said. "But Satan can deceive even those who listen to God." A translucent hand stroked a pale chin in thought. "I could be mistaken," he said.

MacDonald took half a step toward Jeremiah, starting a gesture that he stopped in mid-air. "If you change your interpretation now, it would only confuse the faithful. Give us a chance to decipher the Message. I don't ask you to stop telling the truth as you see it, but at least do not incite your followers against the Project."

Jeremiah looked at MacDonald's hand until it dropped to his side. "What do you hope to decipher? The voices?"

"The voices from the Thirties?" MacDonald said and shook his head. "Those bits and snatches of the radio shows of that time, rebroadcast to us from the direction of Capella, are just the wave of the hand, the attention-getter."

"Then what is the Message?"

"We're not absolutely sure. We think it's in the bursts of static between the Voices. Slowed down, filtered for noise, for real static, it can sound like a real message—dots and silence, dots and silence."

Jeremiah looked skeptical. "You could read anything you wished into dots and silence."

"We haven't. Not yet. But we're trying. The computers are working on it, trying to make some intelligent pattern out of it. We'll get it done. It just takes time. That's what we need—time."

Jeremiah said, "I can't promise anything."

"We'll let you know first."

"I can't promise anything," Jeremiah said again, but this time it was like a promise. "Now leave me alone. And, Judith! You must not see this man again!" He motioned toward Mitchell. "I have told you so before, but I tell you now. You must choose between us. If you choose him, if you choose to disobey me, then I will not see you again."

"Damn it!" Mitchell began, stepping forward.

Judith stopped him. "Go on, Bill," she said. She stepped outside the door with them. "I'm not going to see you again, Bill, not alone."

"I need you," Mitchell said. "We made plans—"

"He needs me," Judith said. "He's old. He's not well. He's not good with people." She went back inside.

"What a strange mixture," Thomas said. "He can make thousands believe he speaks with God, and he can't talk to another human being without trying to push him away, without rejecting the communication."

"You should try to understand him, Bill," MacDonald said gently. "He's asking for understanding in his way. He's asking for help. And you two are a lot alike."

"Damn him!" Mitchell muttered, his soul filled with disgust for the human race. "Damn everybody!" He looked around. "Well, nearly everybody," he said.

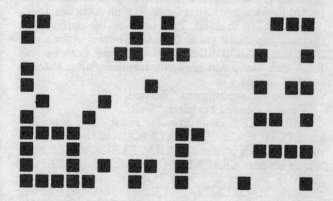

The taxi rolled silently through the traffic toward the airport.

Seated between Thomas and Mitchell, MacDonald said, "You've done a good job."

"Hah!" Thomas said.

MacDonald raised a hand to emphasize his sincerity. "I mean it. You and Bill and the others, with your articles and releases and interviews and programs and all the other techniques of communication, have won general acceptance for the Project. No, not just acceptance—enthusiasm. The news that we have received a message from intelligent beings who live on a planet which probably circles one of the twin suns of Capella has been received without skepticism—with excitement but no panic. I don't know how it could have been done any better."

"I do," Mitchell said.

"You're setting your goals too high," MacDonald said. "After all, for fifty years nine persons out of ten had never heard of the Project, and those who had mostly thought it was a waste of time and effort. And for more than fifty years experts have predicted that people would become hysterical when they were presented with proof of the existence of other intelligent creatures in the universe."

"Experts!" Thomas said.

MacDonald shook his head and chuckled. "All right, gentlemen, accept credit for bringing back radio." He leaned forward and twisted a knob until it clicked.

Music filled the taxi, first some of the current folk revival, then dance music from the Thirties. After a moment that faded and the sound that came back up was filled with static and broken transmissions. . . . Mitchell reached to turn it off.

"Some accomplishment," he said.

Thomas stopped his hand. "Wait!"

"CRACKLE," came over the radio. "Say goodnight grace POPPOP music CRACKLEPOP could have knocked me over with a fender POPCRACKLECRACKLE knee this is rochest CRACKLEPOP music CRACKLEPOP-POPPOP matinee idol larry POPPOP music: au revoir pleasant CRACKLECRACKLE the little theater off POP-POPCRACKLE eye doodit CRACKLEPOP music POP-POPPOP who knows what evil POPCRACKLEPOP . . ."

"That's it, isn't it?" Mitchell said. "The Message itself." He found a strange kind of conviction in the poor quality of the reception.

"Part of it," Thomas said.

His voice was a little shaken, Mitchell thought, as if he were reliving that moment in Puerto Rico when he had heard it first, when he had changed from a skeptic with a muckraker's tools raised to bury the Project to a dedicated Project partisan with a self-assigned mission to convince a great variety of publics that the Message was real, that it was good, that there was nothing to fear. His friends had not believed the change in Thomas, not at first, but then they too had listened to the Message and to George and had agreed to help. Mitchell had joined in the first month.

"Those are the sounds of yesterday and today," the radio announcer said. "Those are the sounds of the stars. That is part of the Message being received from Capella, forty-five light-years away from Earth. If you have any suggestions for deciphering the Message, send them to Robert MacDonald, the Project, Arecibo, Puerto Rico. And now—another episode from a story begun ninety years ago. . . ."

The voice faded and eerie music came up, modulated, and a deep voice asked, "Who knows what evil lurks in the hearts of men?" The music came back up and faded. "The Shadow knows—"

Thomas twisted the knob until it clicked.

"A brilliant idea," MacDonald said, "but I don't know how we're going to answer all the mail."

"Any worthwhile suggestions?" Thomas asked.

MacDonald shook his head. "Not yet. But who knows what brilliance lurks in the minds of men?"

"Well," Thomas said, "we didn't expect any. Tell you what—we'll send somebody down to draft some standard replies, set them up on your computer."

"Good," MacDonald said.

"What are you going to do about the Chinese?" Thomas asked. "They've called the Message a capitalist plot to distract the world from American imperialism. Maybe we should have informed them before the public announcement."

MacDonald shrugged. "Don't worry about it. Their scientists have requested tapes."

"The Russians have announced that they picked up the

Message a year ago," Mitchell said.

"They haven't asked for tapes," MacDonald said. "They're probably picking it up for themselves now that they know where to search."

Thomas sighed. "I'm afraid we're just creating more trouble for you."

MacDonald smiled. "'Law, Brer Tarrypin!' sez Brer Fox, sezee, 'you ain't see no trouble yit. Ef you wanter see sho' nuff trouble, you des oughter go 'longer me; I'm de man w'at kin show you trouble,' sezee."

The taxi pulled up at the airport and MacDonald retrieved his credit card from the meter as he got out.

"Come with me to the gift counter," he called over his shoulder to the others. "I want to pick up something for Maria and Bobby." When they caught up with him as he walked across the vast expanse of imitation marble, he said, "I've switched your reservations. I want you to return to Arecibo with me."

The floor vibrated as the electrical catapult launched another jet. A moment later came a low "whoosh" and a fading thunder.

"I've got things here I should take care of before I leave," Mitchell said.

"For the sake of the Project," MacDonald said, "I think you should stay away from Judith for a while."

"You and Jeremiah," Mitchell said.

"He's a prophet, all right," Thomas said gloomily. "And a danger."

"That's why I want you to come back with me," MacDonald said. "I want you to get the feel of the Project again, the reality, the excitement of the impending breakthrough. If you can communicate this, it might counteract the growing influence of Jeremiah and his followers."

Thomas shook his head. "We won't counteract Jeremiah. He's an honest man possessed by a vision, like a poet. He has his own reality."

"He's an old bastard," Mitchell said.

"He's a man whose basic beliefs have been threatened," MacDonald said, "and he reacts by defending his world. The Solitarians cannot co-exist with the fact of intelligent life on other worlds."

"Then why did you invite him to the Project?" Mitchell asked.

"Because he is an honest man as well as a fanatic," MacDonald said. "I think we have an even chance, or a little less, that if he sees what we are doing, sees the translation, he will accept it and be able to change."

"Or he will reject it or be destroyed," Thomas said.

"Yes," MacDonald admitted. "Those are possibilities."

"How serious is his threat to the Project?" Mitchell asked.

"The most serious since its founding," MacDonald said. "It is ironic—and somehow peculiarly appropriate to the history of the Project—that its most critical moment should come at the time it accomplished what it was created to do. Fifty years without results went unchallenged, but the moment we received a message our existence was threatened."

Thomas laughed. "Scientists are dangerous. They bought you off with toys, but when the toys turned out to be real they began to worry."

"What can the Solitarians do?" Mitchell asked. "Besides talk among themselves."

"They're big," MacDonald said, "and they're growing. They want the Project stopped, and they're putting pressure on Senators and Congressmen. In spite of your good work, in spite of what I've called public acceptance, they still manage to exploit mankind's basic fear of meeting a superior. And there's no doubt that the Capellans are superior."

"How so?" Mitchell asked, and as he heard the words he felt that his tone was a little sharper than he had intended.

The floor shook again. The gift counter was just ahead. MacDonald already was running his gaze along the shelves.

"They're clearly older and more capable than we," MacDonald said. "Their giant red suns are older than our sun by millions—perhaps billions—of years, depending, say my astronomers, on the effect of mass on stellar evolution. In any case, we have not even been able to pick up radio broadcasts from other worlds, much less rebroadcast them so that the original world could receive them again."

"'Who's that little chatterbox?'" Thomas half-sang, half-chanted, his gaze distant. "'Pepsi-Cola hits the spot.'" He shivered.

MacDonald bought a new book, a light romantic novel about love and peril in orbit, for his wife, a three-dimensional scale model of the stars surrounding Earth for a distance of fifty light-years, including, of course, Capella, for his son, and then, admitting that an eight-month-old infant would have little use for the model—at least for a year or two—bought him a large stuffed toy ostrich. It was so big that it had to go into the jet's baggage compartment.

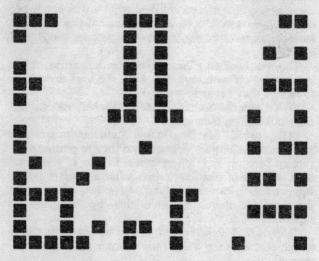

"Robby!" Maria said in the little waiting room of the airport just outside Arecibo. She was frowning as she tried not to laugh at the gigantic bird with the long legs that stood in front of her. "Hush, now, Bobby," she said to the crying child in her arms, "it won't hurt you." And then she said to MacDonald, "What a monstrous bird to give a baby!"

Mitchell thought she was the most beautiful woman he had ever seen. He wondered what she must have been like at twenty or even thirty. Between Maria and his work, MacDonald had two magnificent reasons for remaining in Arecibo as much as possible.

"I'm a fool," MacDonald said, stricken. "I just can't seem to understand my own family."

"Considering," Thomas said, "how well he understands and communicates with everybody else."

"Ah!" MacDonald said deprecatingly. "What of Jeremiah?"

"At least you got him to listen," Thomas said, "and to promise to come."

Maria's smile burst upon MacDonald. "You did, Robby? You won him over?"

"Nothing as final as that," MacDonald said. "Here, now, let me hold him."

He held out his arms to the squalling boy. The baby went to him willingly, trustingly, but not looking at the stuffed bird all the same. In a moment or two the infant's yells turned to sobs and the sobs to silence.

"Now, Bobby," MacDonald said, "you know your father wouldn't bring you anything that would hurt you—though, to be sure, it might frighten you at first. Well, come along," he said to the ostrich with its black eyes enigmatic in their plastic sockets, "we will grow up to you."

He tucked the bird under his other arm, turned toward the door, and stopped. "What am I thinking of?" he asked Maria. "These are my guests. You know George, our own doubting Thomas. And this other handsome gentleman is Bill Mitchell, who is a star-crossed lover."

"Hello, George," Maria said, presenting her cheek to be kissed. "Hello, Bill," she said, extending her hand. "I hope the stars are as kind to you as they have been to me."

"It's not all that serious," Mitchell said, trying to keep his tone light. "You know, a stubborn father, a girl who must choose—it will all work out."

"I know it will," Maria said, and Mitchell was swayed for a moment by her conviction. "Come," Maria said, "I will fix you all a good Mexican supper."

As Maria withdrew her hand from his, Mitchell caught a glimpse of the white scar that crossed her wrist.

"*Querida,*" MacDonald said apologetically, "we ate on the plane."

"You call that eating?"

"Besides," MacDonald said, "we are on our way to the Project. We've still got work to do. Tomorrow—before these gentlemen must fly back to New York—you can fix a big dinner. Okay?"

Partially mollified, she gave him a comic shrug and a broad "Hokay."

They put their bags and the ostrich into the trunk of MacDonald's car. The baby was relieved when the stuffed bird disappeared, and he settled comfortably onto his father's shoulder. Maria drove. She handled the car skillfully. They were well matched, Mitchell thought, Maria and MacDonald—both beautiful, both capable. The old steam turbine hummed peacefully under the hood as they climbed the quiet green hills in the night.

It had been a long day that started in New York and ended in Puerto Rico by way of Texas and Florida, and Mitchell should have been exhausted. But for him the evening was enchanted. He did not know why. Perhaps it was the Puerto Rican quiet after the urban congestion of Texas, perhaps the automobile taking them farther from civilization, perhaps the calm beauty of MacDonald's wife, perhaps their domestic chatter in the front seat. Usually this kind of thing embarrassed him, this talk of food and family in which he played the role of an unwilling eavesdropper, but somehow this was different.

Maybe, he thought, people are not so disgusting.

He looked at Thomas. Even Thomas felt it. This man of tangled nerves, one-time poet and novelist, sometime muckraking reporter, now committed propagandist for the Project and its cause, was staring quietly out a window as if he had packaged all his worries and mailed them back to Manhattan.

The journey in the moonlight went on. Mitchell found himself wishing it would never end, this trip beyond time and space, but then he saw below them a valley that gleamed metallic in the night. Across the valley some giant spider had been busy spinning cables in a precise mathematical pattern; it was a web to catch the stars. Beyond

it they came upon a giant ear cocked to the sky to hear
the whispers of the night. . . .

And then the car drifted onto a broad parking lot that
gleamed phosphorescently in the moonlight, and came to
a stop beside a long, low concrete building. Mitchell
blinked. The spell faded. It faded slowly. Looking back
later Mitchell thought that it continued to color his impressions for as long as he stayed on the island.

They got out of the car. MacDonald placed the sleeping
child gently in the seat and strapped him down. He kissed
Maria and murmured something about his plans.

Thomas and Mitchell took their bags out of the trunk;
MacDonald removed the ostrich. "I'll keep him at the
office for a while," he said, "until Bobby gets used to
him."

The car whispered away. MacDonald opened the door
to the building. "Here we are," he said, as if they had
walked across the street from the Texas airport.

Thomas stopped in the doorway and motioned toward
the distant steerable telescope, moving slowly on its supporting arm. "You're still searching?"

MacDonald shrugged. "Just because we picked up one
message doesn't mean there are no others, that our search
is ended. And we have engineers who are good at listening
but not so good at understanding what they hear—so far,
of course, none of us have been very good at that—and
we don't want to lose them, to see the team broken up
before the game is over."

They entered the building. The corridors were painted
concrete with tiled floors lighted by radiant fixtures in the
ceiling. From the cars in the parking lot Mitchell had
assumed the place was busy, but somehow he was un-
prepared for the bustle. Men walked purposefully along
the halls, papers in their hands, nodding at MacDonald
as if he had never been away, or talking eagerly to each
other and never seeing MacDonald and the strangers. Or
women moved past, more sociable, talking to Mac-
Donald, asking about his trip, about Maria and Bobby,
being introduced to the visitors.

MacDonald smiled at the purposeful scene and quoted
Horace:

"[F]ungar vice cotis, acutum
Reddere quae ferrum valet exsors ipsa secandi."

And then MacDonald led them down the hall to an open door. "Here's our listening post," he said to Mitchell, pulling him by one arm into the doorway. For some reason Mitchell did not mind being guided.

The room was filled with electronic equipment, a computer, recording devices; it smelled of ozone. Two men were in the room, one at a panel against one wall, tinkering with its wiring, the other sitting in a chair with earphones over his head. He looked up and waved and turned one earphone out toward MacDonald in a gesture of invitation. MacDonald waved back and shook his head.

"What's with the bird?" the listener called out.

MacDonald shook his head again. "It's a long story. I'll tell you later." He turned back to Mitchell. "Any other time I'd take you in and show you what we have here. I'd let you listen to the music of the spheres, the sound of the infinite, the voices of the damned who cannot make themselves understood, but right now we don't have time."

"Don't do it," Thomas warned Mitchell, half-seriously. "You'll never be the same. That's what makes them all so strange."

"You want to hear the message," MacDonald said, smiling. "You want to know why we haven't deciphered it in six months of effort. Six months while the Solitarians gather their forces, while Congress grows nervous and thinks about appropriations, while the efforts of clever, dedicated communicators like you and George are being frittered away."

Mitchell shook his head.

"You're right," MacDonald said. "We haven't deciphered the message, and we should have done it by now with all the minds and all the computers we've had working on it. Come on. I'll show you."

They passed other doors, other rooms where doors were open and men and women worked at desks or benches or panels. The computer room was at the end of the corridor. It was called the computer room, apparently, because instead of walls it had computers, and the floor was so filled with data-input keyboards and printers that there was scarcely room to walk between them.

At a keyboard in the midst of the computers, like a witch surrounded by familiars, sat a middle-aged man with salt-and-pepper hair cut short.

"Hello, Oley," MacDonald said.

"You brought me a present," the other said.

MacDonald sighed, took the ostrich out from under his arm and put it in a distant corner, and said, "No, Oley, I brought you some guests." He introduced Mitchell to Olsen, his computer expert. Thomas had met him before.

Mitchell looked around at all the machines, trying to guess what they all did.

"Any breakthroughs?" MacDonald asked.

"We're lucky we haven't lost ground," Olsen said.

"Play your best selection for our visitors," MacDonald said.

Olsen pressed two keys on his keyboard. A visual display appeared on a window in front of him, broken rows of white numbers on a gray background, but Mitchell looked at it only for a moment. Then he was listening to sounds that came from concealed speakers—a soft hiss, then silence, then a noise, silence, more noise. Sometimes the noise would be loud, sometimes soft, sometimes brief, sometimes extended, sometimes a click, sometimes a buzz or a plop.

Mitchell looked at Thomas and they both looked at MacDonald. "I can get better messages from a thunderstorm," Mitchell said.

"That's part of the problem," MacDonald said. "Part of what we get between the rebroadcasts of our old radio programs is static. Add the effect of distance, of interruption, of fading. But part of what we pick up, we think, is message. The problem is how to tell one from the other. Tell them what we're trying to do, Oley."

"First we try to clean up the transmission," Olsen said, "to filter out the natural noise electronically. We try to eliminate what is clearly casual and then run a series of variables on what is questionable, hardening up the signals, reinforcing them where necessary...."

"Show them what we get when we clean it up," MacDonald said.

Olsen pressed two more keys. From the speakers came

a firm series of sounds and silences; like the buzz of an old-fashioned international code without the dashes, a dot and another dot, a long silence, and then six more dots, a silence, seven more dots, silence, dot, silence, dot....

They listened, Mitchell and Thomas, trying to make sense out of it, and finally looked up, sheepishly, for there was no way they could decipher the message just by listening to it. "There's something hypnotic about it all the same," Mitchell said.

"But it's no better than the other," Thomas said, "and it's not real. This isn't the way it sounds."

Olsen shrugged. "The other isn't either. That's just the way our particular speakers interpret the small packets of energy we have picked up on our radio telescopes in space between rebroadcasts of our own radio programs of ninety years ago. With the help of the computers, we have reinterpreted the message in sounds that seem more familiar or more meaningful."

"And you still can't read it," Thomas said.

Olsen nodded. "We've still got problems. We're trying to find duplications, repetitions, patterns. We don't know where the message starts or where it ends, whether it's one message given over and over again or a series of messages. Sometimes we think we've found something, it works for a while, and then it falls apart."

"Like what?" Mitchell asked. "A statement?"

"In what language?" Olsen asked.

"Well, mathematics, maybe. Like one and one equal two, or the Pythagorean theorem or something."

MacDonald smiled. "That would be useful for catching our attention, for demonstrating that it was a message sent by intelligent beings, but they've done that, don't you see? With the rebroadcast of our radio programs."

"What kind of message could they send that would mean anything?" Mitchell asked.

"Sound and silence," Thomas mused. "Sound and silence. It must mean something."

"Dots and silence," Mitchell said. "That's what Mac told Jeremiah. Dots and silence. That's what it sounds like, too. Dots and no dashes. Dots and blanks."

MacDonald looked quickly at Mitchell. "Say that again."

"Dots and silence. That's what you said. To Jeremiah."

"No," MacDonald said. "What you said after that."

"Dots and no dashes," Mitchell repeated. "Dots and blanks."

"Dots and blanks," MacDonald mused. "What does that remind you of, Olsen? A crossword puzzle? Do you suppose—? The old Drake game?" He turned to Olsen. "Let's try it. For all the combinations of prime numbers."

He turned to Mitchell. "Bill, you send a message to Jeremiah over my signature. Three words. 'Come. Message deciphered.'"

"Are you sure you have the answer?" Thomas asked. "Can't you wait and make certain?"

"You've felt that confidence before," MacDonald said, "the feeling that you know you have the answer even

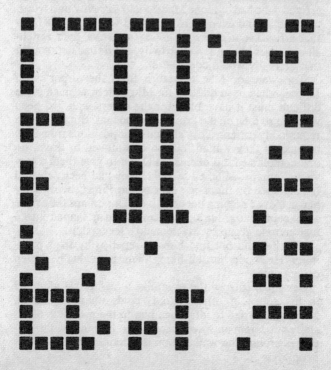

before you try it out, a kind of instant communication?"

"Yes," Thomas said. "Jeremiah knows that feeling too."

"And I want Jeremiah to be here when we run it off for the first time," MacDonald said. "I think that may be very important."

Mitchell paused at the door. "You aren't going to try it until then?" he asked incredulously.

MacDonald shook his head slowly. Maybe Thomas understood MacDonald, but MacDonald was not communicating with him, Mitchell thought.

The room already was crowded with people when Jeremiah and Judith and MacDonald came through the door. Thomas was there and Olsen and a dozen more of MacDonald's colleagues on the Project.

Mitchell had been surprised when Jeremiah's message arrived—he had outdone MacDonald's brevity by a word, "I come"—and even more surprised when Judith's message arrived soon afterward giving the arrival time. Mitchell had never known Jeremiah to fly, and he had not thought that he really would come at all.

The wait for Mac to return from the airport with Jeremiah had been difficult for Mitchell; how much more difficult must it have been for the others who had been working so long on the Project, he thought. But they were remarkably patient. They shifted their positions from time to time as they waited, but no one moved to leave, no one complained, no one urged Olsen to give them a preview. Perhaps, Mitchell thought, they had been selected for patience by the long years of the Project when they had achieved nothing but negatives. Or perhaps they were an exceptional group of men and women shaped into a high-morale group by MacDonald's leadership.

Mitchell did not find himself repelled by their proximity. He found himself liking them individually—even collectively.

Jeremiah entered the room like a high priest wrapped in his robes of office, aloof, cold, unapproachable. MacDonald tried to introduce him to the members of his staff, but Jeremiah waved him away. He studied the machines around the wall and on the floor, and ignored the people.

Judith followed him, nodding at the people they passed as if to make up for her father's absence of humanity. Mitchell's skin turned cold as he saw her again, and he wondered again why it was Judith, why it was this one girl among many, who made him shiver.

Jeremiah stopped in front of MacDonald as if they were the only two persons in the room, and said, "It takes all this to read one small message? For the faithful it requires only a believing heart."

MacDonald smiled. "One small difference between us makes necessary all the apparatus. Our faith requires that all data and results must be duplicable by anyone using the same equipment and techniques. And with all the believing hearts in the world, none, I think, has received identical messages."

"It isn't necessary," Jeremiah said.

"I understand that your communications are highly personal," MacDonald said, "but wouldn't it be wonderful if the important messages were received by all the faithful?"

Jeremiah looked at MacDonald. It seemed to Mitchell that these two men were alone in the room and that they were battling for each other's souls. He reached out and took Judith's hand. She glanced at him and then down at their hands and then away, not speaking. But she didn't take her hand away, and Mitchell thought he felt her fingers tighten.

"You did not bring me here to scoff at my faith," Jeremiah said.

"No," MacDonald said, "to show you mine. I, too, have had my revelation. I do not compare it with yours. It has no identifiable source. It is an inner conviction that has grown from a small thought to a large certainty that there is other life in the universe, that to prove its existence is the most gloriously human thing man can do, that to communicate with it would make this vast, incomprehensible place in which man lives, this unexplored forest of the night, a friendlier, happier, more wonderful, more exciting, holier place in which to be."

Mitchell looked at the other faces in the room. They were staring at MacDonald, and Mitchell had the feeling that they, too, were hearing MacDonald's credo for the first time, that he had lived it but never explained it like this before. Now he was exposing himself before this skeptical stranger as if Jeremiah's belief in him mattered more than anything else. Mitchell's hand tightened on Judith's.

Jeremiah was frowning. "I did not come all this way to argue theology," he said harshly.

"I'm not arguing," MacDonald said earnestly. "And I'm not dealing in theology, not the way I see it, although it may infringe upon those areas you have declared sacred to your beliefs. I'm trying to explain myself, you see—"

"Why?" Jeremiah asked.

"Because it's important to me that you understand," MacDonald said. "I want you to know that I am a man of good will."

"Most dangerous of all are men of good will," Jeremiah said, looking like a prophet in his old-fashioned black suit, "for they are easily deluded."

"I am not easily deluded," MacDonald said.

"You want to believe. You are easily deluded. And you will find what you wish to find."

"No," MacDonald said, "it cannot be that way. I will find what anyone can find, whatever his beliefs and desires, what you would find if you should look and listen. What I am trying to tell you is that no matter what my intentions, my hopes, my fears, my message is not like yours. It can be checked. It must read the same to everyone, every time, or it is wrong and will be discarded."

Jeremiah's lips curled. "You do not interpret? You read it directly as it comes to you?"

MacDonald sighed. "We clean it up," he admitted. "The natural universe makes a great deal of noise, somewhat like the noise of a city, and we must filter that out."

Jeremiah smiled.

"We have techniques," MacDonald said. "They are verifiable. They work. And then there is the signal itself. It must be identified, analyzed."

Jeremiah nodded. "And then?"

"And then," MacDonald admitted, "we must interpret the message. It is not a simple matter, you understand, because the message comes from far away, so far it takes forty-five years for the signal to reach us, and it comes from an alien mind."

"Then you will never read your message," Jeremiah said, "or you will read into it whatever you wish, because there is no possible communication between alien minds."

"What about man and God?"

"Man is made in God's image," Jeremiah said.

MacDonald made a gesture of frustration and then continued. "What alien minds have in common is intelligence and the natural universe. Everywhere in the universe, matter reacts in the same way, forming the same elements which combine in the same way to form molecules, the same kinds of energy are available, all obedient to the same physical laws. Everywhere beings must cope with their environment in the same basic ways to satisfy the same basic needs. And if they communicate with each other in a variety of ways, they will find ways which compare with the experience of other intelligent creatures, and if they try to communicate with other worlds they will refer to these common experiences: measurements, mathematics, sensory impressions, images, abstractions...."

"Faith?" Jeremiah asked.

Judith's hand tightened on Mitchell's.

"Perhaps—" MacDonald began.

"Don't patronize me—" Jeremiah said.

"But we would not know how to depict faith," MacDonald went on without pausing.

Jeremiah gestured impatiently. "I believe you are sincere. You may be deluded, but you are sincere. Show me what you brought me here to see, and let me return to my mission."

"All right," MacDonald said. He seemed like a defeated man. Mitchell felt sorry for him, but he could have told him that any effort to reason with Jeremiah would never succeed. Mitchell had tried it too often in the past. Jeremiah was immovable. How can you reason with a fanatic? "I just want you to understand what we have done," MacDonald continued, "so that the result is intelligible to you when it comes from the computer. Olsen?"

"We kept searching for a meaningful pattern in the brief bursts of energy we were receiving," Olsen began.

"You tell me!" Jeremiah said to MacDonald.

MacDonald shrugged. "Dots and silence. That's what I said to you. Dots and silence. And then Bill here said, 'Dots and blanks,' and something fell into place. The Capellans might be trying to send us a visual message with the sounds standing for black dots and the silences for white spaces. Frank Drake suggested the possibility more than fifty years ago. He sent a message to fellow scientists made up of a series of ones and zeroes and his colleagues made a picture out of it. Perhaps we should have thought of it. Our excuse, I suppose, is that we didn't have a neat little row of binary symbols; instead we had dots and long silences, and we weren't sure when the message began or when it ended. Now I think we can do it. We have asked the computer to plot the Message onto a grid, using prime numbers for the sides of the grid, breaking up the silence into signals equaling the dots in duration, like a switch turning on and off."

"Or like a computer," Olsen interjected, "with only two numbers, one and zero."

"If we plot the signals as dark and light," MacDonald said, "then we may come up with a recognizable picture."

"May?" Jeremiah asked. "You haven't tried it yet?"

"Not yet," MacDonald said. "Sometimes a man has a conviction—you might call it a revelation—that he has found the answer. I think we have found it. I wanted you to see it with us, the first time."

"You had a revelation?"

"Perhaps. We'll see."

"I don't believe it," Jeremiah said, turning away. "You are trying to deceive me. You would not bring me here without having tested your theory first."

MacDonald put out a hand as if to touch Jeremiah and stopped. "Wait. You have come this far. At least see what we have to show you."

Jeremiah stopped. "Do not tell me any more lies," he said harshly. "Show me your deception from the machine and let me go."

"For God's sake," said someone from among Mac-

Donald's colleagues, "let's get it over with." The man's voice was shaky.

In the corner the stuffed ostrich looked over the proceedings with inscrutable eyes. There were some advantages, Mitchell thought, to not caring if you understood others or they understood you.

MacDonald sighed and nodded at Olsen. The computer expert punched a sequence of buttons on the keyboard in front of him. The tapes turned on one of the computer consoles and then on another. In front of Olsen a series of ones and zeroes appeared on the screen, faded, and were replaced by others. In front of Jeremiah a continuous roll of paper began to reel silently out of the printer.

The first few grids were meaningless.

"Folly," Jeremiah muttered and again began to turn.

MacDonald was in his way. "Wait!" he repeated. "The computer is running through the small prime numbers across and down and then the other way, exploring all the possibilities."

The computer reached nineteen plotted against all the smaller prime numbers and then the larger ones. Suspense grew at the same rate as disappointment. The computer hummed. Paper reeled from the printer.

Then it began, something that looked intelligible, printed from the bottom, line by line.

"There's something," MacDonald said. "Look!"

Sourly, skeptically, Jeremiah looked and then with growing disbelief continued to look.

"That square in the corner," MacDonald said, "that could be a sun. Those dots on the right. They look like—look like—"

"Binary numbers," Olsen said.

"But not quite," MacDonald said.

"They read from the right. Look, one, three, five, or maybe that's the way this message writes one, three, five...."

"Of course," MacDonald said, exultation growing in his voice, "why should we expect them to read from the left, why not the right, like the Japanese, or from the bottom up?"

"This is ridicu—" Jeremiah began.

"But what are those symbols on the left-hand side?" MacDonald asked. "And on the right-hand side of the sun?"

"Measurements?" someone suggested.

"Formula?" said another.

"Words?" suggested a third.

"Maybe words," MacDonald said. "Numbers on the right, printed horizontally, words on the left with a vertical component. It looks like they're building up a vocabulary of numbers and words."

"Legs," Jeremiah muttered. "Feet."

"Yes," MacDonald said. "Long legs, and a body, arms— more than one set of arms, and over there at the right— what?"

"If those are words on the left," someone said, "then one of them is repeated three times."

"Must be important," someone else said. "It looks like the creature is pointing at two of them."

And then the picture was complete. Olsen pressed a key. The printer stopped. The computer stopped. In silence they stared at the picture.

"If that's a sun in the lower left, then that's another sun in the upper right," someone said. "Of course. Two suns. Capella."

"And that set of dots below it," MacDonald said, "—a large planet, perhaps a super-Jovian, with four satellites, two of them larger, perhaps Earth size, and the being is pointing at one of them with one of his four arms."

"Not arms," Jeremiah muttered. "Two are wings."

"But what's that thing on its head?" someone asked.

Jeremiah put his hands together in front of him and lowered his face to them, his eyes closed. "Forgive me," he said. "Forgive me for doubting. It is a message from God."

"What is he talking about?" Mitchell said to Thomas.

"Quiet!" Thomas said softly.

The others in the room quieted, too, their comments dwindling one by one until the room once more was silent.

Finally Jeremiah lifted his head from his hands. "I will not stand in your way," he said to MacDonald. "I will tell my people that I have seen the Message and the Message

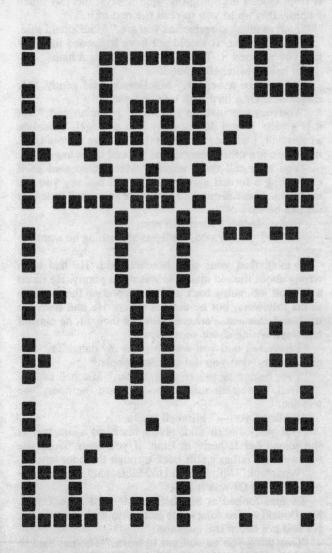

is from God. I do not know what it says, but this much I know. It is up to you to read the rest of it."

"I am as much surprised as you are," MacDonald said.

"I believe that. It would not have happened this way had you planned it. This is an angel. It has a halo."

"A halo," Mitchell echoed.

"It could be a helmet," MacDonald said gently. "Or earphones. Or a bird with a large head."

"You may speculate as you wish," Jeremiah said. "But it is a halo. If you do not deny it is an angel, speculate as you will, I will not deny that the Message is from God, that there are other beings, that we call them angels."

"You may call them angels," MacDonald said as if expressing a formal agreement. "I will not say you are mistaken. There is much to speculate about and little that we can be sure of."

"Come, Judith," Jeremiah said.

"Father," Judith said, "Bill has something he wants to say."

"I misjudged you, sir," Mitchell said. He had been wrong about the old man. He was not a phony. He faced a difficult job, going back and reinterpreting the message to his followers, but he did not flinch. He had seen the truth and changed. Perhaps, Mitchell thought, he himself had been wrong about some things.

"I have felt that you were bad for my daughter," Jeremiah said, "that you did not like people."

"I am beginning to like them better," Mitchell said.

"Well," Jeremiah said, turning toward the door, "we will see."

"I'll drive you—" Mitchell began.

"Not yet," Judith said, giving his hand a squeeze as she joined her father. "In time. If you wish." And she followed her father's stiff back through the doorway.

"What luck!" Mitchell said to MacDonald. "What magnificent luck! Or was it luck?"

Thomas looked at Mitchell and then at MacDonald. MacDonald was looking at the picture drawn by the printer. He had not heard the question.

"One thing you've still got to learn," Thomas said to Mitchell, "is that no two people are alike. To understand

Mac you must understand that he wouldn't cheat."

"Not even to save the Project?" Mitchell said skeptically. "Not even to do tremendous good for man and Capellan? Not even to counteract stubborn mysticism and ignorance?"

"It sure looks like a big bird," someone said.

"If it's a bird," someone else said, "maybe that dot under its feet is an egg."

"One of the three identical words on the left, if they are words, is opposite the egg, if it is an egg," Olsen said.

"Not even then," Thomas said. "Not because he wouldn't be tempted, not even because he would be found out, but because of what he is and because he can't be what he is and be expedient and because he knows it."

"Look," someone said, "the two suns are different."

MacDonald did not move from the spot where he could look directly down upon the print-out. The conversation flowed around him, but he did not seem to hear it. He looked as if he too had seen an angel.

Mitchell watched the others in the room. Each one was reacting differently; each one, like Jeremiah, was seeing the same message but reading it with his own particular interpretation.

Mitchell shook his head and saw the stuffed ostrich in the corner. He walked to it and looked into its black pupils. "You're the only one I really understand," he said. And he turned and looked at the room and all the people clustered about the Message, and he thought about all the equipment and personnel and time that had gone into receiving the Message. His vision broadened to include the steerable radio telescope outside cocked to the night sky and the big array in the valley catching stardust, and he imagined himself traveling across great, dark infinities alone in space for long years, and he shivered.

"Who," he thought desperately, "will understand me?"

COMPUTER RUN

LIFE HAS A STATUS IN THE PHYSICAL UNIVERSE. IT IS PART OF THE ORDER OF NATURE. IT HAS A HIGH PLACE IN THAT ORDER, SINCE IT PROBABLY REPRESENTS THE MOST COMPLEX STATE OF ORGANIZATION THAT MATTER HAS ACHIEVED IN OUR UNIVERSE. WE ON THIS PLANET HAVE AN ESPECIALLY PROUD PLACE AS MEN; FOR IN US AS MEN MATTER HAS BEGUN TO CONTEMPLATE ITSELF....GEORGE WALD, 1960–61...

INCARNATION IS UNIQUE FOR THE SPECIAL GROUP IN WHICH IT HAPPENS, BUT IT IS NOT UNIQUE IN THE SENSE THAT OTHER SINGULAR INCARNATIONS FOR OTHER UNIQUE WORLDS ARE EXCLUDED. ...MAN CANNOT CLAIM TO OCCUPY THE ONLY POSSIBLE PLACE FOR INCARNATION....THE MANIFESTATION OF SAVING POWER IN ONE PLACE IMPLIES THAT SAVING POWER IS OPERATING IN ALL PLACES.... PAUL TILLICH, 1957...

IT MIGHT WELL BE THE CASE THAT THE UNIVERSE HAS PRODUCED AND WILL CONTINUE TO PRODUCE COUNTLESS MILLIONS OF... HISTORIES ANALOGOUS TO HUMAN HISTORY....TO ATTEMPT TO DRAW ULTIMATE CONCLUSIONS ABOUT GOD AND THE UNIVERSE FROM A FEW EPISODES OF THE HISTORY WHICH HAS BEEN ENACTED ON THIS PLANET WOULD SEEM TO BE A MOST HAZARDOUS IF NOT IMPOSSIBLE PROCEEDING....JOHN MACQUARRIE, 1957...

OUR IGNORANCE AND OUR PREJUDICE SHOULD NOT INHIBIT OUR THOUGHTS FROM TRANSCENDING OUR EARTH AND OUR HISTORY AND EVEN OUR CHRISTIANITY....PAUL TILLICH, 1962...

FAR AND FEW, FAR AND FEW
ARE THE LANDS WHERE THE JUMBLIES LIVE;

THEIR HEADS ARE GREEN, AND THEIR HANDS ARE BLUE;
AND THEY WENT TO SEA IN A SIEVE....

                         EDWARD LEAR, 1846...

CITIZENS HELD IN SOME FORM OF DETENTION IN THE UNITED STATES HAVE DECREASED IN TOTAL NUMBERS BY MORE THAN NINETY PERCENT IN THE PAST FIFTY YEARS, THE BUREAU OF EDUCATION ANNOUNCED TODAY. FIFTY YEARS AGO THE BUREAU OF PRISONS WAS ABOLISHED AND THE BUREAU OF EDUCATION TOOK OVER ADMINISTRATION OF THE CRIMINAL REHABILITATION PROGRAM. BU ED POINTED OUT THAT DECREASE HAS OCCURRED IN SPITE OF A VASTLY INCREASED RATE OF ARREST AND CONVICTION DUE LARGELY TO NEW COMPUTERIZED METHODS OF SURVEILLANCE, DETECTION, AND TESTIMONY.

THE BUREAU ASCRIBES THE DECREASE IN THE DETAINED POPULATION TO NEW BREAKTHROUGHS IN CHEMICAL LEARNING AND BEHAVIORAL REINFORCEMENT, AND PREDICTS THAT SOON THE DETENTION CENTERS THEMSELVES MAY BE ELIMINATED IN FAVOR OF NEIGHBORHOOD ANALYSIS AND TREATMENT CENTERS, MUCH AS THE DRUG PROBLEM WAS SOLVED SOME THIRTY YEARS AGO BY REDEFINITION AND LOCAL REEDUCATION.

IN THE BLACKNESS A PHOSPHORESCENCE WAS APPARENT. IT RIPPLED AND ROSE IN THE DARK WITH THE PULSING BEAT OF THE JELLYLIKE MASS. AND THROUGH IT WERE SHOWING TWO DISCS. GRAY AT FIRST, THEY FORMED TWO BLACK STARING EYES....OUT OF THE MASS SHOT A SERPENTINE ARM. IT WHIPPED ABOUT HIM, SOFT, STICKY, VISCID—UTTERLY LOATHSOME....CHARLES W. DIFFIN, 1930...

DID YOU SEE THE PICTURE THEY RECEIVED FROM SOME STAR THE OTHER DAY?

PICTURE? WHAT KIND OF PICTURE?

YOU KNOW—A KIND OF CROSSWORD-LOOKING PICTURE, BLACK AND WHITE SQUARES LIKE.

YEAH, NOW YOU MENTION IT, I REMEMBER SOMETHING LIKE THAT.

WHAT DO YOU THINK? THINK THERE'S REALLY PEOPLE THERE?

PEOPLE WHERE?

THIS STAR.

YOU KNOW WHAT I THINK? I THINK THEY JUST MADE IT UP. HOW COULD PEOPLE LIVE ON A STAR? AND IF THEY DID, HOW COULD THEY SEND US A BUNCH OF BLACK AND WHITE SQUARES?

YEAH...

———

THE RESPEN CONCEPT APPLIED TO THE LEARNING SITUATION HAS BEEN ACCLAIMED AN OUTSTANDING SUCCESS BY EDUCATORS WHO HAVE STUDIED EXPERIMENTAL RESULTS FROM INSTALLATIONS IN SCHOOLS LOCATED IN BROOKLYN, TOPEKA, KANSAS, MONTGOMERY, ALABAMA, AND OAKLAND, CALIFORNIA....

THE ESSENTIAL CHARACTERISTIC OF THE INTEGRATED WORLD IS EXTENSIVE AND SUCCESSFUL WORLD ORGANIZATION FOR PROGRESSIVE AND WELFARE PURPOSES, WITH A SUBORDINATION OF POLITICS AND IDEOLOGY TO PRAGMATISM....LARGE AMOUNTS OF CAPITAL CAN BE ACCUMULATED WITHIN THE UNDERDEVELOPED NATIONS BY THE YEAR 2000. IF WE ASSUME THAT IT TAKES ABOUT $4 OF CAPITAL TO GENERATE AN INCOME OF $1 PER CAPITA, THEN $1 TRILLION OF ADDITIONAL CAPITAL IS SUFFICIENT TO INCREASE THE INCOME OF ONE BILLION PEOPLE BY AN ADDITIONAL $250 PER CAPITA (OVER THE $100–$300 OTHERWISE TO BE EXPECTED). THUS BY THE YEAR 2000 THERE COULD BE ENOUGH CAPITAL AVAILABLE TO PUT MOST OF THE UNDERDEVELOPED NATIONS OVER $500 PER CAPITA AND ALL OF THEM OVER $300 TO $500 PER CAPITA....HERMAN KAHN AND ANTHONY J. WIENER, 1967...

NEBULA...
  NEBULUS...
    NEBULOSITY...
  BUBBLE NEBULA IN CEPHEUS
  RING NEBULA IN LYRA
  VEIL NEBULA IN CYGNUS
        AND NGC 3242 IN HYDRA...
  TRIFID NEBULA IN SAGITTARIUS
  OWL NEBULA IN URSA MAJOR
  CRAB NEBULA IN TAURUS
        AND THE NEBULOUS CLUSTER M16 IN SERPENS...

PLANETARY...
  DIFFUSE...
    DARK...
  HORSEHEAD NEBULA IN ORION
  CONE NEBULA IN MONOCEROS
  LAGOON NEBULA IN SAGITTARIUS
        AND THE NORTH AMERICAN NEBULA IN CYGNUS
  COAL SACK NEBULA IN CRUX

HORSESHOE NEBULA IN SAGITTARIUS
TARANTULA NEBULA IN THE LARGE MAGELLANIC CLOUD
    AND THE HELICAL PLANETARY NEBULA IN AQUARIUS...

GAS...
  DUST...
    BANG...

HOLOVISION TODAY BECAME A REALITY AS GENERAL ELECTRIC
UNVEILED THE FIRST COMMERCIAL MODEL IN THE NEW PRODUCTS
DISPLAY AT MADISON SQUARE GARDEN. THE PRICE IS NOT YET ES-
TABLISHED, BUT IT IS EXPECTED TO BE IN THE TENS OF THOUSANDS
OF DOLLARS AND ONLY GOVERNMENT AND INDUSTRY WILL BE ABLE
TO AFFORD IT FOR THE FIRST YEAR. AFTER THAT, IF PAST EXPERIENCE
IS A GUIDE, THE PRICE WILL DROP RAPIDLY AND OLD-STYLE TELEVI-
SION WILL BECOME OBSOLETE. CERTAINLY THE DISPLAY TODAY WAS
BREATHTAKING, AND THE THREE-DIMENSIONAL QUALITY AND THE AB-
SENCE OF APPARATUS—HOW IT IS DONE IS STILL A COMMERCIAL
SECRET—IS FAR SUPERIOR TO ANY PROJECTION SYSTEM YET DE-
VELOPED....

THE HISTORY OF THE HUMAN RACE IS A CONTINUOUS STRUGGLE
FROM DARKNESS TOWARD LIGHT. IT IS THEREFORE OF NO PURPOSE
TO DISCUSS THE USE OF KNOWLEDGE—MAN WANTS TO KNOW AND
WHEN HE CEASES TO DO SO HE IS NO LONGER MAN....FRIDT-N-JOF
ANSEN, EARLY TWENTIETH CENTURY...

ONCE A CIVILIZATION MADE CONTACT WITH ANOTHER WORLD ITS
OWN LIFE EXPECTANCY WOULD BE GREATLY INCREASED; FOR,
THROUGH THE KNOWLEDGE THAT OTHERS HAVE WEATHERED THE
CRISIS AND, PERHAPS WITH GUIDANCE AS TO HOW THIS WAS DONE,
THE NEW MEMBER OF THE GALACTIC COMMUNITY WOULD BE ABLE
TO SOLVE ITS PROBLEMS BETTER....SEBASTIAN VON HOERNER, 1961...

EVEN RADIO CONTACT WITH A SUPERIOR CIVILIZATION WOULD LEAD
TO PROFOUND UPHEAVALS....COMMITTEE ON LONG-RANGE STUDIES
OF NASA, 1960...

ANTHROPOLOGICAL FILES CONTAIN MANY EXAMPLES OF SOCIE-
TIES, SURE OF THEIR PLACE IN THE UNIVERSE, WHICH HAVE DISIN-
TEGRATED WHEN THEY HAVE HAD TO ASSOCIATE WITH PREVIOUSLY

UNFAMILIAR SOCIETIES ESPOUSING DIFFERENT IDEAS AND DIFFER-
ENT LIFE WAYS; OTHERS THAT SURVIVED SUCH AN EXPERIENCE USU-
ALLY DID SO BY PAYING THE PRICE OF CHANGES IN VALUES AND
ATTITUDES AND BEHAVIOR.

SINCE INTELLIGENT LIFE MIGHT BE DISCOVERED AT ANY TIME VIA
THE RADIO TELESCOPE RESEARCH PRESENTLY UNDER WAY, AND SINCE
THE CONSEQUENCES OF SUCH A DISCOVERY ARE PRESENTLY UN-
PREDICTABLE BECAUSE OF OUR LIMITED KNOWLEDGE OF BEHAVIOR
UNDER EVEN AN APPROXIMATION OF SUCH DRAMATIC CIRCUMSTAN-
CES, TWO SEARCH AREAS CAN BE RECOMMENDED:

1. CONTINUING STUDIES TO DETERMINE EMOTIONAL AND INTEL-
LECTUAL UNDERSTANDING AND ATTITUDES—AND SUCCESSIVE AL-
TERATIONS OF THEM IF ANY—REGARDING THE POSSIBILITY AND
CONSEQUENCES OF DISCOVERING INTELLIGENT EXTRATERRESTRIAL
LIFE.

2. HISTORICAL AND EMPIRICAL STUDIES OF THE BEHAVIOR OF PEO-
PLES AND THEIR LEADERS WHEN CONFRONTED WITH DRAMATIC AND
UNFAMILIAR EVENTS OR SOCIAL PRESSURES. . . . COMMITTEE ON LONG-
RANGE STUDIES OF NASA, 1960. . .

IF TWO OR MORE STABLE SOCIETIES HAVE MADE CONTACT ONCE
SOMEWHERE IT MAY HAVE INITIATED A CHAIN REACTION, WITH NEW
CIVILIZATIONS BEING LOCATED AND SAVED BEFORE THEY DE-
STROYED THEMSELVES. THOSE WHO HAVE TASTED THE EXCITEMENT
OF SPEAKING TO ANOTHER WORLD MIGHT BE INSPIRED TO LONG AND
PATIENT EFFORTS TO BROADEN THE NETWORK OF COSMIC WISDOM.
. . . SEBASTIAN VON HOERNER, 1961. . .

SUCH STUDIES SHOULD CONSIDER PUBLIC REACTIONS TO PAST
HOAXES, "FLYING SAUCER" EPISODES AND INCIDENTS LIKE THE MAR-
TIAN INVASION BROADCAST. THEY SHOULD EXPLORE HOW TO RE-
LEASE THE NEWS OF AN ENCOUNTER TO THE PUBLIC—OR WITHHOLD
IT, IF THIS IS DEEMED ADVISABLE. THE INFLUENCE ON INTERNATIONAL
RELATIONS MIGHT BE REVOLUTIONARY, FOR THE DISCOVERY OF ALIEN
BEINGS MIGHT LEAD TO GREATER UNITY OF MEN ON EARTH, BASED
ON THE ONENESS OF MAN OR ON THE AGE-OLD ASSUMPTION THAT
ANY STRANGER IS THREATENING. . . . COMMITTEE ON LONG-RANGE
STUDIES OF NASA, 1960. . .

PITTSBURGH—A MAN RETURNED HOME IN THE MIDST OF THE
BROADCAST AND FOUND HIS WIFE, A BOTTLE OF POISON IN HER HAND,

SCREAMING, "I'D RATHER DIE THIS WAY THAN LIKE THAT."

SAN FRANCISCO—ONE EXCITED MAN CALLED OAKLAND POLICE AND SHOUTED, "MY GOD! WHERE CAN I VOLUNTEER MY SERVICES? WE'VE GOT TO STOP THIS AWFUL THING!"

BREVARD, NORTH CAROLINA—FIVE BREVARD COLLEGE STUDENTS FAINTED AND PANIC GRIPPED THE CAMPUS FOR A HALF-HOUR WITH MANY STUDENTS FIGHTING FOR TELEPHONES TO INFORM THEIR PARENTS TO COME AND GET THEM.

INDIANAPOLIS—A WOMAN RAN INTO A CHURCH SCREAMING, "NEW YORK DESTROYED; IT'S THE END OF THE WORLD. YOU MIGHT AS WELL GO HOME TO DIE. I JUST HEARD IT ON THE RADIO." SERVICES WERE DISMISSED IMMEDIATELY.

ATLANTA—REPORTS TO NEWSPAPERS FROM LISTENERS IN THE SOUTHEAST HAD IT THAT A PLANET STRUCK IN NEW JERSEY, WITH MONSTERS AND ALMOST EVERYTHING, AND ANYWHERE FROM FORTY TO SEVEN THOUSAND PEOPLE WERE KILLED.

BOSTON—ONE WOMAN TOLD THE *BOSTON GLOBE* THAT SHE COULD "SEE THE FIRE" AND THAT SHE AND MANY OTHERS IN HER NEIGHBORHOOD WERE "GETTING OUT OF HERE."

KANSAS CITY—ONE TELEPHONE INFORMANT SAID HE HAD LOADED ALL HIS CHILDREN INTO HIS CAR, HAD FILLED IT WITH GASOLINE AND WAS GOING SOMEWHERE. "WHERE IS IT SAFE?" HE WANTED TO KNOW. . . .

THIS IS ORSON WELLES, LADIES AND GENTLEMEN, OUT OF CHARACTER TO ASSURE YOU THAT THE *WAR OF THE WORLDS* HAS NO FURTHER SIGNIFICANCE THAN AS THE HOLIDAY OFFERING IT WAS INTENDED TO BE. THE MERCURY THEATRE'S OWN RADIO VERSION OF DRESSING UP IN A SHEET AND JUMPING OUT OF A BUSH AND SAYING BOO!...

> *THE ORANGE KNIVES OF THE SUN*
> *ARE CHOPPING OFF MY HANDS.*
> *THE COSMIC TEMPLES, FALLEN,*
> *ARE CRUSHING MY SHOULDERS.*
> *LIGHT ABANDONS US.*
> *EARTH PULLS US BACK*
> *INTO DARKNESS AND EAST*
> *AS HORIZONS RETREAT*
> *AND OUR TILTING HEARTS TIP*
> *INTO THE EYES*
> *OF THE FRIGHTENED STARS.*
> *KIRBY CONGDON, 1970...*

BIGGEST MOTION PICTURE HIT OF THE YEAR, SAYS DAILY VARIETY, IS NEWEST ONE HUNDRED MILLION GROSSER "UNDER TWO SUNS," WITH SALES TO TELEVISION—OR HOLOVISION, IF THE PRODUCERS DECIDE TO HOLD OFF FOR A BIGGER PRICE WHEN THE NEW DEVELOPMENT TAKES OVER—AND THE MERCHANDISING OF CAPELLAN TOYS, MASKS, HELMETS, T-SHIRTS, AND INTERSTELLAR COMMUNICATION SETS YET TO COME.

CREATURES IN WHICH WE ARE INTERESTED, BESIDES HAVING MINDS, MUST BE ABLE TO MOVE ABOUT AND TO BUILD THINGS. THAT IS, THEY MUST HAVE SOMETHING COMPARABLE TO HANDS AND FEET. THEY MUST HAVE SENSES, SUCH AS SIGHT, TOUCH, AND HEARING, ALTHOUGH THE SENSES THAT EVOLVE ON ANY GIVEN PLANET WILL BE DETERMINED BY THE ENVIRONMENT....CREATURES FULFILLING SUCH REQUIREMENTS MIGHT BEAR LITTLE RESEMBLANCE TO MAN. ...WALTER SULLIVAN, 1964...

THEY MAY BE BLUE SPHERES WITH TWELVE TENTACLES....PHILIP MORRISON, 1960...

THE SEMANTICIST HAD EVIDENTLY MADE A GOOD GUESS IN ALIEN PSYCHOLOGY, FOR NO HOSTILE MOVE WAS MADE TOWARD THE MACHINE. THE NATIVES LAY THERE STUDYING IT, MAKING OCCASIONAL GUARDED GESTURES TO EACH OTHER. THEY STIFFENED AS THE NEXT PICTURE FLIPPED INTO VIEW. IT WAS A TERRESTRIAL FAMILY WITH TWO CHILDREN. IT WAS THE PICTURE STUART KEPT BESIDE HIS BUNK, AND WAS THE BEST THING HE COULD THINK OF TO PUT ACROSS THE CONCEPT OF A PEACEFUL PEOPLE....ROBERTSON OSBORNE, 1949...

4

Andrew White—2028

*"Tell them I came and no one answered,
That I kept my word," he said.*

The office was big. Too big, Andrew White thought. Across the broad, blue, deep-piled carpet with the woven seal in the middle to the carved, white door by which visitors entered was a good twenty yards—that was bigger than the entire flat in which he had been born—and people who came in that door were diminished, like Alice.

That was the way it was intended, no doubt. Space equals importance. And who was more important than the President of the United States?

Everybody, White thought.

The President of the United States is a lonely man, White began to compose in his head. He takes unto himself all the loneliness of the people he serves. And he is a lowly man. Every citizen is higher than he is. He exists to sign his name to other men's decisions, to accept the blame when things go wrong. He is a figurehead and a scapegoat. Fellow Americans, I have made my decision: I will not run for a second term. . . .

But he would, he knew. He would not run away from his duty, and his duty was to complete the job his predecessors had begun more than fifty years ago. The job was not done, God knew, and it was becoming harder all the time to tell people what was wrong, to show them the way it had been, to convince them that the battle needed to be fought anew each day, that peace was an illusion. . . .

Maybe, he thought, it is the ghosts of the other men who have occupied this chair that haunt me today, that make me feel small. He stretched his shoulders and felt the long, flat muscles rippling under the layer of fat too many chicken dinners had put there, and he knew he was a big man, an imposing President, six-feet-six from the soles of his feet to the top of his 'Fro, and the physical equal of any of them, of anyone who came through that door.

Perhaps it was the smell of the place, the smell of fresh air untainted by the odors of cooking food or of other people, the smell of paper and ink, the smell of electrical gadgets functioning noiselessly to bring information or send orders, the smell of power—everything was changed from what he had known as a boy, as a young man. And he smelled the freshly mown grass and turned his back on the door and looked out the broad windows behind the desk toward the green lawn and the leafy trees and the fence, and beyond that the broad streets and tall towers of Washington, which had replaced the familiar ghetto that he had fought to escape and found himself remembering frequently now as if he had been fond of it, as if it had been a happy home.

He thought how wonderful it would be if he could take off his shoes and walk barefooted in the grass the way he used to do in the park when he was a boy. What a fine picture that would be—the President walking barefooted on the White House lawn—and he knew if he did it the picture would be reproduced in one hundred million homes across the nation and the world and it would win him votes. The people liked to think of the President being a bit impulsive when it came to matters of the heart, a bit comic in domestic affairs, a bit inferior to each of them in some way. . . . But he knew he wouldn't do it. He would not have time. He had no time for anything now that he liked to do. He wished he were back in the ghetto, where there was time for everything, time for eating and sleeping and playing and loving, time for being a father or a son, time for joy and indignation. . . .

He heard the door open and he turned. John was standing in the doorway. He was a good-looking man, White thought. He got his good looks from his mother and his size from his father. Maybe a little conservative in his dress and hairstyle but a good-looking brother all the same.

"Dr. MacDonald is calling from the Project," John said. His tone was stiff.

He still recalled last night's conversation, White thought, and he knew now why he felt depressed, why he felt like resigning, why he felt like giving up. It was because of John.

"Who is Dr. MacDonald?" White asked.

"The director of the Project in Puerto Rico, Mr. President," John said. "The one that's been listening for radio communication from the stars, listening for more than fifty years. They picked up something a few months ago that sounded like a message from—some star or other, I forget. From what MacDonald says I gather they've got a translation."

"Good Lord!" White said. "Have I met him?"

"Once or twice, I think—at a reception, at least."

White sighed. "Put him on." He had a feeling of impending disaster. Maybe that was what everything had been leading up to today.

As he felt his stomach sinking under a cold weight, a window opened between his desk and the distant fireplace, unused now with the rigid laws on pollution, and the face of a man a bit past middle age looked at him from a desk. The man's hair was sandy with little apparent gray, unlike his own, and his face was calm and patient and worn. White had seen the face before, he recognized, and he liked the man immediately and sympathized with the man's problem, whatever it was, and caught himself before he went too far.

"Dr. MacDonald," he said. "So good to talk to you again. How are things in Puerto Rico?"

"Mr. President—" MacDonald said, and caught himself and then continued in better control. "Mr. President, this is a moment as historic as the first atomic reaction. I wish I had some memorable phrase to announce it, but all I can say is that we have a message from other intelligent beings on a world circling one of the twin suns of Capella, and we have a translation. We are not alone."

"Congratulations, Dr. MacDonald," White said automatically. "How many people know about this?"

"I was going to tell you—" MacDonald began, and then broke off. "Fifteen," he said. "Perhaps twenty."

"Are they all there?" White asked.

"They've scattered."

"Can you get them back together? Immediately?"

"All except Jeremiah and his daughter. They left a few minutes ago."

"Jeremiah, the Solitarian evangelist?" White asked. "What was he doing there?"

MacDonald blinked. "His opposition to the Project was a threat. He saw the message translation come off the computer print-out; he is no longer opposed. Mr. President, the message—"

"Get him back to your office," White said. "He must not reveal the message, whatever it is, nor will you or any member of your staff."

"And what about an answer to the message?" Mac-Donald asked.

"Out of the question," White said brusquely. "There will be no announcement, no leaks, no answer. The effects of this are incalculable. I must get busy with my staff. I suggest you do the same."

"Mr. President," MacDonald said, "I think you are making a serious mistake. I urge you to reconsider. Let me give you the background, the goals, the significance and meaning of the Project."

White paused and thought. There weren't many people who told him he was wrong—John and this man Mac-Donald, and they both could be difficult. He knew he should cherish the nay-sayers, but he found them a trial; he disliked being told he was making a mistake.

Teddy Roosevelt, someone had written (Lincoln Steffens?), made up his mind somewhere in the region of his hips, and that was the way with Andrew White, he thought. He didn't always know where his decisions came from, but they almost always were right.

He had to believe in his hips. "I'll come to the Project," he said. "You can try to convince me." There—that's all the scientists really wanted, a chance to be heard. "For security reasons I can't specify the time, and you will not tell anyone else. But it should be within a few days." He broke the connection.

Another burden, he thought. One more weary bale to tote.

"John!" he called.

John appeared in the doorway. "I'm making the arrangements now," he said, "and I'm having a brief history of the Project put together for you."

"Thank you," White said. He was a good man and an indispensable assistant, he thought. "You'll go with me, won't you?" he asked humbly.

John nodded. "If you wish," he said. But he was still reserved.

After the door was closed again, White thought, perhaps this would let them get back together again, give them a chance to talk to each other, to really communicate instead of using words like stones.

And then John was in the doorway again. "Dr. MacDonald called back," he said. "The private plane carrying Jeremiah and his daughter back to Texas already had taken off."

White thought briefly about the possibility of intercepting the plane, of having Jeremiah put into custody as he landed, or having the plane shot down at sea on some pretext or other. But it felt all wrong. "Leave an urgent message for him at whatever his destination is: that I want to talk to him before he does anything, to do nothing about the message until I talk to him. And reroute us through Texas."

John hesitated in the doorway. "Father," he said, paused, and then continued, "Mr. President, Dr. MacDonald is right. You're making a mistake. This is a scientific decision, not a political decision."

White shook his head slowly, sorrowfully. "Everything is political. But that's why I'm going to the Project, to give Dr. MacDonald a chance to convince me I'm wrong."

That was only a half-truth. He was going to Puerto Rico to make his decision stick. And for other reasons he had not yet fully explored himself. He knew it, and John knew it.

Damn it! Why couldn't the boy realize that it wasn't intelligence or even wisdom he was talking about; it was just living: he had been there, he had been young and he knew what it was like, and he wanted to save John the pain. And John had never been middle-aged.

* * *

"Those times are done, Father," John had said. "They were fine; they were great; they were necessary like the pioneers; but they're done. You've got to know when the frontier is gone, when the battle is over. You've made it; you've won. There's nothing so unnecessary as a soldier when the war is over. It's time to do something else now."

"I've heard that all my life from people like you, from quitters," White had said, yelling now. "It isn't over; the inequalities haven't been removed— they've just been hidden better. We've got to keep fighting until we've got a final victory, until there's no chance of it slipping away from us. You've got to help, boy! I didn't raise you to pass...."

But that was all wrong. What he should have said was, "I need you, son. You're my link to the future, the reason for it all."

And John would have said, "I never thought of it like that, Father...."

Why didn't the boy ever call him "Dad"?

The trip from Washington to Texas, from catapult to touchdown, was short and uneventful, no longer than it took for John to read to White the brief report on the Project. White sat in his chair, his head leaned back, his eyes closed, listening to the muffled whine of the air trying to find a hold on the polished metal skin a few inches away, and he hated it. He hated mechanical and electrical devices that kept him away from people, that hurtled him here and there, that insulated him from the world, and he was surrounded by them; he couldn't get away from them.

And he listened to John's voice reading the report, heard the boy become interested, get involved, and he wanted to say, "Stop reading! Stop telling me these dull things that I don't want to hear, that will only confuse me! Don't waste your passion on these pointless projects; save it for me! Stop reading and let us talk about matters more suited for a father and son, about love and the past, about love and the future, about us!" But he knew John would not approve; he would not understand. And he listened to John's voice....

The first three decades of the Project had been troubled. Enthusiasm had leaked away over the years as all the efforts, all the imagination, produced nothing for the listeners but silence; directors came and went; morale was a constant problem; funding became perfunctory. Then MacDonald came to the Project and a few years later was named director. Still no messages were received—or recognized, if received—but the Project was pulled together, the long-term nature of the task was recognized, and the search went on.

Then, fifty years after the Project was begun, a Project scientist was checking tapes of the routine radio telescopy from the giant radio telescope in orbit around the Earth, the Big Ear, when he thought he heard voices. He filtered them, subtracted noise and interference, reinforced the information, and heard snatches of music and voices speaking English.

The plane landed in Houston. White's first question to the officials who were waiting to greet him was, "Where's Jeremiah?"

They were embarrassed. One of them finally gave him Jeremiah's message, "If the President wants to see me, he knows where he can find me."

White sighed. He hated airports, too, with all their comings and goings, their noises and their smells, and he wanted to get away. "Take me to Jeremiah," he said.

They argued, but they took him through the clean wide streets of Houston and up to the incredible dome that was called the temple of the Solitarians and down underground passages, dusty and dark, until they reached a small room which seemed even smaller under the oppressive weight of the stadium above.

The old man looked up from the old makeup table and mirror. His hair was white, his face was lined, and his eyes were dark, and White knew as he saw him that he would not be able to move the evangelist. But he had to try.

"Jeremiah?" he said.

"Mr. President?" Jeremiah said in a "render-unto-Caesar" tone.

"You have returned from Arecibo," White said, "with a copy of a message."

"I have returned with nothing," Jeremiah said, "and

any message I received was addressed to me alone. I cannot speak for any other man."

"I speak for many other men," White said sorrowfully, "and in their name I ask that you not reveal your message to anyone else."

"So might Pharaoh have said to Moses when he came down from Mt. Horeb."

"But I am not Pharaoh and you are not Moses and the message is not the Ten Commandments," White said.

Jeremiah's eyes burned. His voice, in contrast, was curiously gentle. "You speak with a greater certainty than I can pretend to. You have legions"—his glance flicked briefly over the guards and assistants who crowded the doorway and the hall outside—"and all I have is my solitary mission. But I will fulfill it unless I am physically restrained, and I will fulfill it this evening." At the end his voice had not seemed to change, but now it was smooth, hard steel.

White tried one more time. "If you do this," he said, "you will be sowing the dragon's teeth of dissension and strife which may well destroy this country."

A smile twisted across Jeremiah's face and was gone. "I am not Cadmus and this is not Thebes, and who knows God's plan for man?"

White started to leave and Jeremiah said, "Wait!" He turned back to his dressing table and picked up a piece of paper. "Here!" he said, holding it out. "You will be the first to receive the message from the hands of Jeremiah."

White took it and turned and walked the long, dark, echoing corridors back to the cars and said to the anonymous men who escorted him, "I want full coverage," and got into the plane to continue his journey to Puerto Rico.

John had a recording of the voices. First there were whispers. The whispers were faint but complex as if they were the whispers of a thousand lips and tongues blended together. Only maybe they were made without lips and tongues, by creatures who had no familiar organs but communicated by humming in their thoraxes or rubbing their antennae together.

White thought about the long years of listening to this,

and he wondered how men had endured it.

Then the whispering grew louder and became the sound of static, miscellaneous sound, noise, and then something more, something coming clearer, something almost intelligible, beginning to come through, almost like the times when you were very small and lying in bed half asleep and people were talking in the next room, and you couldn't make out what they were saying and couldn't rouse yourself enough to listen, but you knew they were saying something. . . .

And then White heard snatches of music and bits of voices saying broken sentences between the static, and the voices were saying pointless things but they were saying something.

"POPCRACKLEPOP," they said. "Voss you dare shar CRACKLEPOP you have a friend and adviser in CRACK-LECRACKLE music POPCRACKLEPOP another trip down allens POPPOPCRACKLE stay tuned for POP-CRACKLE music: bar ba sol bar POP you termites flop-house CRACKLEPOPPOPPOP at the chime it will be ex CRACKLECRACKLEPOP people defender of POPPOP music POPCRACKLE the only thing we have to fear CRACKLE and now vic and POPPOP duffy ain't here CRACKLEPOP music POPCRACKLEPOP information plea CRACKLECRACKLE music; boo boo boo boo POPPOPCRACKLE can a woman over thirty-five CRACKLEPOPPOPPOP adventures of sher POP-CRACKLECRACKLE music POPPOP it's a bird CRACKLE only genuine wrigley's POPCRACKLE born edits the news CRACKLECRACKLEPOP hello every-body POPCRACKLEPOP music POPPOPCRACKLE that's my boy CRACKLE check and double POP. . . ."

"The voices," White said after the silence returned.

"The voices," John agreed.

White noticed that they had said the words differently, that John's tone had been excited and pleased. White was not pleased. He was disturbed at the thought of creatures somewhere out there with apparatus—forty-five light-years from here—listening to the sounds of Earth, alien ears listening to the voices of Earth, and sending them back again transmuted, dirtied. He had been on television, often, and recently on radio as well, since its revival, and he didn't like to think of his voice and picture fleeing on restless waves through space for anyone or anything to intercept and thus possess a part of him. He wanted to disbelieve it.

"Maybe it's just a reflection," he said.

"From forty-five light-years away?" John said. "We'd never pick up a thing."

White tried to imagine the incredible distances between the stars that the voices must have traveled to reach that far place and return, and he could not imagine the endless way, the emptiness between. He thought about an ant walking from Washington to San Francisco, and then coming back, and that was not enough.

"Maybe it's closer," he said.

"Then we wouldn't be getting the program from ninety years ago," John said.

"Maybe it's been floating around in the air all these years," White said, waving his hands in the air as if he could brush these concepts away like cobwebs. "Oh, I know. That's impossible, too. Only it's no more impossible than thinking of aliens out there sending us messages."

Or this, he thought. He looked at the piece of paper Jeremiah had given him. There was a drawing on it, black ink on white paper; it looked as if it had been done by a talented amateur; perhaps it had been drawn by Jeremiah himself. It was a drawing of a stylized angel, its wings spread behind it, a halo around its head, its arms outstretched in a kind of welcome or acceptance, its face peaceful. . . . It was an angel of mercy, of love, carrying a message of God's love, and it was surrounded by a border of entwined flowers. . . .

By what impossible magic, White thought, had the voices changed into this?

"The whole cosmological picture," John was saying, "made it believable. There had to be intelligent life out there. It would be impossible if there were not other creatures in the galaxy, intelligent enough, curious enough, and capable of communicating with us across the light-years, wanting, needing to find other creatures like them-

selves who could look at themselves and at the stars and wonder...."

White was caught in John's vision for a moment and then he looked at his son's face and saw the excitement in it and the rapture, and he thought, "You are a stranger to me, and I cannot speak to you."

He loved he boy, that was the trouble. He didn't want to see him get hurt the way he had been hurt.

He wanted to save him the torment, save him from learning things the hard way. That was the essence of humanity, being able to learn from the mistakes and successes of others, not having to learn it all over again each generation. He knew what John would say. "That's no better than instinct. Being human is being able to do something different."

Why was it always like this? The boy was an alien, but somehow he had to communicate.

Puerto Rico was silent. As they went looping over the dark roads in the powerful black car that was waiting at the airport, all White could hear was the quiet hum of the steam turbine. He had asked that the windows be opened, and he could smell the trees and the grass and the more distant salt and fish of the sea.

This was better than Washington, he thought, and better than Houston. Or any place else he could think of that he had been recently. The concern that kept coiling tighter in his stomach like the spring of a wind-up toy began to relax.

What had happened to all the wind-up toys he had known when he was a child? he wondered. Replaced, he thought, by battery-powered toys. Perhaps he was the last of the wind-up toys. A wind-up President, he thought, wound-up in the ghetto and now working out all the frustrations and aggressions that had pushed him into the White House. Wind him up and see him right the ancient wrongs—but carefully, carefully, so that domestic tranquillity is not disturbed, so that international peace is not threatened. . . .

He laughed, a bit ruefully, and he thought, there was something in that office in Washington which did not let a man be what he had been, what he wanted to be, but forced him to be a President.

John was looking at him, and he realized that John had not heard him laugh for a long time. He leaned over and put his hand on John's.

"It's all right," he said. "It was just a passing thought." And he thought, I could be a better man here. Maybe not a better President, but a better man.

"We're almost there," John said.

White took his hand away. "How do you know?"

"I've been here before," John said.

White settled back in his seat. He hadn't known that. He wondered why he hadn't known about John's visit to the Project. What else about John was a secret, a mystery?

The mood had passed, and when the Project appeared out of the night, glimmering and vast and strange in the moonlight, White turned from it and would not look at it. The car pulled up beside a long, low concrete building.

By the time they were inside the building, MacDonald was waiting for them. It did not seem to White as if he had rushed there, for he was not out of breath or nervous but as if he always was where he was needed. Again, but even stronger, White felt a surge of empathy toward the man. No wonder, he thought, MacDonald had kept the Project alive for so long.

White felt sorry that he must kill what this man had given his life to.

MacDonald was escorting the Presidential party down the painted concrete corridor. "Mr. President," he had said, "you do us honor." But he walked casually and talked easily as if he did this every day and this party were no different than any of the others.

The corridors were busy with men and women moving purposefully on errands as if it were the middle of the day instead of the middle of the night, and then White realized that this was the busy part of the twenty-four hours for the Project, the nighttime when the listening was best. What would it be like, he wondered, to have the days and nights always reversed? To have light and dark turned around like a bat or an owl? And he thought, he should know the answer to that as well as anybody.

The people passed. MacDonald did not introduce any of them, feeling without being told, perhaps, that this was an unofficial visit—or perhaps not wanting to stir up speculation in the Project about his visit. But some of the staff members glanced at them and then glanced a second time with a shock of recognition. White was used to that. And there were some who were busy talking to each other and glanced at them and continued their conversations without a pause. White was not used to that. He discovered that he didn't like it. He had thought that it was his loss of anonymity that he disliked, but he realized that he disliked more not being recognized at all.

He also disliked the sterile corridor, echoing with footsteps and voices, and the room filled with electronic equipment through which he was ushered. He recognized oscilloscopes and recorders, but much of it was alien to him and he was pleased that it should remain so. A man was sitting in front of a panel with earphones over his head. MacDonald waved to him as they passed, and he waved back, but his eyes were glazed as if they were focused on something hundreds of miles away. Billions of miles, light-years, White corrected.

They passed through another room that was virtually all computer. Instead of walls, there was a computer, cables snaked into other rooms, apparently to other computers or units of the same one, and the floor was crowded with data-inputs and printers. It was the biggest computer setup White had ever seen, bigger even than the Pentagon or State Department's simulators or the Information Department's data files. The place smelled of oil and electricity, and it talked to itself of information and events and correlations, of shoes and ships and sealing wax, and it added one and one and one very fast, over and over again. Being in that room was like being inside a computer, a modern Jonah inside a great fish not yet born, and he was relieved when it opened a mouth and spat them out into an office.

The office did not reveal the evidences of a man's life, of twenty years of effort and dedication. Like the rest of the building it was plain, a simple desk set in front of tall bookshelves built into the wall, and the shelves had real books on them with leather bindings. Some of the books had titles in foreign languages, and White remembered from John's briefing that MacDonald had been a linguist before he became an engineer.

"Set up my information center," he said to John.

"You can plug it right into the computer," MacDonald said. "My assistant will show you where."

They were alone. They faced each other, and White hardened his heart against the man.

If MacDonald recognized the situation, he did not acknowledge it. Instead he said casually, "Jeremiah?"

White shook his head. "He refused to be moved. He is going to release the message to the faithful. His message, he called it."

MacDonald motioned him to a chair. "And so it is," he said. "His message, my message, your message."

White shook his head. "Not my message. Here is a copy of his message." He handed MacDonald the piece of paper Jeremiah had given him.

MacDonald looked at the drawing of Jeremiah's angel, pursed his lips, and nodded. "Yes, that's what Jeremiah saw. You didn't stop him?"

"There are some things a President can do and should do, there are some things he can do and should not do, and there are some things he cannot do. Stopping Jeremiah falls somewhere between the second and the third. But that"—he indicated the piece of paper—"cannot be the message."

"How much do you know about the Project?" MacDonald asked.

"Enough," White said, hoping to forestall a repetition of John's briefing.

"You know about the long listening without results?" MacDonald asked.

"I know all that," White said.

"And then the voices?" MacDonald continued, and pushed a button on his desk.

"I've heard them," White said, but it was too late. The voices had already started.

The acoustics were better here or something had been lost along the path of reproduction. The whisperings that began it were more urgent here; they held a note of pleading, of insistence, of anger, of despair, and they shook White so that when they became the voices he relaxed as if the effort to hear and understand had taken all his strength. The voices, too, were a little different, as if they started at another point in an endless loop, and they were more distinct.

POPCRACKLE ice regusted CRACKLEPOP music: that little chatterbox the one with the pretty POPPOPCRACKLE wanna buy a duck POPCRACKLEPOP masked champion of justice CRACKLEPOPPOP music POPPOPPOPCRACKLE ter eleven book one hundred and POPCRACKLEPOP here they come jack POPPOP music CRACKLE yoo hoo is anybody POPCRACKLE is raymond your POPCRACKLEPOPPOP music POPPOPCRACKLE music: wave the flag for hudson CRACKLEPOP um a bad boy POPPOPPOP lux presents holly CRACKLECRACKLE music POPPOPCRACKLE rogers in the twenty POPCRACKLEPOP music: cola hits the spot twelve CRACKLE. . . .

White shook himself to break the spell. "That wasn't the message," he said.

MacDonald adjusted a dial on the desk. The voices continued in the background like a distant Greek chorus commenting on their predicament. "That was only what they used to attract our attention."

CRACKLECRACKLEPOP hello everybody POPCRACKLEPOP.

"The message was in the static between the voices," MacDonald continued. "When we slowed it, stretched it, the static turned into a sound and silence pattern that we tried to decipher for months."

POPCRACKLE ice regusted CRACKLEPOP.

"I'se regusted," White repeated in a deep voice and laughed.

"You know that one?" MacDonald asked.

"One of our folk heroes," White said in a self-deprecating tone. "Does it bother you to have a black President?"

"About as much," MacDonald said, "as it bothers you to have a white Project director."

MacDonald was not only wise; he was shrewd. He knew that there were differences between men and these differences inevitably affected how they felt about each other, about themselves. White had liked MacDonald from the start; now he was beginning to admire him, and that was dangerous.

*   *   *

*What John wanted to do was even more dangerous.
He thought there were no more differences, that he
could forget his color and his people, that he could
live like a white man, concerned with himself alone.
How could he be so blind to the realities of racism?
You still had to be on guard; to trust yourself in their
world without the protection of power or of righ-
teous anger was to risk your soul. His son—Andrew
White's son—could not go over.*

"Finally it came to us," MacDonald said. "Those dots
and silences between the voices could be translated as
spaces filled and unfilled, like a crossword puzzle, and
the computer finally worked it out, figured out the length
of the message and where it began and where it stopped,
and what was false message—static, noise—and what
was the real message endlessly repeated, and it printed
out the message for us."

MacDonald reached for a frame that until now had been
face down on his desk. White had not noticed it before.
How much else had he not noticed? he wondered. How
much of the message had he missed?

"Here it is," MacDonald said. He turned it over and
reached it out to White. "This is the original message, the
first one transferred from electronic signals in the computer onto paper. We had it framed for you; we thought
you might like to keep it for a while, to look at, to wonder
about a bit, perhaps, and when you're finished with it,
when you're tired of showing it to visitors, you might
send it over to the Smithsonian."

White took the frame reluctantly as if the message were
one he did not really want to receive, like a summons or
a subpoena or a warrant. He did not want to look at it;
he did not want to wonder about it; he did not want it
translated for him. He wanted to destroy it, to forget it;
it was bad news, and he understood the Egyptian tradition
of executing the messenger who brought evil tidings.

He looked at the message. It consisted of little marks
scattered in random fashion across a blank sheet of paper.

White looked up. "This is a message?"

MacDonald nodded. "I know it's not impressive at first

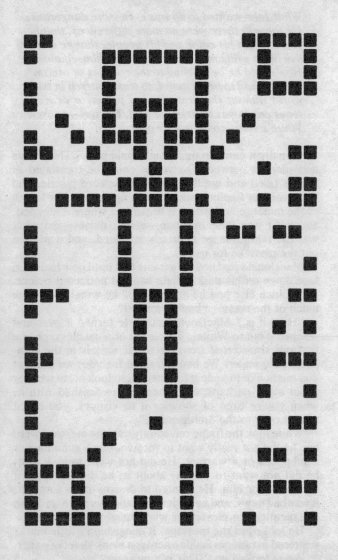

glance. What is impressive is its origin in the minds of alien creatures born under two alien suns—red giants—forty-five light-years from here. That's how far it traveled to reach us, to reshape itself into the picture you hold in your hands."

"It's still not much," White said, turning the frame over to look at the blank back as if there might be something more important, more revealing, on that side.

"Perhaps it doesn't seem like much," MacDonald said patiently, "but the information contained in that sketch is surprising. 'A picture is worth a thousand words,' the Chinese are reputed to have said, and we can learn at least that much more from this than from words—in some arbitrary symbols—even if we could read the symbols. What we have is 589 dots and dashes, dots and blanks, a grid made up of nineteen spaces across and thirty-one spaces down, and in those spaces the Capellans have drawn a portrait of themselves."

White looked at it again. He was beginning to see forms and shapes in it, and he realized that his first reaction was conditioned by his desire to believe that the computer marks were random, that the message was in fact meaningless. "Damn poor portrait," he muttered. "Like the stick figures children draw."

"Or like the figures adults draw for children, the kind of images children can identify because they can draw them—the kind of pictures you must draw with a blunt crayon or a grid. It looks like something intelligible even to the unsophisticated."

White glanced up, amused. "Like me?"

"Like you. But unlike most stick figures, this picture rewards study. Much about it still is ambiguous, but some of what it means seems reasonably clear. In the lower left-hand corner is a square four spaces to a side; another one is in the upper right. Those probably are suns."

"Two suns?" White said and then felt foolish. "Of course. Capella has two suns. John told me and you told me, but I can't seem to remember things like that."

"'My words fly up, my thoughts remain below,'" MacDonald quoted.

"'Words without thoughts never to heaven go,'" White

continued, and enjoyed the look of admiration and new respect in MacDonald's glance, and knew he was being subtly flattered and appreciated the skillful way it was being handled.

"Below the symbol in the upper right is a smaller square with single marks and double marks seemingly grouped around it. If a large square is a sun, a smaller square is a—"

"A planet," White supplied.

"That's right," MacDonald said.

White felt as if he were back in school and had just received the teacher's approval.

"And those single and double marks," MacDonald continued, "probably are satellites of the big planet. Theory suggests that only large superjovian planets would be able to maintain an orbit in a double-sun system. Life on a superjovian seems unlikely. But a superjovian could have Earth-sized satellites on which an intelligent race of creatures could evolve. And the Capellan—if that is what he is—seems to be pointing with two of his, or her, arms— or an arm and a wing—toward one of the suns, the one in the upper right-hand corner, and one of the satellites, if that is what they are. The implication is: this is its sun, not the other, which may be at considerable distance, and this is its home world."

White nodded. In spite of himself he had become involved. "Ingenious. Almost like a detective story." He felt MacDonald's eyes on him and realized he was being played upon and enjoyed it.

"We've been working at it, trying to put together the clues and solve the mystery," MacDonald said. "I have an excellent staff, Mr. President—dedicated, brilliant, much more capable than I; my job is to keep them supplied with pencils and rubber bands and paper clips."

"I know that feeling," White said dryly. How much about him did MacDonald know, he wondered. How much did he guess? How much was common to all administrators?

"Below the satellites are numbers from one to nine written in a binary system, establishing a system of counting, the beginning of a common mathematics, and the fact that the Capellans' intellectual processes are similar to ours. Down the left-hand side is what appears to be words; numbers on the right, words on the left; numbers written horizontally, words with a vertical component."

"Why words?"

MacDonald shrugged. "We're still guessing about a lot of things. Perhaps they're building a vocabulary for later use when a word may be worth at least one picture, perhaps they're necessary to make a statement in the message that we have not yet deciphered, or perhaps it is because they help explain the picture."

"What are the words?"

MacDonald pointed at the picture in White's hands. "They seem to apply to something that is on the same line or lines with them, usually to their right. Let's skip the top one for a moment. The next one is repeated three times. Two of them the Capellan is pointing at with his right upper limbs. Perhaps they are the Capellan word for 'Capellan.' You will notice that the third time the word appears it is opposite the dot underneath the Capellan, which—if it is not an accidental dot, or meaningless noise—may mean that this, too, is a Capellan—or a Capellan in embryo." He looked at White expectantly.

"An egg?" White ventured.

"Very likely. It may be trying to tell us that it breeds by laying eggs."

"It's a bird."

"Or a reptile. Or an insect. But most likely a bird, which would explain the second pair of limbs."

"They really are wings?" White said.

"Working wings or vestiges."

White glanced at Jeremiah's drawing on MacDonald's desk and back to the framed computer read-out. He was beginning to see how one could become the other, how Jeremiah could have seen the stick figure as an angel, the square thing on its head as a halo. The situation became more understandable, though no less serious. "And the other words?" he said.

"These are even more speculative," MacDonald said. "The third word may mean 'wing,' the fifth, 'body' or 'chest,' the sixth, 'hips' or 'legs,' the seventh, 'legs' or 'feet.' They may mean something else entirely, refer to function rather than parts. Some of these we're filing away until we have some repetitions."

White was startled. "More messages are being received?"

MacDonald shook his head. "The same message over and over. As if, having attracted our attention, the Capellans want to tell us only the important things about themselves, and these it wants to be sure we understand before they go on."

"Like programmed learning," White said. He was relieved that there were no more messages, that he had to cope with one alien communication, one problem, not a continuing series.

"Or maybe," MacDonald said, "they do not wish to go further, to send more messages of whatever kind, until they know we are receiving them and understand, until we have replied."

White quickly changed the subject. "What important things are they trying to tell us?"

"Who they are. Where they live. What they call themselves. How they reproduce. How they think."

"How do they think?" White asked.

"In words and numbers and images," MacDonald replied, "the way we do."

White studied the picture as if by looking at it he could force it to yield up its secrets, but it clung to them stubbornly. "Do they think the same way we think—in terms of advantage and disadvantage, in terms of profit and loss, in terms of victory and defeat, in terms of what's in it for me?"

MacDonald looked at White much, White thought, as he had been looking at the picture. He shook his head. "They seem very peaceful to me. All of us don't think in terms of advantage, of conflict. Increasingly, I think we become more uncompetitive. And birds always have been a symbol of peace."

"Only the dove," White said gloomily. "Did you ever see a bluejay attacking other birds or cats or even people? What about hawks and eagles and vultures? Any creature that becomes the dominant species on its world has to be aggressive. How does a bird think?"

How does a man think? A person you have raised within your home, within your arms, within your love—how does he think? How can one reach him, tell him, make him see what he is, what the world is like? What he wanted to say was, "Look, son, you see the world as a benign, smiling place of peace and opportunity and fair play, but it's not like that. You go on thinking it is, and the first chance it gets it's going to bite your black ass off."

And John would say, "Stop talking like a nigger, Father!"

White lifted his eyes from the picture in his hands to MacDonald's face. "Do you have a son?" he asked, and hearing himself say it realized he had let slip something about himself. Not "Do you have any children?" but "Do you have a son?" In an age when one child was the norm, perhaps MacDonald would not notice.

MacDonald's face softened. "Yes," he said.

That had got through to him. "We're a lot alike," White said. "That was my son who came in with me."

"I know," MacDonald said.

"He acts as my personal assistant. He is very much interested in your Project," White heard himself saying.

"I know," MacDonald said.

White hastened on. "I wouldn't know what to do without him," he said, and it sounded in his ears almost like a plea. Perhaps it was.

"My son is only eight months old," MacDonald said.

White raised his eyebrows.

MacDonald chuckled. "I've spent my life waiting. For that I almost waited too long."

White thought of MacDonald waiting here at the Project among all these alien machines with their alien smells, listening for a message from the stars that never came, listening without results for fifty years. Bosh! He was sentimentalizing again. That wasn't this man. The Project itself was fifty years old, but MacDonald had been with it only twenty years, and he was an engineer—no doubt he liked machines and their smells and their meaningless noises. Still, twenty years. . . . And now the message had come, and it would never be acknowledged. White felt a new flash of sympathy for MacDonald and all the people who had given their lives to the search.

"You don't look like a man who has been told that his life's work can't be completed," White said.

MacDonald smiled. It was the kind of patient smile he must have maintained throughout the long listening, White thought. "I've waited a long time," MacDonald said. "So have the Capellans. We can wait some more, if necessary. But I hope that your decision can be changed. You're still here, and you're still listening."

"I owe you that," White said. MacDonald waited. "He could have said, 'You don't owe me anything, Mr. President. We owe you for your sacrifices,'" White thought with fleeting irritation, and dismissed it as childish. "Those other words," he said, "the ones you passed over—what about them?"

"If those are words at the bottom," MacDonald said, pointing out the two symbols at the bottom of the page beneath the egg, "the one in the upper left-hand corner is repeated below. It could mean 'sun.'"

"And the other word at the bottom?"

"We don't know," MacDonald said. "Perhaps 'more sun.' You will notice that the sun at the bottom left has rays at each of its corners. The one at the top has only a single beginning of a ray. Perhaps the distant sun is hotter and they're trying to tell us this in case we have the astronomical capability to distinguish between them."

White studied the picture again. "All that from this?"

"As you said, a detective story. We're detectives hunting for clues, and we have a great many clues. And a great research tool." He waved his hand toward the wall beyond which was the computer room. "Virtually the entire written history and literature of humanity—in all its written languages—is stored in there. Everything we do or say within the Project is recorded. It's that kind of computer. It learns and compares and translates and stores and works cryptograms and breaks codes. And of course, what we are working with is not cryptography but anticryptography, the designing of a code impossible to misunderstand. . . ."

"Our earlier conversation, your call," White said. "That is recorded." It was half a question.

"If we wished, we could recall the information upon voice command or eliminate it from the record upon written command."

White waved a negligent hand. "It doesn't matter. What I have done and said is a matter of record throughout the world, and when my term of office is over it will all be ferreted out by scholars and dissected and buried in a library somewhere.... What I can't understand is why Jeremiah was here."

MacDonald was thoughtful. "Until you spoke, the Project was not a secret. One of my responsibilities was to keep the Project going, and one way I fulfilled that responsibility was to tell people what we were doing, to show them what it meant, how important it was."

Just as you are doing with me, White thought. "Public relations?" he said. "Promotion?"

"Yes," MacDonald said.

Meaning, White thought, call it what you will; it is the function all administrators must perform effectively if they are to administer successfully; they must develop public (and internal) acceptance for what they are doing—public acceptance through public understanding. "Communication?" he said.

"I like that best," MacDonald said.

"I do too," White admitted.

John opened the far door. "Mr. President," he said, "we have a report from Houston."

"Let's have it," White said.

MacDonald pushed a button on his desk.

As the familiar window opened in front of them, White said, "I hate this stuff."

"Me too," MacDonald said. "It's a filtered communication; most of the sensory clues are missing."

White looked at MacDonald in mild surprise, and then the scene came alive. The view was in mid-air—perhaps from a hovering jet—outside the Houston temple. Men and women were marching back and forth in the street. They were carrying signs. The signs had words on them; at first they were unreadable and then, as the view zoomed in, the words became clear: THE MESSAGE IS PHONY; JEREMIAH LIES; NOT ANGELS BUT ANGLES; SHUT DOWN THE PROJECT; DESTROY RADIO

TELESCOPES; NO COMMUNICATION WITH ALIENS....

Between the pickets other men and women passed and entered the building in an irregular but persistent flow. Beyond the pickets, as the view pulled back again, were silent figures massed like a cloud around the building and waiting for something, a word, an event, a signal, and from their appearance it was difficult to determine whether the figures were spectators or participants waiting for their moment.

The scene changed. Now the viewpoint was inside the giant dome. The view looked up at the distant ceiling and then slowly panned the seats. Every one was filled, and more people were sitting and standing in the aisles. Below them, in a circle of light, like a gleaming stick figure in black and white, was Jeremiah. He was not alone. A creature was behind him, an evanescent, transparent figure, but clearly an angel, with halo and wings outspread, and it had its right hand on Jeremiah's shoulder. And the stick figure raised his left hand to the crowd, and the crowd came to its feet in one simultaneous movement. White could not hear anything—he supposed there was sound with this transmission, but it was not turned up—but he could feel the shock wave that exploded from more than one hundred thousand throats and shook the distant ceiling of the temple....

"Trouble," White said as the scene faded and MacDonald turned it off.

"Excitement," MacDonald said.

"Disturbance, dissension," White added, "trouble. We have solved many of the problems that threatened to tear this nation apart at the time the Project was started and trouble will keep us from solving the others. We need calm, serenity, and this angel of Jeremiah's means trouble. It will bring back the old problems of the chosen peoples and the outcasts, the favored and the fallen, the elect and the nonelect.... This angel of Jeremiah's brings not peace but a sword. I don't see how he could have read that into the message," he said, forgetting his earlier perception.

MacDonald picked up a piece of illustration board from his desk—something else he had missed, White thought, and held it out. "I had a staff artist prepare this for you. Something comparable to what I thought Jeremiah would describe."

White accepted it, turned it over, looked at it. It, too, had a drawing, but this one was a drawing of a tall bird-like creature with vestigial wings. On its head was a transparent helmet. At opposite corners of the drawing was a stylized representation of a sun; below the one in the upper right-hand corner was a Jupiterlike planet with four satellites, two small ones like the moon and two larger ones, one resembling Venus, the other resembling Earth. Numbers from one to nine were written underneath along the right-hand edge. Running down the left-hand side were words that said, "Sun—Capellan—wing—Capellan—chest—hips—legs—Capellan." And below the figure was a large, well-shaped egg; below that were two more words—"sun" and "hotter sun."

Through the creature's transparent helmet could be seen the face of an alien obviously avian in evolution but also intelligent, and intelligence had molded its features into a distant relative of man. The bird looked interested, gentle, benevolent....

"I suppose," White said, "one is just as reasonable as the other."

"That's one reason I couldn't tell Jeremiah he was wrong," MacDonald said. "He had just as much right to his interpretation as I to mine."

"Another reason," White said, "his acceptance of the message was an advantage for the Project."

MacDonald shrugged. "Certainly. Although what I was trying to tell him was that the message was no threat to him or his religious beliefs. And that is true."

White was a little surprised at MacDonald's cynicism. Not much, because he was never really surprised by anyone's opportunism, but somehow he had been building a different image of MacDonald. "What you are saying is that you allowed him to deceive himself."

"No," MacDonald said steadily. "We don't know what the message says. We're interpreting it on a simple mechanistic basis, reading it at a kind of childish, stick-figure level; Jeremiah is interpreting it at a more adult level,

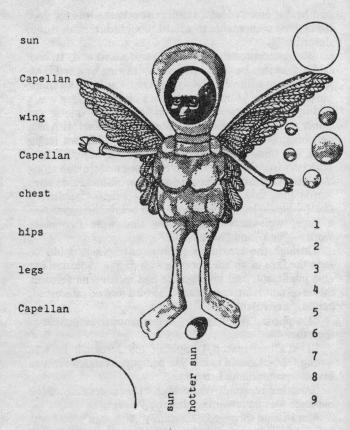

sun

Capellan

wing

Capellan

chest

hips

legs

Capellan

1
2
3
4
5
6
7
8
9

sun   hotter sun

translating symbols into images. The two drawings—ours and Jeremiah's—are of roughly equal value. The only reality we have is the computer grid."

White said softly, "Such a small thing. So much disturbance."

"Temporary," MacDonald said. "If you allow us to release what we believe is the substance of the message, let the knowledgeable scientists of the world supply their interpretations, let us come up with an answer and transmit it to the Capellans...."

White looked at the drawing in his hand. He did not

answer MacDonald directly. "Do you have a pencil?" he asked. "Or a crayon or pen?"

MacDonald rummaged in his desk and produced a broad-tipped pen. White worked over the face of the bird for a moment and then handed the illustration board to MacDonald.

Now the bird was no longer humanoid. Its beak was longer and curved at the end, a beak made for biting and tearing. The bird's eyes were hooded and cruel. It was a bird of prey looking for its next meal. "What if it really looks like that?" White asked.

"The question," he should have said, "is what the world is really like. Is it the world you see or the world I know? If some doubt remains, wouldn't it be better to consider the past, to learn the history of your people, to be black until you are certain the present has changed its old ways, its old habits of mind?"

But he hadn't said that. "By God, I know the world, John, and you don't. You've got to take my word for it if you can't see for yourself."

And John had told him, "The past is irrelevant."

But even that was a statement out of the past.

Time was running out, White felt. Soon he would have to terminate this conversation and decide what to do about the trouble that was coming, that he could feel in his hips. But he hated to cut off this man—this good man, he thought—until he was satisfied.

"What difference can it make," MacDonald was saying, "forty-five light-years away? They want to communicate. They're looking for other minds, for fellow intelligent creatures in the universe."

"But why?" White asked. "Why go to all the trouble?"

"So they won't be alone. For the same reason we've listened. So we wouldn't be alone. It is a terrible thing to be alone."

What does he know? White thought. "Yes," he said.

"Besides," MacDonald said, "they already know we're here."

"What?" White asked, surprised, a little alarmed.

"The voices," MacDonald said.

The voices. Of course. The aliens had picked up the old radio broadcasts, so they knew there were people at the other end. "They don't know who we are or what we are," White said. "They don't know whether we have received their message or whether we have deciphered it or whether we will respond to it—or whether we can do any of these things."

MacDonald put his fingertips together. "Does it matter?"

White shrugged a bit impatiently. "You and your colleagues are the experts in aliens and in alien potentials, but even a layman can imagine a situation in which it might matter."

MacDonald smiled. "The boogeyman from the stars?"

"There are boogeymen," White said. "The tribe from the East or the North. The bad men from the hills. The lynch mob from the village."

"None of them civilized," MacDonald said. "None of them trying to communicate."

"I can find examples of that, too. Maybe the Capellans are signaling a number of different worlds, and they will determine which one to invade according to which one responds."

"Even if interstellar travel is possible—which it probably is not—even if interstellar warfare is possible—which it almost certainly is not," MacDonald said, "even then, why would they want to do it?"

White spread his hands wide. "Why would they want to expend the effort to signal us in the first place?" MacDonald started to speak but White continued. "'Dear Miss Lonelyhearts, I have been waiting here for a million years. . . .' Perhaps they need to be sure we have not ruined our planet with radioactivity since we discovered radio. Perhaps they intend to send us instructions for constructing a matter transmitter. Perhaps they require a certain level of technology to make us worthwhile as a subject world."

"If all this were possible," MacDonald said, "then we must also remember that they have put themselves and their world in our hands, as much as we would put ourselves in theirs. That demonstrates a certain amount of trust."

"Or confidence. Or arrogance."

"I cannot believe—" MacDonald began.

"But can you conceive?" White broke in. "You have spent your life among scholarly men of good will. To you the universe is a benevolent place; it has treated you with kindness, or, at least, neutrality. I have seen passion and malice and greed, and I know that intelligence is not necessarily benevolent; in fact, in my experience, it is more likely to be merely an instrument in the persistent search for advantage, in weighing profit and loss and finding a means of maximizing profit and minimizing loss."

MacDonald did not respond as White had expected. "Logic is our assurance," MacDonald said calmly. "The only thing worth sending from star to star is information, and the certain profit from such an exchange far outweighs the uncertain advantage from any other kind of behavior. The first benefit is the knowledge of other intelligent creatures in the universe—this alone gives us strength and courage. Then comes information from an alien world; it is like having our own instruments there, even our own scientists, to measure and record, only with the additional advantage of a breadth and duration of measurements under a variety of conditions. Finally comes the cultural and scientific knowledge and development of another race, and the treasure to be gained from this kind of exchange is beyond calculation."

White changed his approach. "What if it changes us? We have seen problems of cultural shock, when a more advanced race meets a more primitive one. Some of the societies that have gone through it here on earth have disintegrated; some have become slaves; and the ones that survived did so by changing their values, attitudes, behavior...."

MacDonald studied White as if estimating his ability to understand. "I should think you would not find conditions so perfect that you would not welcome change."

Not understanding; reaction. "My kind of change," White said.

"Besides," MacDonald said, "the anthropological examples you have cited refer to societies that are unsophisticated or isolated, that could not imagine anything superior to themselves, even anything different—"

"As a tearful old medicine man once said to Carl Jung," White said, as if he were remembering, "we might find ourselves 'without dreams.'"

"We are not so naive," MacDonald said. "We know that there are other intelligent beings in the universe; we know that they will be different from us, and we hunger for the exchange. Our dreams are of spaceflight and alien contact; an entire literature has developed it, and our myths reinforce it with their flying saucers and visitations. We have been listening now for fifty years, and people are prepared to hear something. They are psychologically ready for contact. Now they know we have been contacted; they have heard the voices, and they have seen one version of the message...."

John opened the door again. "More information coming in, Mr. President."

MacDonald looked at White. White nodded, and MacDonald pressed a button.

The first scene showed police battling a mob outside the Solitarian temple. Stains could be seen on the streets when the conflict swirled an opening into view. Bodies could be seen, too, and some of the bodies wore uniforms. Men and women were streaming out of the temple endlessly, trying to get through the battle—or to join it.

MacDonald turned up the sound. The conflict rumbled like distant thunder.

The second scene revealed a smaller mob in the street in front of a neoclassical building; around it, like a moat, was a reflecting pool which kept the mob at a distance. But there was fist-shaking and shouts; the shouts were in some foreign language.

The third and fourth and fifth scenes were similar: the only changes were the architectural styles of the buildings, the color and dress of the mob, and the language of the shouts. Some of the shouts were in English.

The sixth scene showed a group of people, men, women, and children, gathered on a dark hilltop around a man in dark robes. They were looking up at the stars in silence.

The seventh scene revealed something fleshy, and bloody, and visceral spread out on pavement like an abstract painting. The view tilted up the side of the building until it reached the distant concrete peak.

The eighth scene showed ambulances pulling up to a hospital emergency entrance.

The ninth scene was a morgue.

The tenth scene revealed an impenetrable traffic snarl as cars and copters tried to leave a city. . . .

What would John be like in the kind of world White knew, the kind of world that existed out there? Unconsciously, White knew now, he had sheltered John from it. John had not been exposed to the passions and the violence, the ignorance and the prejudice. White had wanted to spare his son the kind of hurt that he had felt, the kind of bitterness that even now twisted his guts in secret sorrows. That had not been a kindness; it had been a mistaken sentimentality that now was turning on him. Even the basic political facts, the kinds of bargaining and trades that politics forced on a man, he had shielded John from; he had not wanted his son to be touched by that kind of pitch. Or was it that he did not want his son to know what made his father's skin black?

To be black—and without a son?

"They don't understand," MacDonald said. "They're reacting out of fear."

White took a deep breath. It was a habit when he was forced to make a decision, as if he could draw in the situation and force it down where his decisions were made. He soon would have to make a statement, to commit himself in a way he could never review, to unleash forces he could never recall. "It seems," he said quietly, "like the start of something—religious riots, perhaps even a religious war—or the end of something."

"People are reacting to a lack of information," MacDonald said. "Let us communicate with them. People are uncertain. An official announcement and a planned campaign of information about the Project and the Message and the Answer...."

"Might ease the fears," White said, "and might reinforce them."

"The fears are not logical. Facts will dispel them. The Capellans cannot come here. Matter transmission is fantasy, and we cannot imagine any kind of propulsion system which could even approach the speed-of-light limit."

"What we cannot imagine," White said, "has had a habit of coming true the last few centuries. And what was considered impossible by one generation was the next generation's commonplace. Tell me: why do you insist on responding to this message? Isn't it enough that your search has been successful, that you have demonstrated the existence of intelligent life in the universe?"

"I could give you rationalizations," MacDonald said. "There are many good reasons—I have given you the most important one: communication between aliens could result in incalculable benefits to both—but behind all the rationalizations, as you suspect, is the personal motivation. Before our answer could reach Capella I will be dead, but I want my efforts to be rewarded, my convictions to be proved correct, my life to have been meaningful. Just as you do."

"We come down to fundamentals at last," White said.

"Always. I wish to leave a legacy to my son and to the world. I am not a poet or a prophet, an artist, a builder, a statesman, or a philanthropist. All I can leave is an open door. An open line to the universe, hope, the prospect of something new, a message to come from an alien world under two strange, distant suns...."

"We all want that," White said. "The only question is how to get there."

"Not all of us," MacDonald said. "Some of us wish to pass on our hatreds, our battles, not something new but something old. But life changes, time passes, and we must give our children the future, not the past—or if the past, only the past as it affects the future. The past is not irrelevant, but we can't live there; the only place we can live in is the future, and it is the only thing we can change. Believe me: once the answer is sent, peace will come to the world."

"Why then?"

"For one thing, it will be done, over. The people who are quarreling now will realize that they are human beings, that the different creatures are out there; that if we can talk with them, why shouldn't we communicate with each other, even those who speak different languages and believe in different gods...."

John said, "The Chinese Ambassador is calling, Mr. President," and White realized that he had been so involved in MacDonald's argument that he had not noticed the door opening.

"I don't have my translator with me," he said.

"Don't worry," MacDonald said. "The computer will take care of it."

After White and MacDonald had changed places and White found himself behind MacDonald's desk staring into the window, the Chinese face above the colorful tunic said, in English, with almost exact lip synchronization, "Mr. President, my country respectfully requests that you control the disturbances within your borders, and that you cease the provocative news announcements which threaten the peace of other friendly nations."

"You may tell your Premier," White said carefully, "that we regret these disturbances more than anyone, that we hope to bring them under control soon, and that we have no mechanism for controlling news announcements, as he has."

The sleek Chinese head nodded politely. "My country also requests that you make no answer to the message you have received from Capella, now or in the future."

"Thank you, Mr. Ambassador," White said politely, but before he could turn to MacDonald the Chinese face was replaced by a Russian.

"The Russian Ambassador," John said.

"The Soviet Union is greatly disturbed by the suppression of this message," the Russian said brusquely. "We wish you to know that we, too, have received the message and are composing a reply to it. We will announce this shortly."

And the window was empty and shimmering.

"No more," White said. The window winked out. He put his hands on the desk. It was a good, solid working desk, not a ceremonial desk like the one in the White House, and he felt as if he could work here. Here, seated at the desk, looking at MacDonald, he felt as if their roles had been reversed, as if he were in charge here.

"Nothing human beings can speak," MacDonald went on, as if he had not been interrupted, "is so foreign as the language of the Capellans; nothing they can believe is so strange as what the Capellans believe."

"I think you knew about the Russians and the Chinese," White said.

"The fraternity of science is closer than the fraternity of birthplace or of language."

"How did they learn about the message?"

MacDonald spread his hands in a gesture of helplessness. "Too many people knew about it. If I had suspected that we would not be permitted to release the information as a matter of course, that there would be any question about our replying, then I would not have assembled that group for our moment of triumph. But once they knew, the information could not be entirely suppressed. We were not a secret project; we were a scientific laboratory committed to sharing our findings with the world. Why, we even have some Chinese and Russian exchange scientists working with us. At this late date—"

"Nobody thought you would succeed," White said.

MacDonald looked at White in surprise. It was the first time White had seen MacDonald surprised at anything.

"Then why did you fund us?" MacDonald asked.

"I don't know why the Project was started," White said. "I haven't looked up its historical origins, and perhaps the real answer isn't there, anyway. But I suspect that the answer is much the same as our rationalization over the past few years: it was something scientists wanted to do, and nobody saw any harm in it. After all, we live in the age of welfare."

"Public welfare," MacDonald corrected.

"Welfare of all kinds," White said. "This nation—and other nations, some of them before us, some of them after us—set out on a conscious policy of eliminating poverty and injustice."

"The function of government is 'to promote the general Welfare,'" MacDonald said.

"It is also a deliberate policy. Poverty and injustice are evils, but they are endurable evils in a world where other problems are greater. They are not endurable in a complex, technological society where cooperation is essential, where violence and rioting can destroy a city, even civilization itself."

"Of course."

"So we turned ourselves around and set this nation to the task of eliminating poverty and injustice—and we have done it. We have established a stable social system where everyone has a guaranteed annual income and can do pretty much what he pleases except procreate without limit or harm others in other ways."

MacDonald nodded. "That has been the great accomplishment of the past few decades—the welfare movement."

"Except we don't call it welfare anymore," White said. "It's democracy, the system, the way things are, what people are entitled to. What makes you think that science is not part of the system?"

"It creates change," MacDonald said.

"Not if it is unsuccessful," White said. "Or if it is successful in certain limited, anticipatable ways like the space program. God knows, we thought the Project was safe enough. Certainly it is part of the welfare program, and the diversion of public funds to support it over the years has been a dole to the scientists to keep them busy and out of mischief. The important task of government, you see, is to keep conditions stable, to hold down disturbances and unrest, to maintain itself, and the best way to do that is to give everybody the opportunity to do what they want—except change things. Don't tell me you haven't suspected this all along, that you haven't used it."

"No," MacDonald said, and then, "yes. I guess so. I knew that if we made ourselves difficult it was easier to get money. I guess I realized it without facing it. And now you want us to stop, just like that."

"Not just like that," White said kindly. "Wind it down.

Pretend to be considering an answer. Keep searching for other messages. Set up another project somewhere, to do something. You've had experience. Put your mind to it: you'll know what to do."

But the battle against injustice and poverty was not won, White knew. John thought it was; he thought he could be discharged from it. But it was desertion. That was what White had called John: "deserter."

Welfare wasn't enough. Too many blacks were satisfied with their guaranteed annuals, were unwilling or afraid to compete for more. They had to be educated; they had to be led; they needed figures like himself to model themselves after, like John could be if he stayed in politics. Oh, there were some models: there were black scientists, black doctors, black artists, even some black members of the Project. But there weren't enough; the percentages still said that inequality was a reality.

He had presided over the welfare state, but he hadn't thought welfare would get John.

MacDonald was thoughtful, as if he were weighing something deep inside himself. Does he think in his hips like Teddy and me? White thought.

"I've spent my life in search of truth," MacDonald said. "I can't lie now."

White sighed. "Then we will have to get someone who can."

"It won't work. The scientific community will act, when suppressed, the same way as any other minority."

"We must have tranquillity."

"In a technological world," MacDonald said, "change is inevitable. What you must have for tranquillity is reasonable change, manageable change."

"And the change the Message brings is unmanageable, incalculable."

"That is because you have not allowed us to manage it—I do not like that word—you have not allowed us to communicate our reality to the people, to explain it to them in such a way that they see it as an adventure, as a promise, as a gift of understanding and awareness and information and insight yet to be delivered.... Besides, how can you know what the world or this nation will need ninety years from now?"

"Ninety years?" White laughed shakily. "I think no farther ahead than the next election. What does ninety years have to do with it?"

"That is the length of time it will take an answer to reach Capella and for their response to return," Mac-Donald said. "That is what I meant when I said I wished to leave a legacy for my son—and his son. Why, by the time our answer reaches Capella, you and I will be dead, Mr. President. Most of the people now alive will be dead; your son will be elderly and my son will be middle-aged. And by the time the response reaches us from Capella, virtually everyone now alive will be dead. What we do we do not for ourselves but for future generations. We bequeath you," MacDonald said softly, "a message from the stars."

"Ninety years," White repeated. "What kind of communication is that?"

"As soon as people understand," MacDonald said confidently, "the disturbances will disappear. Fear, anger, hatred, distrust—these do not last. Tranquillity lasts, and tranquillity will return, along with a vague sense of something pleasant which will happen in the indefinite future, like the promised land: not now, not tomorrow, but sometime. And those who threaten the tranquillity, from nation to individual, consciously threaten a definite future good—and will refrain."

White looked around the room once more, this small, bare simple place where a man had worked for twenty years and left few marks behind. Perhaps, he thought, MacDonald had left his mark elsewhere, on people, on ideas, on a project, on the stars, and he still felt that sense of unease in his hips that said "no, this is wrong," and he felt sorry for everybody, and he hoped that it was not just because he was not an intellectual, because he felt uncomfortable with ideas, because he could not think in terms of centuries....

"I can't take the chance," he said. "You will not send

an answer. You will begin the dismantling of the Project. Can you do it?" He stood up. The discussion was over.

MacDonald rose thoughtfully. "Is there nothing I can say to change your mind?"

White shook his head. "You have said it all. Believe me, you have done everything any man could do."

"I know what kind of legacy I wish to leave my son," MacDonald said. "What kind of legacy do you wish to leave yours?"

White looked at him sadly. "That's unfair. I do what I must. Will you do what you must?"

MacDonald sighed, and White saw the life go out of him, and felt sad. "Let me handle it my way," MacDonald said. "We will continue to study the message, continue to riddle its meaning. Gradually I will shift the listening to other locations."

"You want a chance to wait me out?" White said. "You hope for better luck with my successor?"

"Our time scale is different. The Project can wait."

"You have in me," White said, "someone who still believes in change. My successor will believe in none, and his successor will want to take conditions back the way they used to be." He shrugged with regret, and held out his hand to be shaken, protecting it automatically the way he had learned to do in campaigning. "But perhaps your way is best. Keep hoping; keep your Project going; keep your men working. But do not—I will put this in writing immediately, even though it has been recorded by your computer—do not send an answer. I have my own men on your project, and they have their instructions."

MacDonald hesitated and then took White's hand. "I'm sorry," he said.

White didn't know why MacDonald was sorry. Perhaps he was sorry that he had to preside over the betrayal of the Project, perhaps he was sorry for a President who had to compromise himself and his country's ideals, perhaps he was sorry for the human race which would receive no more messages from the stars, or perhaps he was sorry for the Capellans who would receive no answer to their hopeful message. . . . Perhaps he was sorry for all of them. "I never asked you," White said, "what you would have answered if you had been permitted to send an answer."

MacDonald reached past White and picked up the last sheet of paper on his desk. He handed it to White. "It's very simple, very obvious," he said, paused, and added, "anticryptography. It's not even very original. Bernard Oliver suggested something like this more than fifty years ago. It tries to tell the Capellans pretty much the same things they told us: who we are, where we live, what we call ourselves, how we breed, how we think. . . ."

White looked at the sheet of paper.

"You're holding it sideways," MacDonald said. "We had to stretch it out the other way to keep the same grid dimensions."

White turned the sheet of paper around and looked at it for several seconds. Then he began to laugh.

After a few moments, MacDonald said, "What's funny?"

White's laughter stopped as quickly as it had begun. He wiped his eyes and blew his nose. "I'm sorry," he said. "I wasn't laughing at the answer. I don't begin to understand half of what's here. But that's obviously a father and a mother and a son—a child—and the Capellans would have no way of knowing whether they were white or black."

When he and John had returned to Washington, what would he say to John? That he had ordered a great man to hide his greatness, to destroy what he had built? He knew what that would do to John, what it would do to their relationship. On the one hand he preached leadership of the revolution; on the other, he rejected leadership in others.

"It's only your own vision you can see," John would say. "To others' visions you are blind."

What would he say? What if John was right? What if the revolution were done, as much as leaders could do for it, and now it was up to the individual? What if the important battle now was to allow individual greatness once more to be expressed, to open up society again?

What was it John had said? What was it he had tried to forget? He remembered. He remembered too well.

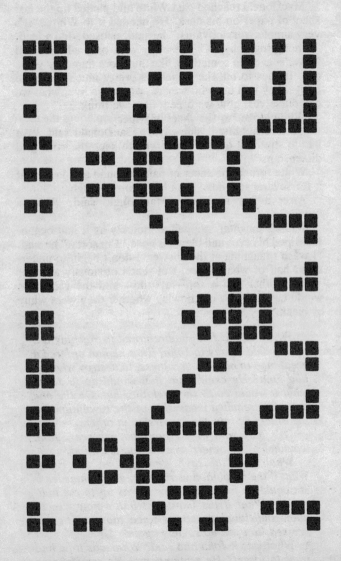

"Politics is dead, Father," John had said. "Don't you understand that? Why do you think they let you be President? Being President doesn't matter anymore!"

The speakers on either side of the room were saying, "Mac! Mac!"

"Yes, Oley," MacDonald said.

"John White has just had an inspiration about the message," the speakers said. "I hate to break in on your conference, but I don't think it ought to wait."

"That's all right," MacDonald said, glancing questioningly at White. "We were just finishing."

Almost before the words had faded, a stocky, sandy-haired, middle-aged man was in the room. John followed him.

"Olsen," MacDonald said, "this is—"

"I know," the other said. "Mr. President," he said, giving it the least possible break in the flow of his enthusiasm. "It falls into place like the last piece of a puzzle."

White looked at his son. John was clearly pleased and excited but reluctant to speak. "Is this your idea?" White said skeptically. "Really your idea?"

John nodded. "Yes."

"You tell them," Olsen said, turning to John.

"You," John said.

Olsen turned back to MacDonald. "The symbols for the two suns were different, right?" he said, speaking rapidly, not waiting for an answer. "The sun in the upper right-hand corner had a single mark extending from it. The one in the lower left had two marks at each corner, like rays. The words in the upper left and at the bottom to the right of the lower sun seem to be the symbol for 'sun.'"

"Yes," MacDonald said, looking at White and then back at Olsen.

"And the next symbol at the bottom we interpreted as 'more sun,' or 'bigger sun,' or 'hotter sun.' I was showing it to John, and he said, 'Maybe that isn't just an idle description. Maybe it's the answer to another question about themselves they want us to know: what's happening to them. Maybe the distant sun is increasing its energy output, radiating more heat, turning nova perhaps.'"

"What does that mean?" White asked. He was asking the question of anyone, but he was looking at John. His voice was troubled, he realized, and he didn't know why. And then he thought that to have the sun change in the sky was a basic alteration in the scheme of things that would be frightening beyond terror. He tried to imagine what it would be like on earth if the sun began to glow brighter, hotter. What would men do? Would they tell other intelligent races in the universe about themselves? Or would they hide?

MacDonald was saying something. "—which may explain the helmets, if that is what they are. Perhaps they have to wear the helmets—and protective suits as well—whenever they go outside. To keep out of the heat."

"I'm sorry," White said. "What did you say?"

"The temperature increase from the more distant sun," MacDonald said, "may not be a great problem. But now their sun—the sun the superjovian planet orbits around—shows signs of going nova as well."

"They're going to die," White said.

"Yes," MacDonald said.

White realized that MacDonald believed it, the man named Olsen believed it, John believed it—they all were convinced that it was true, mourned the Capellans as if they were friends. Perhaps they were: MacDonald had lived with them in anticipation for twenty years now. And now that he had found them, and communicated with them, he had discovered that they were doomed.

"The message carries no suggestion of an attempt to escape. The helmet, if that is what it is, implies an acceptance of conditions as they exist," MacDonald said. "Spaceships are a possibility for the few, perhaps," he went on, "and with the other satellites of the superjovian, they surely must have developed spaceflight, but there are no ships in the message. Perhaps their philosophy breeds acceptance...."

"They're going to die," White said again.

"That changes the situation," John said. "You feel it, don't you, Father?"

"We can't go there any more than they can come here,"

MacDonald said. "We can't help them, but we can let them know that they did not live in vain, that their last great effort to communicate was successful, that someone knows and cares and wishes them well."

He picked up the sheet of paper from the desk where White had placed it and the broad-tip pen and over the head of the child sketched in the head and shoulders of a Capellan arm in arm with the humans.

White looked at the picture and considered the question, but he knew in his hips what the answer was. The public would accept this message; it would please the people that an answer would be sent, and the exchange would enlarge their vision and their understanding, bring them closer together, give them courage and a belief in themselves.

"Yes," he said. "Send the answer."

Later, as he and John stood at the entrance of the building, he realized that John was hanging back. "What is it, son?" he asked.

"I'd like to stay for a while," John said. "I'd like to find out what I would have to do to join the Project, to be able to contribute something." He hesitated and then he added, "If it's all right, Dad."

Something froze inside White's chest and then slowly went away like ice melting. "Of course, son," he said, "if that's what you want to do."

In a moment John was gone, and White looked out across the phosphorescent white parking lot to where a slowly moving radio telescope was outlined against the night sky, held aloft on an arm like a searchlight ready to be turned on, ready to pierce the night with its brilliance and thrust its way to the stars.

Some time soon the answer to a message from the stars would be flinging upward in wave after wave started on its long journey to a distant world. Or if not from this particular antenna, some other.

He imagined it going now and tried to feel in his hips that he was right, but he wasn't sure. He hoped he was right—right for John, right for the black people, right for his country, right for all humanity now and to come, right for intelligent life everywhere. . . . And his vision fled outward and upward into the infinite where there were other creatures incredibly different from him, and he thought they said, "Well done, Andrew White."

COMPUTER RUN

WOULD BEINGS FROM ANOTHER WORLD COVET OUR GOLD OR OTHER RARE SUBSTANCES? DO THEY WANT US AS CATTLE OR AS SLAVES? HARDLY, CONSIDERING THE ASTRONOMICAL COST OF TRANSPORT BETWEEN SOLAR SYSTEMS. ANY CIVILIZATION ABLE TO COVER INTERSTELLAR DISTANCES WOULD HARDLY NEED US FOR FOOD OR RAW MATERIAL, WHICH THEY COULD FAR MORE EASILY SYNTHESIZE AT HOME. THE MOST INTERESTING ITEM TO BE TRANSFERRED FROM STAR TO STAR IS INFORMATION, AND THIS CAN BE DONE BY RADIO....RONALD N. BRACEWELL, 1962...

ONE OF THE PRIMARY MOTIVATIONS FOR THE EXPLORATION OF THE NEW WORLD WAS TO CONVERT THE INHABITANTS TO CHRISTIANITY—PEACEFULLY, IF POSSIBLE; FORCEFULLY, IF NECESSARY. CAN WE EXCLUDE THE POSSIBILITY OF AN EXTRATERRESTRIAL EVANGELISM? WHILE AMERICAN INDIANS WERE NOT USEFUL FOR ANY CONCRETE TASK IN THE COURTS OF SPAIN AND FRANCE, THEY WERE NONETHELESS TRANSPORTED THERE FOR PRESTIGE PURPOSES.... OR PERHAPS HUMAN BEINGS HAVE SOME RELATIVELY UNCOMMON TALENT, OF WHICH THEY ARE THEMSELVES ENTIRELY UNAWARE.... WHILE ANY ORGANISM OR ARTIFACT OF EARTH COULD BE DUPLICATED BY AN ADVANCED EXTRATERRESTRIAL SOCIETY, THE ORIGINAL AND THE DUPLICATE ARE STILL DIFFERENT....FINALLY, CAN WE EXCLUDE EVEN DARKER MOTIVES? MIGHT AN EXTRATERRESTRIAL SOCIETY WANT TO BE ALONE AT THE SUMMIT OF GALACTIC POWER, AND MAKE A CAREFUL EFFORT TO CRUSH PROSPECTIVE CONTENDERS? OR MIGHT THERE EVEN BE THE "COCKROACH RESPONSE"—TO STAMP OUT AN ALIEN CREATURE SIMPLY BECAUSE IT IS DIFFERENT....CARL SAGAN, 1966...

THE MILKY WAY,

        SOMBRERO, WHIRLPOOL,

OUR LOCAL GALAXY,

        AND THE GREAT SPIRAL IN ANDROMEDA

IS ONLY ONE

        (NOT TO MENTION NGC 819)

AMONG BILLIONS.

        BLACK EYE, THETA ORIONIS,

NOT ONLY STARS

        AND THE GLOBULAR CLUSTER M. 3

WITHOUT NUMBER

        (NOT TO MENTION NGC 253)

BUT GALAXIES—

        PLEIADES, COMA HYADES,

ELLIPTICAL, SPIRAL,

        PRAESEPE, STEFAN'S QUINTET

BARRED SPIRAL, GLOBULAR—

        (NOT TO MENTION FLEET 3C295)

GREAT GATHERINGS

        HERCULES, COMA-VIRGO,

OF STARS

        LARGE AND SMALL MAGELLANIC CLOUDS

WITHOUT

        (NOT TO MENTION NGC 3190,

NUMBER.

        7331, 1300, 5128, 2362, 4038, 4039, 3193, 3187...)

THE RESPEN MANUFACTURING COMPANY TODAY PUT ON THE MARKET A HOME MODEL CAPABLE OF MOST RESPONSES AVAILABLE FROM COMMERCIAL INSTALLATIONS. IT REQUIRES NO MORE SPACE THAN THE AVERAGE BATHROOM AND SELLS FOR ONLY $50,000.

IT WAS THE FACE THAT MADE OTIS STARE. THE MOUTH WAS TOOTHLESS AND PROBABLY CONSTRUCTED MORE FOR SUCKING THAN CHEWING. BUT THE EYES! THEY PROJECTED LIKE ENDS OF A DUMBBELL FROM EACH SIDE OF THE SKULL WHERE THE EARS SHOULD HAVE BEEN, AND FOCUSED WITH OBVIOUS MOBILITY. PEERING CLOSER, OTIS SAW TINY EARS BELOW THE EYES, ALMOST HIDDEN IN THE CURLING OF THE NECK....H. B. FYFE, 1951...

INTELLIGENCE MAY INDEED BE A BENIGN INFLUENCE CREATING ISOLATED GROUPS OF PHILOSOPHER-KINGS FAR APART IN THE HEAV-

ENS AND ENABLING THEM TO SHARE AT LEISURE THEIR ACCUMU-LATED WISDOM. ON THE OTHER HAND, INTELLIGENCE MAY BE A CANCER OF PURPOSELESS TECHNOLOGICAL EXPLOITATION, SWEEPING ACROSS A GALAXY AS IRRESISTIBLY AS IT HAS SWEPT ACROSS OUR OWN PLANET. ASSUMING INTERSTELLAR TRAVEL AT MODERATE SPEEDS, THE TECHNOLOGICAL CANCER COULD SPREAD OVER THE WHOLE GALAXY IN A FEW MILLION YEARS, A TIME VERY SHORT COM-PARED WITH THE LIFE OF A PLANET.

WHAT OUR DETECTORS WILL PICK UP IS A TECHNOLOGICAL CIV-ILIZATION, BUT IT WILL NOT NECESSARILY BE INTELLIGENT, IN THE PURE SENSE OF THE WORD. IN FACT, IT MAY EVEN BE THAT THE SO-CIETY WE ARE INHERENTLY LIKELY TO DETECT IS MORE PROBABLY A TECHNOLOGY RUN WILD, INSANE, OR CANCEROUSLY SPREADING THAN A TECHNOLOGY FIRMLY IN CONTROL AND SUPPORTING THE RATIONAL NEEDS OF A SUPERIOR INTELLIGENCE. IT IS POSSIBLE THAT A TRULY INTELLIGENT SOCIETY MIGHT NO LONGER FEEL THE NEED OF, OR BE INTERESTED IN, TECHNOLOGY. OUR BUSINESS AS SCIENTISTS IS TO SEARCH THE UNIVERSE AND FIND OUT WHAT IS THERE. WHAT IS THERE MAY CONFORM TO OUR MORAL SENSE OR IT MAY NOT.... IT IS JUST AS UNSCIENTIFIC TO IMPUTE TO REMOTE INTELLIGENCES WISDOM AND SERENITY AS IT IS TO IMPUTE TO THEM IRRATIONAL AND MURDEROUS IMPULSES. WE MUST BE PREPARED FOR EITHER POSSIBILITY AND CONDUCT OUR SEARCHES ACCORDINGLY.... FREEMAN J. DYSON, 1964...

IN A DIRECT CONFRONTATION WITH SUPERIOR CREATURES FROM ANOTHER WORLD, THE REINS WOULD BE TORN FROM OUR HANDS AND WE WOULD, AS A TEARFUL OLD MEDICINE MAN ONCE SAID TO ME, FIND OURSELVES "WITHOUT DREAMS," THAT IS, WE WOULD FIND OUR INTELLECTUAL AND SPIRITUAL ASPIRATIONS SO OUTMODED AS TO LEAVE US COMPLETELY PARALYZED.... CARL GUSTAV JUNG, EARLY TWENTIETH CENTURY...

WHAT WOULD HAPPEN IF ALL GALACTIC CIVILIZATIONS WORKED ONLY ON RECEIVING AND NOT ON TRANSMITTING INTERSTELLAR RA-DIO SIGNALS?... I. S. SHKLOVSKY, 1966...

AFTER FIFTY WEEKS, A BOY AND HIS BIRD STILL NESTS ATOP THE BEST-SELLER LIST. ALTHOUGH CRITICAL REACTION TO THE NOVEL HAS BEEN MIXED, WITH SOME REVIEWERS CALLING IT "THE WORST BOOK OF THIS OR ANY OTHER YEAR" AND OTHERS DESCRIBING IT AS "A BOOK FOR OUR TIMES" AND "A FRANK ACCOUNT OF PASSION BE-

TWEEN ALIENS," THE PUBLIC REACTION HAS BEEN UNANIMOUS: THE
PUBLIC LOVES IT.

THE GROSS NATIONAL PRODUCT REACHED $4.5 TRILLION YES-
TERDAY, THE UNITED STATES BUREAU OF ECONOMICS ANNOUNCED
TODAY. TOTAL GROSS WORLD PRODUCT REACHED ALMOST $28 TRIL-
LION, NEARLY TEN TIMES ITS VALUE FIFTY YEARS AGO.

THE BUREAU ATTRIBUTES THE SOLUTION OF MANY OF THE PROB-
LEMS THAT TROUBLED THE WORLD A HALF CENTURY AGO TO THE
DRAMATIC GROWTH IN THE GROSS WORLD PRODUCT THROUGH AU-
TOMATION, FUSION POWER, GREATER USE OF COMPUTERS AND CY-
BERNATION, AND NEW EDUCATIONAL METHODS.

IT MAY BE THAT THESE GRUESOME POSSIBILITIES ARE REAL. OR
THE FACT THAT WE CAN IMAGINE THEM MAY BE ITSELF ONLY A RE-
FLECTION OF HOW MUCH FURTHER WE HAVE TO GO BEFORE WE WILL
BE READY FOR FULL MEMBERSHIP IN A GALACTIC COMMUNITY OF
SOCIETIES. BUT IN EITHER CASE, THERE IS NO WAY BACK. IT IS NO
USE TO MAINTAIN AN INTERSTELLAR RADIO SILENCE; THE SIGNAL HAS
ALREADY BEEN SENT. FORTY LIGHT-YEARS OUT FROM EARTH, THE
NEWS OF A NEW TECHNICAL CIVILIZATION IS WINGING ITS WAY AMONG
THE STARS. IF THERE ARE BEINGS OUT THERE, SCANNING THEIR SKIES
FOR THE TIDINGS OF A NEW TECHNICAL CIVILIZATION, THEY WILL
KNOW OF IT, WHETHER FOR GOOD OR FOR ILL. IF INTERSTELLAR
SPACEFLIGHT BY ADVANCED TECHNICAL CIVILIZATIONS IS COMMON-
PLACE, WE MAY EXPECT AN EMISSARY, PERHAPS IN THE NEXT SEV-
ERAL HUNDRED YEARS. HOPEFULLY, THERE WILL THEN STILL BE A
THRIVING TERRESTRIAL CIVILIZATION TO GREET THE VISITORS FROM
THE FAR DISTANT STARS....CARL SAGAN, 1966...

HOLOVISION, UNTIL NOW AVAILABLE ONLY TO GOVERNMENT, IN-
DUSTRY, AND THE VERY RICH, NOW HAS BEEN PRODUCED IN A SET
CAPABLE OF BEING INSTALLED IN THE HOME AT A PRICE THE AVERAGE
CITIZEN CAN AFFORD. LIKE ITS LARGER AND MORE EXPENSIVE PRE-
DECESSORS, THE HV, AS GENERAL ELECTRIC CALLS IT, OPERATES
WITHOUT AN IMAGE TUBE; IT MAKES ITS PICTURE VISIBLE BY EXCITING
THE AIR PARTICLES IN FRONT OF THE CONCEALED PROJECTOR. THE
EFFECT IS LIKE HAVING A PERSON OR A SCENE IN THE ROOM WITH
YOU. EXPERTS PREDICT THAT IT WILL TAKE OVER ALL BROADCASTING
AS SOON AS SUFFICIENT SETS CAN BE MANUFACTURED.

THAT, OF COURSE, IS WHAT THE EXPERTS SAID ABOUT TELEVISION AND RADIO, AND WE HAVE JUST SEEN A REMARKABLE RESURGENCE IN RADIO...

ASSUMING THAT THE ENERGY OF THE SOLAR-FUSION PROCESS COULD BE USED WITH 100 PERCENT EFFICIENCY, IT WOULD STILL REQUIRE: 16 BILLION TONS OF HYDROGEN FUEL TO ACCELERATE A TEN-TON CAPSULE TO 99 PERCENT OF THE SPEED OF LIGHT, AND TO SLOW IT DOWN FOR THE LANDING WOULD REQUIRE ANOTHER 16 BILLION TONS.... EVEN WITH THE PERFECT MATTER-ANTIMATTER FUEL, MY HYPOTHETICAL JOURNEY WOULD STILL REQUIRE 400,000 TONS OF FUEL, EQUALLY DIVIDED BETWEEN MATTER AND ANTIMATTER.... WELL, THIS IS PREPOSTEROUS, YOU ARE SAYING. THAT IS EXACTLY MY POINT. IT IS PREPOSTEROUS. AND REMEMBER, OUR CONCLUSIONS ARE FORCED ON US BY THE ELEMENTARY LAWS OF MECHANICS.... EDWARD M. PURCELL, 1960...

A WAY OUT OF THESE DIFFICULTIES WHICH APPROACHES ELEGANCE IN ITS CONCEPTION HAS BEEN PROVIDED BY THE AMERICAN PHYSICIST ROBERT W. BUSSARD... AN INTERSTELLAR RAMJET WHICH USES THE ATOMS OF THE INTERSTELLAR MEDIUM BOTH AS A WORKING FLUID (TO PROVIDE REACTION MASS) AND AS AN ENERGY SOURCE (THROUGH THERMONUCLEAR FUSION).... CARL SAGAN, 1966...

AN INTAKE AREA ALMOST 80 MILES IN DIAMETER WOULD BE NEEDED TO ACHIEVE THE NEEDED VELOCITY FOR A SPACESHIP OF ABOUT 1,000 TONS. THIS IS VERY LARGE BY ORDINARY STANDARDS, BUT THEN, ON ANY ACCOUNT, INTERSTELLAR TRAVEL IS INHERENTLY A RATHER GRAND UNDERTAKING.... R. W. BUSSARD, 1960...

IN ORDINARY INTERSTELLAR SPACE, WITH ONLY ONE HYDROGEN ATOM PER CUBIC CENTIMETER, THE SWEEPING SYSTEM WOULD HAVE TO BE 2,500 MILES IN DIAMETER. PERHAPS STARSHIPS DART FROM ONE DUST CLOUD TO ANOTHER.... INTERSTELLAR VEHICLES MAY BECOME FEASIBLE FOR US WITHIN THE NEXT FEW CENTURIES. WE CAN EXPECT THAT IF INTERSTELLAR SPACEFLIGHT IS TECHNICALLY FEASIBLE—EVEN THOUGH AN EXCEEDINGLY EXPENSIVE AND DIFFICULT UNDERTAKING, FROM OUR POINT OF VIEW—IT WILL BE DEVELOPED. ...CARL SAGAN, 1962...

INTERSTELLAR FLIGHT IS ESSENTIALLY NOT A PROBLEM IN PHYSICS OR ENGINEERING BUT A PROBLEM IN BIOLOGY.... FREEMAN J. DYSON, 1964...

AND THE GOLDEN GLOW BUILT UP, DROWNING OUT THE GREEN RADIANCE FROM FLOOR TO ROOF, SETTING THE MULTITUDE OF CASE-SURFACES AFIRE WITH ITS BRILLIANCE. IT GREW AS STRONG AS THE GOLDEN SKY, AND STRONGER. IT BECAME ALL-PERVADING, UNENDURABLE, LEAVING NO DARKNESS IN WHICH TO HIDE, NO SANCTUARY FOR LITTLE THINGS.

IT FLAMED LIKE THE RISING SUN OR LIKE SOMETHING DRAWN FROM THE HEART OF A SUN AND THE GLORY OF ITS RADIANCE SENT THE COWERING WATCHER'S MIND AWHIRL.... ERIC FRANK RUSSELL, 1947...

OH CAPELLA, OH CAPELLA,
WE HAVE HEARD YOUR VOICES TELL US,
OVER SPACES INTERSTELLAR
THAT WE ARE NOT ALONE.
BROTHERHOOD—THIS YOU HAVE FOR US;
WE WOULD LIKE TO JOIN THE CHORUS,
BUT WE MUST SING ALONE.
FOR YOU THE WORDS, FOR US THE
SONG,
BUT DISTANCES ARE MUCH TOO LONG.
A CAPPELLA, A CAPPELLA...

THE MOST MASSIVE ENGINEERING CONSTRUCTION FORCE EVER ASSEMBLED FOR A PEACETIME JOB TODAY BEGAN THE DECADE-LONG TASK OF BUILDING A DAM ACROSS THE STRAIT OF GIBRALTAR. WHEN THE DAM IS COMPLETED THE LEVEL OF THE MEDITERRANEAN IS EXPECTED TO RISE, THE WATER OF THE SEA WILL BECOME FRESH WITHIN A FEW DECADES, AND POWER WILL BE AVAILABLE FROM WATER POURING THROUGH HYDROELECTRIC GENERATORS INTO THE ATLANTIC FOR A VARIETY OF USES, INCLUDING THE PUMPING OF WATER INTO THE SAHARA FOR IRRIGATION AND INDUSTRY.

AS DIFFICULT A CONSTRUCTION JOB AS THE DAM IS SCHEDULED TO BE, THE POLITICAL, SOCIAL, ECONOMIC, AND ORGANIZATIONAL PROBLEMS WERE EVEN MORE DIFFICULT. EXPERTS IN THOSE FIELDS HAVE CONCLUDED THAT ONLY IN PEACEFUL TIMES LIKE THE PRESENT WOULD AGREEMENT HAVE BEEN POSSIBLE....

THE BREAK IN THE SAWTOOTH PATTERN OF CATASTROPHE AND RECOVERY MAY FINALLY COME ABOUT THROUGH THE ESTABLISHMENT OF CONTACT WITH A MORE ADVANCED SOCIETY—ONE THAT HAS ALREADY ACHIEVED STABILITY.... FRED HOYLE, 1963...

THE YEAR 2000 CONDITIONS COULD PRODUCE A SITUATION IN WHICH ILLUSION, WISHFUL THINKING, EVEN OBVIOUSLY IRRATIONAL BEHAVIOR COULD EXIST TO A DEGREE UNHEARD OF TODAY. SUCH IRRATIONAL AND SELF-INDULGENT BEHAVIOR IS QUITE LIKELY IN A SITUATION IN WHICH AN INDIVIDUAL IS OVERPROTECTED AND HAS NO SYSTEMATIC OR OBJECTIVE CONTACT WITH REALITY. FOR EXAMPLE, THERE ARE PROBABLY MANY PEOPLE FOR WHOM WORK IS THE PRIMARY TOUCH WITH REALITY. IF WORK IS REMOVED, OR IF IMPORTANT FUNCTIONS ARE TAKEN FROM WORK, THE CONTACT THESE PEOPLE HAVE WITH REALITY WILL BE TO SOME DEGREE IMPAIRED. THE RESULTS—MINOR OR WIDESPREAD—MAY BECOME APPARENT IN FORMS SUCH AS POLITICAL DISRUPTION, DISTURBED FAMILIES, AND PERSONAL TRAGEDIES—OR IN PURSUIT OF SOME "HUMANISTIC" VALUES THAT MANY WOULD THINK OF AS FRIVOLOUS OR EVEN IRRATIONAL. ... HERMAN KAHN AND ANTHONY J. WIENER, 1967...

IMAGINE THAT A REPLY TO ONE OF YOUR MESSAGES WAS SCHEDULED TO BE RECEIVED FORTY YEARS FROM NOW. WHAT A LEGACY FOR YOUR GRANDCHILDREN.... EDWARD M. PURCELL, 1961...

5

Robert MacDonald—2058

Never the least stir made the listeners,
Though every word he spake
Fell echoing through the shadowiness of the still house...

Robert MacDonald waited patiently for the ship that would take him from Miami to Puerto Rico.

He had plenty of time. Nothing was waiting for him at Arecibo anymore but memories.

Why hurry? *Nous n'irons plus aux bois, les lauriers sont coupés.*

He threw his fishing line back into the clear blue water off the pier and smelled the salt, sea air and watched the white sails of the freighters slide along the horizon and off the edge of the world.

A day later MacDonald had a string of eating-size fish wiggling in the water beneath the pier, a new computer program for translating Mandarin into Senegalese worked out in his head, and the trimaran had coasted up to the pier, its nylon sail like a drift of snow across the brown deck. A Viking in a ragged pair of blue-denim shorts stood on the deck next to the pier. He threw a nylon line to MacDonald. "Take a turn around the bitt there, will you, Mac?" the sailor asked. MacDonald looked up in surprise. The sailor continued calmly, "That upright pole there, Mac, like a piling."

MacDonald looped the line twice around the rope-slicked bitt. The ship slowed its forward drift against the slow stretch of the line, stopped, and settled back against the woven rope bumpers that kept its fragile sides away from the pier.

"Thanks, Mac," the sailor said. "May all your messages be answered."

"And yours," MacDonald said. "You sail that all by yourself?" He nodded at the trim ship with the single cabin across the triple hulls, all shining white in the hulls and the sail and the cabin, gleaming stainless steel in the masts, glowing brown teak in the deck.

"Me and any passengers I might have," the sailor said. On his head, on his face, on his body and legs, his hair was bleached the color of his sails, and where there was no hair his skin was as dark as his deck. "Me alone, if I have to. I got a computer on board can set the sails in seconds, predict a blow, measure the bottom, read a map, navigate, sail a course, and find a school of fish if I've a mind to."

"Heading back to Puerto Rico soon?" MacDonald asked casually.

"This afternoon—tomorrow—the next day. Depends," the sailor said. He looked at MacDonald. "Been waiting long?" He jumped easily to the pier.

MacDonald shrugged. "Couple of days."

"Sorry," the sailor said. "I had a passenger coming back from Arecibo who heard the swordfish were biting off Bermuda, and we made a swing up that way."

"Any luck?" MacDonald looked around the deck for a sign of the passenger.

"He caught one off the stern and had a hell of a good battle with it before we cut it loose. Decided to stay and try his luck off a small boat. President of some computer company, I think he said—IBM, GE, Control Data, one of those."

"Short, wiry man with a trimmed dark beard and a receding hairline?" MacDonald asked.

"Yeah," the sailor said. "You know him?"

"Friedman," MacDonald said. "IBM. I know him." But he hadn't known Friedman was going to Puerto Rico. He didn't have to search hard for a reason Friedman hadn't told him.

"You going over?" the sailor asked.

MacDonald shrugged again. "I started down this way from New York ten days ago," he said. After heading the other way for twenty years, he added to himself. "Bicycle and bus." The other time it had been jet all the way. "If I'd been in a hurry I'd have taken a jet or at least the ferry."

Across Biscayne Bay he saw the Puerto Rico ferry

come in now, its air-support fans spraying sea water to
each side. It looked, MacDonald thought, like a giant
many-legged water bug.

"A couple days more won't make much difference,"
he said.

"And we all got sixty years to wait, right?" the sailor
said. He held out a sun-darkened hand. "I'm Johnson,
master of the Pequod." His sun-bleached eyebrows slid
up his forehead when he smiled. "Funny name for a trimaran out of Miami, right? But I used to teach college
English, and contrasts appeal to me. I'm no Ahab, you
see, and I'm not looking for a white whale or anything
else, I guess."

"I'm MacDonald," MacDonald said, taking the hand,
feeling as if he were shaking hands with the sea itself. He
grinned. "But you can call me Ishmael."

"I've heard that name before," Johnson said.
"MacDonald, I mean. Wasn't he—?"

"Yes," MacDonald said, and a wave of grief swept over
him like nausea. He fought it back, blinking his eyes to
hold back the tears. He didn't mind weeping in front of
this friendly seaman, but not for nothing. There was nothing to weep about, no reason to feel sad. . . .

"I'll check the shipping deck to see if there's some
freight for Puerto Rico," Johnson said. He started off.
"We'll head back as soon as we can get it loaded and put
aboard water and provisions."

"No hurry," MacDonald called after him. But there
was hurry. He could feel it now, what he had pushed down
and kept down, the urgency to get to Arecibo, the burning
need to end the waiting. . . .

*He had a persistent dream—maybe it was a
memory rather than a dream—of waking up in a
big bed all alone. It was his mother's bed, and she
had let him climb into her bed and press himself
against her soft warmth, and he had fallen asleep.
Now he was awake and alone, and the bed was cold
and he was afraid.*

*He got out of bed in the darkness, carefully, lest
he step on something terrible or fall into a bottomless hole, and he ran through the darkness, feeling*

deserted and afraid, down the hall to the living room, screaming, "Mama-mama-mama!"

A light loomed ahead, a small light holding apart the darkness, and in the light his mother was sitting, watching the door, waiting for his father to come home, and he felt alone....

He had met a girl on his trip south. They met in a bicycle shop in Savannah. They both wanted the same bicycle—it was the only rental bicycle left in the place except for a tandem—and they argued good-naturedly over whose need was greater.

Actually they were both dividing their journey between bicycle and bus, peddling until they got tired and then turning in their bicycle and taking a bus to the next town, and either one of them could have shifted modes at this point. But to MacDonald, at least, the trip so far had been uneventful—a beautiful, up-and-down-hill journey through a timeless land where people moved with careless grace and unconscious courtesy—and he was bored. He enjoyed the moment of conflict with this beautiful girl and the sexual counterpoint that underlay it.

Her name was Mary, and MacDonald liked her right off—which was unusual because he almost always noticed some flaw which spoiled a girl for him. Mary had dark hair and large dark eyes and olive skin with a delicate flush of health underneath and a properly rounded figure with the spring of the athlete to it.

"Tell you what," MacDonald said at last, smiling, "why don't we rent the tandem, the two of us, and ride off together," but as it turned out he was going south, en route from New York to Miami, and she was going north, en route from Miami to New York.

"Destiny has brought us together," MacDonald said.

Her smile and a glance from her dark eyes was encouraging, but she said, "And destiny will pull us apart."

Finally the elderly shopkeeper said, "It's almost dark, and you won't be traveling. I think I'll have another bicycle or two in the morning. One of you can take this one; the other can come back. You'll both get the same start."

MacDonald raised his hands and shoulders in mock

perplexity. "But which shall do which? We still are un-
resolved."

"Tell you what," Mary said, in imitation of Mac-
Donald's Solomonic tone of a moment before, "since the
one of us without a vehicle might have to travel some
distance to find lodging for the night, let us rent the tandem and travel together to the nearest inn where we can
spend the night—"

"Together," MacDonald put in hopefully.

"Where we can spend the night and return tomorrow
to rent our two bicycles and go our separate ways."

And so it was settled, and MacDonald found himself
peddling through the leafy streets of Savannah, his pack
and bedroll upon his back, with the city darkening around
him as the sun disappeared beyond the horizon and Mary
behind him remembering better than he the shopkeeper's
directions.

The inn was pleasant and old-fashioned and hospitable
and redolent with the odor of the evening meal being
prepared in the kitchen. MacDonald and Mary were
greeted at the door by the plump innkeeper.

"We would like—" MacDonald said, and looked at
Mary.

"Two rooms," she said.

The innkeeper's face was round and red and apolo-
getic. "I'm truly sorry," he said, "but we have only one
room left."

"Destiny," MacDonald said softly.

Mary sighed. "All right," she said. "We'll take the
room."

The innkeeper's look of apology turned to one of vi-
carious pleasure.

The evening was a delight. The food was well cooked
and hearty, which suited appetites whetted by a day on
the road. And to everything they ate, to everything that
happened, to everything they said or did not say was
added the spice of knowledge that soon they would be
going upstairs together to spend the night.

"Let us treat destiny like the royalty he is," MacDonald
said as he ordered wine with the meal, "not like a ragged
beggar at the door."

"Sometimes," Mary said, "destiny is hard to recognize,

and it is even harder to know what destiny intends."

"Why," MacDonald said, "destiny intends us all to seek our heart's desire."

"But not," Mary said, "necessarily to find it."

Mary was a seeker. She was on her way to begin graduate study in xenopsychology at a university in New York, and when MacDonald got her talking about her plans she bubbled with the thrill of the search. MacDonald liked the enthusiasm that lifted her voice and flushed her cheek.

"And what are you going to do in Miami?" she asked at last.

"I am going to take a ship to Puerto Rico," he said.

"And there?"

"I don't know. I don't know," he said. "Perhaps to lay old ghosts to rest."

Later, with acute disappointment, he watched Mary spread his bedroll upon the floor. "But—" he said. "I don't understand—I thought—"

"Destiny moves in inscrutable ways," she said.

"We're both adults," he protested.

"Yes," she said, "and if this were only a chance encounter we might both enjoy it and think no more about it. You are an attractive man, Robert MacDonald, but you have a dark, uneasy quality to you that you must resolve; there are answers you must find elsewhere. And there is time. We have lots of time."

He could have persuaded her, he thought. He could have told her about his past and won her sympathy and from there her bed, but he could not talk about it.

In the morning he offered to go back to New York with her, but she shook her head. "Go on with your journey," she said. "Go to Puerto Rico. Put your ghosts to rest. And then—if destiny brings you back to New York—"

They went in opposite directions, the distance between them widening, and MacDonald turned his thought toward Puerto Rico and the past.

"Bobby," his father said, "you can be anything you want to be, go anywhere you want to go, do anything you want to do—if you don't get in a hurry. You can even travel to another star if you want to and you're in no hurry to get there."

"Daddy," he said, "I just want to be like you."

"That's the only thing you can't be," his father said, "no matter how slow you're willing to go. Every person's different, you see. Nobody can be like anybody else in any significant way. And nobody would want to be like me—all I am is a caretaker, a janitor, a waiter. Be yourself, Bobby. Be you."

"You be like your father, Bobby, if you want to be," his mother said. She was the most beautiful woman in the world, and when she looked at him with her large dark eyes he thought his heart would burst. "He's a great man. Never forget that, my son."

"'Es un entreverado loco, lleno de lúcidos intervalos,'" his father quoted. "But your mother is a bit prejudiced."

They looked at each other with eyes of love, and his mother held out her hand for his father to hold, and Bobby felt as if a giant hand were squeezing his chest, and he ran to his mother, crying, and threw himself into her arms, and he did not know why he cried. . . .

The voyage across the Caribbean was a trip through a timeless world of water and sky, with the hiss of the hulls through the quiet water and the occasional slap-slap of a wave the only reminder that they sailed the ocean and not the sky itself—one blue or another, it was all the same—and MacDonald renewed his old acquaintance with the sea that he had bade good-bye to and thought he did not want to see again.

They sailed with their cargo of computer parts and software in the hold, and only the slow arch of the sun marked the passage of the day, and only an afternoon squall broke the oil-smooth surface of the water. They fled before it briefly and then slid away from it, guided by the computer in the cabin. They ate and drank when they were hungry or thirsty, and MacDonald got to know Johnson, the college professor who had wearied of the process which chopped his days into little blocks and escaped to the timeless ocean and its peace. And it was right.

Now MacDonald had time and inclination to consider the uneventfulness of his long trip down the coast, broken only by a brief interlude in Savannah—or was it only more of the same? The country was calm. The world was calm. Like the sea. Waiting. Waiting for what?

Even Miami, like New York, was more like a village than a city. People moved about their daily tasks—if there were tasks—with unhurried grace. It was not that they could not move swiftly if they had to: ambulances occasionally roared emergencies to hospitals; special deliveries sometimes raced along the express lanes; once in a while individuals would speed on unusual errands. But mostly people walked or rode bicycles or took the electric buses which could not go faster than twenty-five miles an hour.

Waiting. For what?

"What are you waiting for?" he asked Johnson during the long evening as they sat studying the sunset, salt spray occasionally drifting over them, sweating bottles of cold beer in their hands, the trimaran under the control and guidance of the computer.

"Me?" Johnson said lazily. "I'm not waiting for anything. I've got what I want."

The sea hissed by under the hulls. "No," MacDonald insisted, "I mean—it's not that you want anything, but you're waiting for something. The whole world is waiting. Time has slowed down, and we're waiting."

"Oh, that!" Johnson said, "It's the Reply. You know. We picked up a Message from creatures out there. They live on a world orbiting one of twin giant red suns. Capella. And we sent an answer, and now we're waiting for a Reply."

"It can't be that," MacDonald said.

"Sure it is," Johnson said and took a long drink from his bottle. "We can't get in any hurry, you see, because it's going to take ninety years for our answer to reach Capella and a reply to return. It's been about thirty years. So we got sixty years to wait, right? We can't speed it up. We must build it in, live with it."

"What difference will it make to you?" MacDonald asked. "By the time the reply gets here you'll be dead—or too old to care. Like me."

"What else have I got to do?" Johnson said. "I wait—
and meanwhile I do what I want. No point in hurrying."

"But what kind of message can the Reply bring that
will be worth the waiting?" MacDonald asked. "What will
it mean to you or me or anybody else?"

Johnson shrugged in the gathering darkness. "Who
knows?"

It was an echo from the past.

Two nights and a day later, the trimaran coasted into
the Arecibo harbor, and by then MacDonald had fallen
into the slow, tidal rhythm of the sea itself, the inhalation-
exhalation pattern which controls the ocean and the lives
of those creatures that live within it and upon it.

Arecibo was quieter, more serene than MacDonald had
remembered, even in his dreams. He rented a bicycle from
an agency where the brown man who waited on him moved
slowly among the spoked wheels that hung from pegs on
the wall and the ceiling beams and spoke to him in the
language of MacDonald's mother.

In a few minutes he was out of the city itself. The
highway stretched in front of him like a white ribbon tying
together the green hills, and he rode through the peace
of the countryside, smelling the mingled odors of luxuriant
tropic green and the salt of the nearby sea, and he remembered how slow time had seemed when he was small.
It was like coming home. It was coming home, he told
himself. And then he corrected himself, "No, I live in
New York, where the rhythms are those of concrete and
construction and the rumble of subway trains through
dark tunnels." That was where his home was. This was
only the place he grew up.

But the magic grew as he peddled through the eternal
summer of this island, and soon he was a boy again,
drifting over the hills like a cloud, weightless, drifting. . . .

A boy's will is the wind's will,
And the thoughts of youth are long, long thoughts.

Before MacDonald knew where he was he came to a
familiar driveway. Automatically the wheel of the bicycle
turned and he was coasting toward a Spanish-style ha-

cienda. He half decided to turn back, but he went on and stopped the bicycle in front of the house and got off and walked up to the heavy, carved, wooden door and pulled the bell. Somewhere inside the house he heard it chime. It was like a signal for another bell to go off inside his chest. Grief rose into his throat, tears welled into his eyes, and he turned away.

"*Si?*" someone said.

He turned back to the door. Half-blinded, he thought for one incoherent moment that his mother was standing there, but he blinked rapidly and it was a stranger, a pleasant, brown-faced woman. "I beg your pardon," he said. And then he repeated his apology in Spanish, although the woman understood the English well enough. "I was—I was born here, and I've been away."

The woman hesitated and then said sympathetically, "Won't you come in and look around?"

He hesitated and then he nodded and went through the familiar door and into the familiar house and looked around. But it wasn't the same. The furniture was all different. The rooms were smaller. Even the air smelled strange. The house was changed; he had changed. It was not the same place he had stood in last, a ten-year-old boy, twenty years ago.

His father stopped just inside the door as if he had forgotten that his son was there, waiting for him. He was old, Bobby thought. He was an old man. Bobby had not realized that truth until now. His father was old, and he was smaller than he had seemed before.

"Bobby," his father said. And then he didn't seem to know what he was going to say, and he stopped and collected himself. "Bobby, your mother is dead. The doctors tried but they couldn't save her. Her heart stopped beating. She used too much of it, you see. On you, on me, on everybody. She cared about things, about people. And she used it all up . . . ."

"You did it!" Bobby said. "You killed her."

He ran toward his father and beat at him with his fists.

His father tried to hold his hands, not trying to keep himself from being hurt, but Bobby. "No, Bobby," he said. "No, Bobby. No, Bobby." But there was no force behind his words. They were like a message that had been turned on and now could not be turned off.

The trip from the hacienda to the Project had seemed long when MacDonald was a boy, even when his father took him in the old turbine car, but the bicycle mounted the hills and coasted through the valleys and MacDonald hardly noticed that time had passed when he reached the valley lined with metal plates like a rusty saucer in the sunlight and beyond it the smaller metal dish held aloft on a framework arm and beyond it the one-story concrete building on the other side of the white parking lot.

As he peddled up to the parking lot he noticed that it was virtually empty, and he wondered if the Project had died. And then he realized that it was noon, and only a few people on the Project worked during the day. Night was the shift for astronomers.

He parked the bicycle in a rack beside the door and opened the glass doors that led into the building. He stepped out of the sunshine and stood blinking in the darker corridor and smelled the old odors of the Project, the oil and ozone of electrical equipment.

As he stood there waiting for his eyes to adjust someone said, "Mac. Mac!"

A bony hand grasped his and shook it up and down. "No, it's not Mac. It's Bobby. You've come back."

MacDonald's vision returned, and an old man swam into view in front of him. "It's Olsen, Bobby," the old man said. MacDonald remembered. Olsen, a stocky, sandy-haired computer scientist, a man of great strength and vitality who used to swing him up on his shoulders and take him through the corridors and rooms of the Project, and he felt taller than anybody. MacDonald had difficulty associating his memories with this frail old man standing in front of him shaking his hand as if he had forgotten how to stop.

"I'm superannuated now," Olsen said. "No use to anyone, including myself. But they let me hang around here for old time's sake, fool around with the computer a bit, you know. You gave me a start, I'll tell you, when you came in that door. Looked just like your father when I first knew him, and I thought for a minute there it was your father—you know?"

"Kind of you," MacDonald said. "But I really don't look much like him." The poor old man was getting senile, he thought.

"Nonsense. Spitting image." Olsen kept on shaking his hand.

"My father's eyes were blue," MacDonald said, "and mine are dark; his hair was blond, mine is black—"

"Got something of your mother in you too, Bobby, but I swear, when you came in that door— Should have been here a week ago, Bobby."

MacDonald started walking down the familiar corridor toward the office that had been his father's. The corridor had been diminished by time, and its concrete block walls had been layered with dust and paint by the years.

"All sorts of people were here," Olsen said, sidling along beside MacDonald to keep pace and still look toward his old friend's son. "Famous people—a president and a couple of ex-presidents, a prime minister or two, and a clutch of ambassadors, and the scientists—Bobby, you would have been proud. I guess every important scientist in the world was here."

"My father was a great man," MacDonald said. He had reached the door of his father's old office.

A black man with grizzled hair looked up and smiled. "Yours, too?" He stood up from behind the desk and came forward. He was a big man, with big shoulders and thick arms.

"Hello, John," MacDonald said. "I thought I might find you sitting here."

They shook hands. "You didn't know?" John White asked.

"I haven't read anything about the Project for twenty years."

Olsen had gone around them toward the desk but he turned back in surprise. "Your father didn't write?"

"I got letters from him," MacDonald said. "I never read them. I just tossed them into a box, unopened."

Olsen shook his head. "Poor Mac. He never hid the fact that he didn't hear from you, but he used to bring in clippings from your school newspaper and the official school reports to show how well you were doing."

"He understood, Bobby," White said. "He didn't blame you."

"Him blame me?" MacDonald said. He said it quietly but there was intensity behind the words.

"Did you keep the letters, Bobby?" Olsen asked.

"The letters?"

"The box full of unopened letters," Olsen said. "They'd be priceless now. In his own hand, unopened." The word "his" almost seemed to be capitalized. "The people who were here—they all were talking about how important the Project was, how important everything connected with it had become. A holographic record of the Project written to his son."

"His only begotten son," MacDonald said. "I don't know. I've moved around a lot." But he knew where they were, all right, in the dusty box on the shelf at the back of the apartment closet. He had moved around a lot, true, but the box had gone with him. Each time he had been about to throw it away, and something had kept him from doing it, and he had frowned and put it back. Perhaps, in spite of everything, he had shared a bit of Olsen's feeling that he had history in his hands, that he would be throwing away not just letters from his father but documents from a Great Man.

"Is the Project dead now?" MacDonald asked.

"Your father is dead," White said. "The Project goes on. It is difficult to imagine it going on without your father, but that it does is a tribute to him. It must. This is his memorial, and we cannot let it die."

"Mac is dead, Bobby," Olsen said. "He's gone, and it's all gone. The spirit has gone out of this place."

The familiar wave of grief surged up in MacDonald's chest, grief, he told himself, not for his father, but for the father he never had.

"John thinks he can keep it going," Olsen said, "but he can't. Mac kept the Project together for fifty years.

For the first fifteen years after he became director he kept it together without results. Nothing. We just kept listening for some kind of communication from the stars, and Mac kept us going, trying new things when we got discouraged, working at different ways of doing the old things, cheering us up, him and Maria."

MacDonald looked around the room where his father had spent his days and many of his nights, the concrete block walls painted a neutral shade of green, an unostentatious wooden desk, shelves built into the wall behind the desk and on the shelves books with leather bindings, dark green, dark red, and brown, cracking a little now, and on either side of the room speakers built into the walls, and MacDonald tried to imagine his father sitting in this room day after day, part of him seeping into the walls and into the desk and into the books he loved, and he could not see him; he could not remember him here. He was gone.

"And then, after the Message, it was a different problem," Olsen said. "We had a result. Oh, that was a great time. We were crazy with enthusiasm. Our fifty years had paid off, like so many coins invested in a slot machine; we hit the jackpot, and we kept counting and gloating and congratulating ourselves. And Mac had to keep us going through that, too, settle us back for the long pull, get us back into harness. And there were problems he handled we didn't even know about at the time; like the Solitarians who felt we were going to destroy their religion and the politicians like John's father, here, who thought we should not answer the Message. And after that, after we had answered, what was there to do? We had to wait for a reply. Ninety years we had to wait. We had to keep going so that when the Reply came we would be here to receive it. Mac put us back to work searching for new signals, new messages. But who will keep us going now? How can we keep going without a MacDonald?

"What gives us nightmares," Olsen said, his voice dropping into a lower range, "is not the fear of dying but the fear that the Reply will come and no one will be here. We'll have stopped listening. The Project will have closed down." Olsen's voice faded away, and he looked down at his old hands.

MacDonald looked at John. It was John whose leadership was being questioned, whose ability was being challenged.

White didn't seem disturbed by the comparison. He moved back and sat down beside Olsen on the edge of the desk. It creaked under him. "What Oley has said is not new. We talk about these things now, how we keep going. We didn't talk about that sort of thing when your father was alive. We didn't need to. As long as Mac kept going the Project would. But now he's dead."

"'The whole world is the sepulcher of famous men,'" MacDonald said.

"Since I've been sitting in that chair," White said, motioning with his head, "five years now, I've learned a lot of things—like what Mac kept bottled up inside him, didn't let out because it would hurt the Project. Questions—will the Project continue, how will the Project continue?—those were questions nobody asked because Mac kept them to himself. Now everybody's asking himself and everybody else, too. I'm not Mac. I can't operate the way Mac did; but I've got to do the same job with what I've got and what I can get. That's why I sent for you."

He stood up and put one big hand on MacDonald's shoulder and looked into his face, as if he could read there the answer to a question he had not yet asked. "Welcome home, Bobby," he said.

They landed at the airport, the olive-skinned, dark-eyed woman and the little boy, and they walked from the airplane to the waiting room because it was only a small airport, the woman walking eagerly, pulling the boy along, and the boy hanging back, tugging at her hand.

And then the big man was there, throwing his arms around the woman, hugging her, kissing her, telling her how glad he was that she was back, how much he had missed her. And finally he knelt to the boy and tried to put his arms around him, too, and the boy stepped back, shaking his head.

The man held out his arms. "Welcome home, Bobby."

"I didn't want to come home," the boy said. "I wanted us to keep going, madre and me, just the two of us forever."

MacDonald shook his head. "This isn't my home. I left it twenty years ago when I was only ten years old, and I haven't been back since. I only came now because you sent a telegram."

White let his hand drop to his side. "I was afraid you wouldn't come just because of your father's death."

MacDonald looked at the desk and the empty chair behind it, its arms worn down by decades of hands and elbows. "Why should he mean more to me dead than alive?"

"Why did you hate him, Bobby?" Olsen asked.

MacDonald shook his head as if he could shake away the old memories. "I didn't hate him. Oh, I had all sorts of Freudian reasons for hating him—I've had enough analysis to recognize those ghosts and live with them— but it was more than that: I needed a father and he was too busy. I never had a father, and I had a mother who worshiped him, and there was not room between them for a little boy."

"He loved you, Bobby," Olsen said. There were tears in the old man's eyes.

MacDonald wished they would stop calling him "Bobby," but he knew he would never be able to tell them so. "He loved my mother, too. But there was no room for her, either, because he loved what he was doing most of all. That was what he lived for, and she knew it and he knew it; we all knew it. Oh, he was a great man, all right, and great men dedicate themselves to their callings, sacrificing everything else. But what of those who get sacrificed? And he was a good man, too. He knew what it was doing to us, to my mother and to me, and he hated it and he tried to make it up to us, but there was nothing left."

"He was a genius," White said.

"'Genius does what it must,'" MacDonald quoted dryly, "'and Talent does what it can.'"

"You sound just like your father," Olsen said. "Always quoting things."

"Why did you ask me to come back?" MacDonald said to White.

"There are things of your father's," White said. "Books." He swept his hand at the shelves behind the desk. "Those were all his. They belong to you now, if you want them. Other things. Papers, letters, files. . . ."

"I don't want them," MacDonald said. "They belong to the Project. Not to me. He had nothing for me."

"All of it?" White asked.

"Everything. But that wasn't why you asked me to return, either."

"I thought you might make your peace with your father," White said. "I did, you know. With my father. Twenty years ago. He finally realized that I wasn't going to be what he wanted, that I couldn't dream his dream, and I finally realized that he loved me anyway. And I told him, and we cried together."

MacDonald looked at the chair again and blinked. "My father's dead."

"But you aren't," White said. "At least you can make peace with his memory."

MacDonald shrugged. "That wasn't why you asked me here either. What am I to you that you should care?"

White spread his hands helplessly. "We do care. That's what's important. We all loved Mac, you see. And so we love Mac's son, and we want his son to love Mac, too."

"All for Mac," MacDonald said. "Mac's son wants to be loved for himself."

"But mainly," White said, "I want to offer you a job with the Project."

"What job?"

White shrugged. "Any job. This one, if you want it." He motioned toward the chair behind the desk. "I'd be pleased to see you sitting there."

"And what of you?"

"I'd go back to what I was doing before Mac got me appointed director in his place, working with the computer. Even though Mac was nearly eighty and officially retired, I never felt like the director while he was around. It wasn't until a few days ago that I suddenly realized I had all the responsibility, that I was the director."

"It wasn't that Mac interfered," Olsen said. "Actually, he wasn't the same after your mother died and you went away to school. He changed. He was detached, somehow, and he kept going only because he was part of this machine for listening and it moved and he moved, and they moved together. After John was appointed, Mac seemed relieved; he never interfered, hardly even spoke unless someone asked him for help."

White smiled. "That's all true. But he was around, and no one ever had any doubt who was the director. Mac was the Project, and the Project was Mac. And now it has to be the Project without Mac."

"You want me because of my name," MacDonald said.

"Partly," White admitted. "You see I've never really had the feeling that I've been director, only that I was sitting in that chair until Mac could come back to fill it again—or at least somebody named MacDonald."

MacDonald looked around the office again as if he were trying to imagine himself in it. "If you're trying to persuade me," he said, "you aren't being very persuasive."

"In this business of anticryptography," White said, "you forget how to say one thing and mean another. And then there's a voice in this place that keeps asking, 'How would Mac have handled it?' And we know he would have been open and honest. Of course I checked up on what you've done since you left here. You're a linguist. You majored in Chinese and Japanese, and traveled extensively while you were in school."

"I had to do something with my vacations," MacDonald said.

"Your father studied languages," Olsen said.

"Yes?" MacDonald said. "But I did it because I wanted to."

"And then you went into computer programming," White said.

"Your father went into electrical engineering," Olsen said.

"I just drifted into it," MacDonald said, "through my work on computer translation."

"And made some original contributions to the art, too," White said. "Don't you see, Bobby, it's as if all these years you've been preparing yourself for us, getting ready to sit in that chair."

"Maybe you and Mac didn't understand each other," Olsen said, "but you were a lot alike. You've been walking in his footsteps, Bobby, and you didn't even know it."

MacDonald shook his head. "All the more reason for me to stop, now that I'm aware of it. I don't want to be like my father." No one can be like anyone else, he thought.

"Twenty years is a long time to carry a hurt," White said.

MacDonald sighed and shifted his feet. He had that bored, impatient feeling he got when he knew, and knew that others knew, that the conversation was over but nobody knew how to stop it. "We carry the load that's placed on us."

"We need you, Bobby," White said. "I need you."

Finally it got down to the personal appeal. "The Project needs me, but not for myself. It needs my father's name, my father's presence. And if I accepted I would be forever buried here in my father's image. The Project would absorb me, the way it absorbed and used up my father, leaving nothing for any other purpose."

White's face was sympathetic. He shook his head. "I know what you're feeling, Bobby. But you've got it all wrong. The Project didn't absorb your father; your father absorbed the Project. The Project was Mac; he made it go. Those radio telescopes were not inanimate—they were his ears listening; that computer was not a machine—it was his brain thinking, remembering, analyzing. And the rest of us—we were just different aspects of Mac with different talents, different ideas, and more time for him to expend. . . ."

"You make it seem worse and worse," MacDonald said. "Don't you understand that's what I've been trying to get away from all my life, the omnipresence, yes, the benevolence of my father . . . ?"

"We've been trying to be honest with you," White said.

"There's some things," Olsen said, easing himself off the desk, "that are bigger than human feelings, more important, like a religion maybe or something a person does for the whole human race, and if you can find something like that and make yourself a part of it and make it happen, why then you've got real satisfaction. Nothing else matters."

MacDonald looked around at the walls as if they imprisoned him. "You're asking me to spend my life here, the next forty years—oh, not here, I'm not qualified to be director, but a part of this place—working with these machines and finding nothing, nothing, and dying probably before the Reply comes from Capella. What kind of life is that? What kind of goal? What kind of satisfaction?"

White looked at Olsen as if to ask what kind of person this was who couldn't understand their dedication, the essence of their being, and how could they get through to him? "Why don't you give Bobby a tour of the place before he leaves?"

To a little boy the Project was a place of mystery and magic. In the daytime it was interesting, but at night it was splendid. Bobby loved to go there when he was allowed to stay up late on special occasions. First he saw the metal valley gleaming in the moonlight, a place where the elves slid to polish the surface to a mirror brightness so that it would catch the stardust the elves bottled to work their spells. And then the Ear, a giant cuplike Ear held up on an arm like an arm of Earth itself to listen to all the whispered secrets of the universe, and they were the secrets a boy had to know if he was going to make his dreams come true. Someday, he told himself, he would find the place where the secrets were stored and he would learn them all and then he could do anything he wanted to.

And one day his father took him to the listening room where you could hear the secrets being whispered, and Bobby was excited to hear them on the earphones, hissing, mumbling, just too low for a boy to understand, and then, when his father turned them up louder, he was disappointed to discover that they were in a secret language that he could not understand.

"No one can understand it, Bobby," his father said.

"I can," Bobby insisted. He couldn't, of course,

but he promised himself that someday he would learn all the languages of Earth and under Earth and above Earth, too, and then he would be able to understand the secrets and know everything there was to know, and when his father wanted to know something he could ask Bobby instead of going off to the Project....

Why does a boy have to grow up? MacDonald asked himself. Life for a boy was so simple and uncomplicated and full of undestroyed hopes. Only it wasn't, he corrected; it was filled with fears and unfulfilled desires and ambitions bigger than the child could ever achieve.

Walking through these old corridors and rooms was like walking through a wonderland deserted by the little people, left to gather dust and tarnish, exposed to the light of the sun to fade and rust.

The building was old: there was no doubt about that—sixty, seventy, maybe eighty years old. And though it had been built to last—like the Project—for centuries, the years had weathered it. Successive layers of paint could not hold the concrete together, and the outsides of the blocks had powdered and come off with the paint, and in some places chunks of concrete had fallen out and been patched. And where generations of clerks and astronomers had walked along the corridors, swinging their arms, the occasional brush of knuckles had worn grooves in the walls. The tiled floors did not show the wear; but then they were more easily replaced.

Olsen introduced him to all the secretaries and maintenance men and occasional astronomers around at this time of day. "This is Bobby MacDonald," Olsen would say, and invariably he would add, "Mac's son, you know."

There would be greetings and shakings of hands and happy sounds and the expectation or hope that MacDonald had come home and would be staying now and the embarrassment when he said "no," so that he finally stopped saying it and merely smiled.

The old listening room had grown a bit shabby as if while nobody had been watching. The glass that covered the dials had been scratched so that in some places they were difficult to read, and dust had collected in places around the rims. The panels themselves had grown worn until in some places the metal gleamed through the dark plastic with which it had originally been covered. Even the earphones had been worn smooth by generations of ears.

Nobody was in the room, although MacDonald had the feeling that someone had just left, and he stopped just inside the door and looked at the place that magic had deserted. It was dead, the spirit that transfigured it fled to some more congenial clime.

"Do you want to hear the Voices, Bobby?" Olsen asked. "Do you want to hear the Message?"

"No," MacDonald said. "I've heard them often enough." And he didn't want to hear them again, not here, not now.

Olsen scurried to the control panel. "We're still listening, you know," he said, as if he had picked up fringes of MacDonald's thoughts. "Still searching for signs in the skies." He chuckled as if it were an old joke. He flipped a worn switch and whisperings filled the room.

And it was as if MacDonald had returned again to the boy he had been. In spite of himself, in spite of his skepticism, in spite of the sunlight and its pitiless exposure of lies and deceits, he was back again listening to the uninterpretable communications from other worlds, the agonies of distant alien creatures trying to make themselves heard and understood. He thought, "God! If I could only help. If I could only answer that cry. If I could only close that broken circuit, tear down that impassable wall of distance, bring intelligence together with intelligence." And he held out his hand as if to take his father's hand and said, "Turn it off!"

It wasn't that the voices were so powerful, he thought, but that he was so weak. He was a spoiled creation, a man ruined in his childhood.

"Have you picked up anything else?" he asked when the whispers were silenced and he had regained control of his imagination.

Olsen shook his head. "It's like before," he said, not discouraged but perhaps a little weary. "We searched for fifty years, you know, before we picked up the message from Capella, and we've only been searching thirty years since then. We picked up the Message the year you were born, Bobby."

"You had better luck with it than with me," MacDonald said. The baby and the Message. There was no question which arrival had meant more to his father, which his father had understood. "Maybe that's all there is," he said.

Olsen shook his head again with a stubbornness that seemed confirmed by occupation and habit. "That's what they used to say, the skeptics, the doubters. Used to say, 'Maybe there's nobody there.' But we kept listening. We had faith. And we proved they were wrong. We picked up the Message, and we deciphered, and we answered it. There's others out there, and we'll pick them up, too. Maybe tonight. Nobody can imagine how vast it is out there, how many stars, how much sky we have to search, how many different ways of signaling we have to explore. If there's one, there's others. And even if there isn't, we still have Capella. That will have made it all worthwhile when we hear from them."

"Yes," MacDonald said. "I suppose it will." He tried to say good-bye to Olsen politely, tried to get away gently, but some of his pain came through, and then Olsen didn't listen.

"I've been saving the best till last," Olsen said. "I want to show you the computer."

MacDonald tried to wave it away. "I've seen computers," he said.

"Not like this one," Olsen said. MacDonald remembered that Olsen was a computer specialist. "And besides, there's something else."

The computer room—the biggest in the entire building—with three and a half of its walls given over to panels and dials and shiny wheels inside glass windows and blinking, many colored lights, and in the center of the room were other units like squat monsters eating data or spitting out wide strips of paper that folded themselves into stacks if nobody was looking at them, and all the while the computer clicked and chuckled to itself.

The only places in the walls the computer did not cover were two doors. One was the entrance from the hall; the other, an entrance from his father's office so that his father, any time he wanted, could ask the computer what he wanted to know, or he could order the computer to do whatever he wanted it to do.

Cables like black snakes reached through the walls into other rooms for more information, and perhaps, the boy thought, the computers went on forever.

And he thought that here was a creature, finally, that knew everything there was to know, even the secrets that were whispered in the listening room, and all you had to do was ask it, and it would tell you.

"Daddy," Bobby said, "why don't you ask the computer what the whispers are saying?"

"We do, Bobby," his father said, "but maybe we don't know the right questions or we don't know how to ask them in the right way, because it doesn't tell us."

With his feet planted wide apart and his hands on his hips, Bobby faced the computer from his father's door, the big and comforting presence of his father behind him, and he said, "When I grow up I'll make the computer tell me everything."

"That would make me very happy and proud," his father said.

Even the computer room had shrunk over the years, and what had once been gleaming glass and painted metal seemed to have melted into the walls with a kind of weary acceptance of time's tyranny. Here and there a unit had been replaced and no doubt memories and readers and printers and even operators had been strung on, but it was basically the same computer that had been standing here for MacDonald's three decades and more.

In terms of memory and linkages, it still was the biggest computer in the world, though by no means the fastest. MacDonald himself had worked on computers that in many ways were superior to this one.

"We've kept up," Olsen said behind him. "It may not look like much in comparison to the newer models with their fancy outsides and micro-miniaturization, but every important new development has been incorporated somewhere. We didn't like to change the memory, that's all, or the looks. After you've worked with a machine for years, it begins to seem almost like a person, and you expect to see a familiar face when you come in here."

A few comfortable chairs had been placed about the room between the readers and the printers and in far corners, and here and there darkness had accumulated in areas where bulbs had burned out and never been replaced. As he turned away from one shadowy corner, MacDonald thought he saw someone sitting there in a chair, but he blinked his eyes and saw that the chair was empty and the room was empty except for MacDonald and Olsen and the computer.

The room was not silent. It clicked and muttered and chuckled, and the air smelled of oil and ozone.

"Sit down," Olsen said, motioning toward one of the chairs in the center of the room. "There's something you should listen to."

"Really," MacDonald said. "I don't want—" But he was sitting down when Olsen pressed a button at the end of a cord and eased himself into the chair beside MacDonald.

"We need to keep reminding ourselves what we are doing," a voice out of the past was saying, "or we'll get swallowed in a quicksand of data. . . .

"Gentlemen, to our listening posts . . ."

Another voice: "These might be something."

The first voice: "Odds."

A third voice, a bit tinny: "Mac, there's been an accident. . . . It's Maria."

A bit later the same voice said, "You can't do this, Mac. . . . This isn't just you. It affects the whole Project."

And the first voice that MacDonald knew too well: "I'm a failure, Charley. Everything I touch—ashes. . . . A poor linguist? An indifferent engineer? I have no qualifications for this job. . . . You need someone with ideas to head the Project, someone dynamic, someone who can lead, someone with charisma."

"You give a good party, Mac," said a voice that sounded like a younger Olsen.

A fifth voice: "Mac, you're what I believe in instead of God."

A sixth voice: "You are the Project. If you go, it all falls apart. It's over."

And the unbearably familiar voice said, "It seems like it always, but it never happens to those things that have life in them. The Project was here before I came. It will be here after I leave. It must be longer lived than any of us, because we are for the years and it is for the centuries. . . ."

And a tinny voice said, "She's going to be all right, Mac."

"They say you're leaving, Mr. MacDonald," said a new voice, a little older and less educated than the others. "Don't go, Mr. MacDonald. . . . You're the one who cares."

The voices went on in the computer room, constructing in MacDonald's imagination a time gone by. Olsen spoke over them. "You see everything that went on here has been recorded since Mac took over as director. 'Who knows,' he said, 'when something one of us says in casual conversation or in jest may be the key that unlocks the locked room, the clue that solves the mystery. We have an unlimited memory and an infinite capacity for creating interconnections. We've got a computer; let's use it.' My job," Olsen said, "was to write the programs that ordered the information so that we didn't keep getting junk when we asked for correlations."

"Everything?" MacDonald said. "From the beginning?"

Olsen swept a wrinkled hand at the walls of computer. "It's all there, every word, and a world of information besides. Everything anyone ever recorded about other worlds or languages or communication or cryptography. 'Who knows,' your father said, 'where imagination interfaces with reality?' He was a great one for 'who knowses.' We had a running joke: 'Pardon me,' someone would say, 'while I blow my who nose.' Mac used to laugh; he said it himself. He was a great man, Mac was. I'm sorry, Bobby—I mean Robert. You get tired of hearing me say things about your father and talking to you as if you were still a boy. You're a man and Mac is dead, and I programmed this for you so you would know what he was like here at the Project, what he did and how he did it."

The old man no longer seemed to MacDonald like a senile fool. He was old but he was still observant. And what he had done—creating a program that could make sense out of that ocean of unrelated data—should be studied by every computer scientist.

"That was your father during his first real crisis," Olsen said, "when your mother attempted suicide and your father almost quit the Project."

MacDonald sat quite still, listening to voices from his past.

"You can listen as long as you wish," Olsen said. "When you've heard all you want to hear just push the button."

MacDonald did not notice him leave. He was listening to the voice of his father: "A man must believe sufficiently in himself—or in his cause—that he persists in spite of disappointments and the inexorable metronome of the years."

And another voice, a dry, skeptic's voice, that said, "Hope and faith keep this Project going—"

His father said, "And scientific probability."

"That's another name for faith. And after more than fifty years even scientific probability becomes more than a little improbable. . . ."

"Fifty years is but the flicker of an eyelash on God's face."

"Fifty years is a man's working life. It has been most of your life. I don't expect you to give it up without a struggle, but it won't do any good. Are you going to cooperate with me or fight me?"

And then, after a bit, the babble-babel of voices like a multitude talking simultaneously, earnestly, confused. . . .

"The sound of the infinite," his father said.

And then another babble, only this one was recognizable and familiar now—the fragments from the radio programs of the Thirties which had been the first interstellar signals picked up, which Capella had rebroadcast as a way of calling attention to the Message it was trying to send, which had been used so effectively on radio and television to build support for the Project. . . .

"We are not alone," a voice said.

The voice of the skeptic now sounded uncertain. "What could they have said to us?"

"We'll find out," his father said.

Time and voices passed in the half-dark room, and MacDonald heard a deep voice say, "It takes all this to read one small Message? For the faithful it requires only a believing heart."

His father said, "Our faith requires that all data and results can be duplicated by anyone using the same equipment and techniques. And with all the believing hearts in the world, none, I think, has received identical Messages."

Minutes later the deep voice said, "Forgive me for doubting. It is a message from God."

The scenes from the past, recorded in holes and tiny magnets and electrons, capable of being recalled completely and infinitely from a vast, frozen storehouse, continued pouring from the computer into MacDonald's mind.

Someone said, "Tell me: why do you insist on responding to this message? Isn't it enough that your search has been successful, that you have demonstrated the existence of intelligent life in the universe?"

His father said, "I could give you rationalizations... but behind all the rationalizations, as you suspect, is the personal motivation. Before our answer could reach Capella I will be dead, but I want my efforts to be rewarded, my convictions to be proved correct, my life to have been meaningful. . . . I want to leave a legacy to my son and to the world. I am not a poet or a prophet, an artist, a builder, a statesman, or a philanthropist. All I can leave is an open door. An open line to the universe, hope, the prospect of something new, a message to come from an alien world under two strange, distant suns. . . ."

He had a persistent dream—maybe it was a memory rather than a dream—of waking up in a big bed all alone. It was his mother's bed, and she had let him climb into her bed and press himself against her soft warmth, and he had fallen asleep. Now he was awake and alone, and the bed was cold and he was afraid.

He got out of bed in the darkness, carefully, lest he step on something terrible or fall into a bottomless hole, and he ran through the darkness, feeling deserted and afraid, down the hall to the living room, screaming, "Mama-mama-mama!"

A light loomed ahead, a small light holding apart the darkness, and in the light his mother was sitting, watching the door, waiting for his father to come home, and he felt alone.

And he remembered: his father came home and was happy to find them waiting for him, mother and son, and they all were happy....

A voice was saying, "You do us great honor by your presence here, Mr. President."

Another voice answered, "No, it is Robert MacDonald who did us the honor with his life and work. It is because of him the world is waiting for a reply from the stars, because of him we have this curious mixed sense of liberation and serenity, as if by contact with creatures who are truly alien we have discovered what it means to be truly human."

A bit later MacDonald heard John White say, "I'm glad you could come, Father."

And an older version of the same voice, "I told MacDonald he could go ahead with his answer, but I never told him it was the right thing to do. I guess I can tell him now."

And other voices said like a Greek chorus:

"Remember when Mac had us put a recorder beside the janitor's false teeth because he said they were picking up messages in the night?"

"And the time he married his secretary to a visiting Congressman—"

"And lost the best secretary he ever had—"

"And the time a reporter came to do an exposé on the Project and stayed to become public relations director?"

"And the time..."

"And the time..."

A bit later there was a more formal chorus:

"He deserved a state funeral."

"In Washington."

"Or in the United Nations building."

"But he wished to be cremated like his wife, and if it were possible and not too much trouble or too expensive, to have their ashes scattered in space."

"Of course."

And someone said:

> *"When he shall die,*
> *Take him and cut him out in little stars,*
> *And he will make the face of heaven so fine*
> *That all the world will be in love with night,*
> *And pay no worship to the garish sun."*

The voice of John White again: "I don't think I know your name."

And a deep old voice: "Jeremiah."

"I thought you were—"

"Dead? Nonsense. MacDonald is dead. Everyone of my generation is dead. I go on. The Solitarians go on, diminished in numbers, perhaps, but not in spirit and rectitude, and they shall see the one God, the God who created man in his image. But I did not come to talk about the Solitarians but to pay my last respects to MacDonald, who was a good man in his lights, though an atheist, a man of great dreams and great deeds whom even a God-fearing man had to respect, and a man about whom it must be said that he was the servant of God though he knew it not...."

And after it was all over, MacDonald sat in the room with the computer staring into the distance. Once his lips moved:

> *In freta dum fluvii current, dum montibus umbrae*
> *Lustrabunt convexa, polus dum sidera pascet,*
> *Semper honos nomenque tuum laudesque manebunt.*

MacDonald did not hear the door open or shut.

John White said, "The memorial is over, Bob." And then, more gently, "I'm sorry. You're crying."

"Yes," MacDonald said. "And the saddest part of it is

that I'm still crying for myself." He could feel the tears roll down his cheeks, and he couldn't stop them from coming. "I never told him I loved him," he said. "He never knew that, and I didn't know it until now."

"He knew," White said.

"You needn't try to comfort me."

"He knew, I tell you," White said.

"One of these days," MacDonald said, "I may be able to weep for him." He shoved himself out of the chair.

White held out his hand. "Thanks for coming. Will you think about it? The job?"

MacDonald took his hand this time without reservation. "I'm not quite ready to think about it. Not yet. There's a girl in New York I want to see again, and something else I've got to do. Maybe then I can think about it."

At the door that led into the corridor, MacDonald turned and looked back at the computer room once more. For a moment, in a distant, shadowed corner, he thought again he saw someone sitting in a chair, someone familiar and ageless, someone composed of memories and old recorded sounds. . . . And he shook his head, and the vision was gone.

Outside the building the day had turned to night and what had seemed tawdry and tarnished had become magical again in the moonlight—the ear of Earth held aloft to overhear the whispered secrets of the universe, the metal bowl polished to catch the stardust—and MacDonald stood, holding his bicycle, looking at the scene once again with eyes cured of the astigmatisms of growing up, and he knew that he would be coming back. For him the waiting was over, though not perhaps for the world; and he wondered if the world was not so much waiting but adjusting its rhythms to the metronome of a conversation with a ninety-year cycle.

He was, MacDonald thought, on his way to living a life of his own at last. He had come home.

"Robert," someone said behind him. It was Olsen standing in the lighted doorway. "Did you see him? Did you see him sitting there?"

"Yes," MacDonald said. "I saw him."

"He'll be there," Olsen said, "as long as the Project

goes on. He'll be there when the reply comes from Capella. Whenever we need him he'll be there."

"Yes," MacDonald said, and turned to go.

"Will you be coming back?" Olsen asked.

"The winds willing," MacDonald said. "But first I've got to go read some letters."

COMPUTER RUN

UPON A SLIGHT CONJECTURE I HAVE VENTURED ON A DANGEROUS JOURNEY, AND I ALREADY BEHOLD THE FOOTHILLS OF NEW LANDS. THOSE WHO HAVE THE COURAGE TO CONTINUE THE SEARCH WILL SET FOOT UPON THEM. . . . IMMANUEL KANT, 1755 . . .

SCIENCE AND TECHNOLOGY HAVE BEEN ADVANCED, IN LARGE MEASURE, THOUGH NOT ENTIRELY, BY THE FIGHT FOR SUPREMACY AND BY THE DESIRE FOR AN EASY LIFE. BOTH THESE FORCES TEND TO DESTROY IF THEY ARE NOT CONTROLLED IN TIME: THE FIRST ONE LEADS TO TOTAL DESTRUCTION AND THE SECOND ONE LEADS TO BIOLOGICAL OR MENTAL DEGENERATION. . . . SEBASTIAN VON HOERNER, 1961 . . .

APPROXIMATELY HALF THE NATION'S WORKING FORCE ARE PUTTING IN A NORMAL 7.5-HOUR WORK DAY AND A 4-DAY WEEK, WITH THE CUSTOMARY 13 WEEKS VACATION, THE UNITED STATES BUREAU OF LABOR ANNOUNCED TODAY. ABOUT ONE-FIFTH OF THE WORK FORCE ARE LABORING 10 HOURS A DAY, 5, 6, OR EVEN 7 DAYS A WEEK, THE BUREAU ADDED. AMONG THIS 20 PERCENT ARE PROFESSIONALS OF ALL KINDS—PHYSICIANS, SCIENTISTS, WRITERS, TEACHERS, MINISTERS, LAWYERS, EDITORS, PRODUCERS AND DIRECTORS, PSYCHOLOGISTS, AND A VARIETY OF BUSINESSMEN AT TOP EXECUTIVE LEVELS. . . .

SPURRED BY THE URGENCY OF HER TONE, HE WENT CRASHING OUTSIDE. HE FOUND MOLLY STANDING RIGID, TRYING TO CRAM BOTH HER FISTS IN HER MOUTH AT THE SAME TIME. AND AT HER FEET WAS A MAN WITH SILVER-GRAY SKIN AND A BROKEN ARM, WHO MEWED AT HIM. . . . THEODORE STURGEON, 1946 . . .

IT MAY BE IMAGINED THAT A HIGHLY DEVELOPED TECHNOLOGICAL SPECIES MIGHT USE WHITE BINARY DWARFS SCATTERED AROUND

THE GALAXY AS RELAY STATIONS FOR HEAVY LONG-DISTANCE FREIGHT TRANSPORTATION.... FREEMAN J. DYSON, 1963...

SUCH A SOCIETY—AFFLUENT, HUMANISTIC, LEISURE-ORIENTED, AND PARTLY ALIENATED—MIGHT BE QUITE STABLE. IT MIGHT, IN FACT, BEAR SOME RESEMBLANCE TO SOME ASPECTS OF GREEK SOCIETY (THOUGH OF COURSE GREEK SOCIETY DID NOT DEVELOP PRIMARILY BECAUSE OF AFFLUENCE). WE CAN IMAGINE A SITUATION IN WHICH, SAY, 70 OR 80 PERCENT OF PEOPLE BECOME GENTLEMEN AND PUT A GREAT DEAL OF EFFORT INTO VARIOUS TYPES OF SELF-DEVELOPMENT, THOUGH NOT NECESSARILY THE ACTIVITIES WHICH SOME FUTURISTS FIND MOST IMPORTANT FOR A HUMANISTIC CULTURE. BUT ONE COULD IMAGINE, FOR EXAMPLE, A VERY SERIOUS EMPHASIS ON SPORTS, ON COMPETITIVE "PARTNER" GAMES (CHESS, BRIDGE), ON MUSIC, ART, LANGUAGES, OR SERIOUS TRAVEL, OR ON THE STUDY OF SCIENCE, PHILOSOPHY, AND SO ON.... HERMAN KAHN AND ANTHONY J. WIENER, 1967...

FEARS THAT THE LIFETIME OF TECHNOLOGICAL CIVILIZATION ON EARTH MAY BE QUITE SHORT ARE NOT GROUNDLESS. HOWEVER, THERE IS AT LEAST THE POSSIBILITY THAT A RESOLUTION OF NATIONAL CONFLICTS WOULD OPEN THE WAY FOR THE CONTINUED DEVELOPMENT OF CIVILIZATION FOR PERIODS OF TIME COMMENSURATE WITH STELLAR LIFETIMES.... J. P. T. PEARMAN, 1961...

IT MUST BE ASSUMED THAT A HIGHLY ADVANCED SOCIETY WOULD ALSO BE STABLE OVER VERY LONG PERIODS, PRESERVING THE RECORDS OF PREVIOUS EXPEDITIONS AND WAITING PATIENTLY FOR THE RETURN OF OTHERS. ACCORDING TO THIS HYPOTHESIS CIVILIZATIONS THROUGHOUT THE GALAXY PROBABLY POOL THEIR RESULTS AND AVOID DUPLICATION. THERE MAY BE A CENTRAL GALACTIC INFORMATION REPOSITORY WHERE KNOWLEDGE IS ASSEMBLED, MAKING IT FAR EASIER FOR THOSE WITH ACCESS TO SUCH INFORMATION TO GUESS WHERE, IN THE GALAXY, NEWLY INTELLIGENT LIFE IS ABOUT TO APPEAR—A PROBLEM VERY DIFFICULT FOR US, WITH ONLY OUR OWN EXPERIENCE ON ONE PLANET TO GO BY.... CARL SAGAN, 1963...

IMAGINE ALL THE MATTER IN EXISTENCE GATHERED TOGETHER
IN THE CENTER OF THE UNIVERSE—
ALL THE METEORS
COMETS

MOONS
PLANETS
STARS
NEBULAS
THE MYRIAD GALAXIES
ALL COMPACTED INTO ONE GIANT PRIMORDIAL ATOM,
ONE MONOBLOC, MASSIVE BEYOND COMPREHENSION,
DENSE BEYOND BELIEF...
THINK OF WHITE DWARFS, THINK OF NEUTRON STARS,
THEN MULTIPLY BY INFINITY....

THE CENTER OF THE UNIVERSE? THE UNIVERSE ITSELF.
NO LIGHT, NO ENERGY COULD LEAVE, NONE ENTER.
PERHAPS TWO UNIVERSES, ONE WITHIN THE GIANT EGG
WITH EVERYTHING
AND ONE OUTSIDE WITH ALL NOTHING...
DISTINCT, UNTOUCHABLE...
IMAGINE!
ARE YOU IMAGINING?
ALL THE MATTER BROUGHT TOGETHER,
THE UNIVERSE A SINGLE, INCREDIBLE MONOBLOC,
SEETHING WITH INCOMPREHENSIBLE FORCES AND
POTENTIALS
FOR COUNTLESS EONS OR FOR INSTANTS
(WHO MEASURES TIME IN SUCH A UNIVERSE?),
AND THEN...
BANG!
EXPLOSION!
BEYOND EXPLOSION!
TEARING APART THE MONOBLOC, THE PRIMORDIAL
ATOM,
THE GIANT EGG HATCHING WITH FIRE AND FURY,
CREATING
THE GALAXIES
THE NEBULAS
THE SUNS
THE PLANETS
THE MOONS
THE COMETS
THE METEORS
SENDING THEM HURTLING IN ALL DIRECTIONS INTO
SPACE

CREATING SPACE
CREATING THE EXPANDING UNIVERSE
CREATING EVERYTHING...
IMAGINE!

YOU CAN'T IMAGINE?
WELL, THEN, IMAGINE A UNIVERSE POPULATED WITH
STARS AND
GALAXIES, A UNIVERSE FOREVER EXPANDING,
UNLIMITED,
WHERE GALAXIES FLEE FROM EACH OTHER,
THE MOST DISTANT SO RAPIDLY
THAT THEY REACH THE SPEED OF LIGHT
AND DISAPPEAR FROM OUR UNIVERSE
AND WE FROM THEIRS....

IMAGINE MATTER BEING CREATED CONTINUOUSLY,
A HYDROGEN ATOM POPPING INTO EXISTENCE
HERE AND THERE,
HERE
   AND
      THERE,
PERHAPS ONE ATOM OF HYDROGEN A YEAR
WITHIN A SPACE THE SIZE OF THE HOUSTON
ASTRODOME,
AND OUT OF THESE ATOMS,
PULLED TOGETHER BY THE UNIVERSAL FORCE OF
GRAVITATION,
NEW SUNS ARE BORN,
NEW GALAXIES TO REPLACE THOSE FLED BEYOND
OUR PERCEPTION,
THE EXPANDING UNIVERSE
WITHOUT END,
WITHOUT BEGINNING....

YOU CAN'T IMAGINE?
WELL, PERHAPS IT IS ALL A FANTASY....

NO DOUBT MANY WOULD FIND THOUSAND-YEAR TRIPS UNAP-
PEALING, BUT WE HAVE NO RIGHT TO IMPOSE OUR TASTES ON OTH-
ERS....FREEMAN J. DYSON, 1964...

———

SPACEFARING SOCIETIES MIGHT SEND OUT EXPEDITIONS ABOUT ONCE A YEAR AND, HENCE, THE STARSHIPS WOULD RETURN AT ABOUT THE SAME RATE, SOME WITH NEGATIVE REPORTS ON SOLAR SYSTEMS VISITED, SOME WITH FRESH NEWS FROM SOME WELL-KNOWN CIVILIZATIONS. THE WEALTH, DIVERSITY, AND BRILLIANCE OF THIS COMMERCE, THE EXCHANGE OF GOODS AND INFORMATION, OF ARGUMENTS AND ARTIFACTS, OF CONCEPTS AND CONFLICTS, MUST CONTINUOUSLY SHARPEN THE CURIOSITY AND ENHANCE THE VITALITY OF THE PARTICIPATING SOCIETIES. ... CARL SAGAN, 1963 ...

WORLD POPULATION LEVELED OFF AT APPROXIMATELY FIVE BILLION PERSONS FIFTEEN YEARS AGO AND SINCE THEN HAS DECLINED BY SEVERAL MILLION, MOSTLY IN THE HEAVILY URBANIZED NATIONS, THE UNITED NATIONS BUREAU OF POPULATION STATISTICS AND CONTROL ANNOUNCED TODAY IN ITS ANNUAL REPORT.

LATEST ITEM TO HIT THE MEDIA STANDS IS A COMPLEX OFFERING THAT BLENDS VISUAL DISPLAY, ODOR, MUSIC, TOUCH, FICTION, AND VERSE INTO ONE MASSIVE COMMUNICATION ABOUT—WHAT ELSE?—COMMUNICATION. THE VIEWER-AUDITOR-SNIFFER-FEELER PURCHASES A BLACK BOX WHICH HAS SEVEN BUTTONS ON ONE SIDE. BY PRESSING THE SEVEN BUTTONS AT RANDOM, THE V-A-S-F IS ASSAILED BY WHAT SEEMS AT FIRST LIKE AN OVERWHELMING VARIETY OF SENSE IMPRESSIONS, BUT HE EVENTUALLY DISCOVERS, IF HE IS LUCKY, THAT THEY ADD UP TO MORE THAN THE MISCELLANEOUS PARTS: THERE IS A COMMUNICATION ABOUT COMMUNICATION, WITH THE MISCELLANY COMMUNICATING NOT ONLY WITH THE USER BUT AMONG THEMSELVES, AND THE SENSITIVITY OF THE USER INCREASED TO THE EVERYDAY PROCESSES BY WHICH WE INFORM OURSELVES ABOUT THE NATURE OF WHAT IS HAPPENING AROUND US AND THE EFFORTS OF OTHERS TO TELL US WHAT THEY WANT US—OR DON'T WANT US—TO KNOW.

HOW CAN I EXPLAIN IT? WORDS ARE NOT THE ONLY, NOR PERHAPS THE BEST, MEANS OF COMMUNICATION. GET ONE FOR YOURSELF. EXPERIENCE!

IF THERE ARE ABOUT A MILLION WORLDS IN THE GALAXY CAPABLE OF SUCH FEATS, THEY WOULD VISIT ONE ANOTHER ABOUT ONCE IN EVERY THOUSAND YEARS AND SCOUTS MAY HAVE VISITED THE EARTH FROM TIME TO TIME IN THE PAST—PERHAPS A TOTAL OF 10,000 TIMES OVER THE FULL SPAN OF THE EARTH'S HISTORY. ... CARL SAGAN, 1963 ...

HE STARED BACK AT THE DOME, A TINY BLACK THING DWARFED BY THE DISTANCE.

BACK THERE WERE MEN WHO COULDN'T SEE THE BEAUTY THAT WAS JUPITER. MEN WHO THOUGHT THAT SWIRLING CLOUDS AND LASHING RAIN OBSCURED THE FACE OF THE PLANET. UNSEEING HUMAN EYES. POOR EYES. EYES THAT COULD NOT SEE THE BEAUTY IN THE CLOUDS, THAT COULD NOT SEE THROUGH THE STORMS. BODIES THAT COULD NOT FEEL THE THRILL OF TRILLING MUSIC STEMMING FROM THE RUSH OF BROKEN WATER....

"I CAN'T GO BACK," SAID TOWSER.

"NOR I," SAID FOWLER.

"THEY WOULD TURN ME BACK INTO A DOG," SAID TOWSER.

"AND ME," SAID FOWLER, "BACK INTO A MAN."...CLIFFORD SIMAK, 1944...

THE REAPPEARANCE IN OUR SOCIETY OF THE DILETTANTE, THE GENTLEMAN-SCHOLAR-PROFESSIONAL, THE PERSON WHO INDULGES HIS PASSION FOR THE ARTS OR THE PROFESSIONS BECAUSE OF THE PLEASURE HE DERIVES FROM IT, IS A PHENOMENON THAT DESERVES FURTHER STUDY. WHEN WORK IS AN AVOCATION DOES IT CEASE TO BE WORK? DOES AN AVOCATION PROVIDE A GREATER POTENTIAL FOR DISCOVERY AND SERVICE? OR LESS?

ADVANCED SOCIETIES THROUGHOUT THE GALAXY PROBABLY ARE IN CONTACT WITH ONE ANOTHER, SUCH CONTACT BEING ONE OF THEIR CHIEF INTERESTS. THEY HAVE ALREADY PROBED THE LIFE HISTORIES OF THE STARS AND OTHER OF NATURE'S SECRETS. THE ONLY NOVELTY LEFT WOULD BE TO DELVE INTO THE EXPERIENCE OF OTHERS. WHAT ARE THE NOVELS? WHAT ARE THE ART HISTORIES? WHAT ARE THE ANTHROPOLOGICAL PROBLEMS OF THOSE DISTANT STARS? THAT IS THE KIND OF MATERIAL THAT THESE REMOTE PHILOSOPHERS HAVE BEEN CHEWING OVER FOR A LONG TIME....PHILIP MORRISON, 1961...

WILL WE BE ABLE TO UNDERSTAND THE SCIENCE OF ANOTHER CIVILIZATION?...OUR SCIENCE HAS CONCENTRATED ON ASKING CERTAIN QUESTIONS AT THE EXPENSE OF OTHERS, ALTHOUGH THIS IS SO WOVEN INTO THE FABRIC OF OUR KNOWLEDGE THAT WE ARE GENERALLY UNAWARE OF IT. IN ANOTHER WORLD, THE BASIC QUESTIONS MAY HAVE BEEN ASKED DIFFERENTLY....J. ROBERT OPPENHEIMER, 1962...

6

The Computer—2118

. . . he felt in his heart their strangeness,
Their stillness answering his cry. . . .

The observers began arriving on Wednesday.

Some had been selected by their governments or by qualified selectors; some had been elected by popular vote; some came by special invitation of a Project committee, signed by the director.

They came from all over the world and in all manners. Many arrived in sailing ships ranging from passenger schooners with two stainless steel masts and elegantly appointed cabins to the smallest of sloops with no cabin at all. An outrigger canoe was paddled all the way from Samoa by a dozen proud Polynesians to demonstrate that they still revered and were capable of the feats of their ancestors.

One man came in his personal submarine with the intention, to be sure, of doing exploration of the ocean floor after the occasion, one man swam from St. Thomas, and a woman peddled a bicycle mounted on two pontoons from Cuba.

The majority arrived on Saturday by ferries spouting their wings of spray, by commercial jet, by private helicopter, by sailplane, or by balloon.

This was the era of the individual when men and women had the opportunity and the time to make their own decisions.

Saturday was the Day of the Reply, a holiday in all parts of the world, the day the world had been awaiting for ninety years, and it was as if the world was awakening from a long sleep—no, not a sleep but a dream, a kind of wonderful slowed-down reality, a dream about humanity and what mankind might be like with a bit more time, a little less urgency, a bit more grace, a little less adrenaline. The Project set up nearly one hundred fifty years before to listen for messages from the stars and the Message from Capella that it had received and deciphered had given Earth and its people ninety years of peace in which to explore the other aspects of humanity besides aggression. The problems which had seemed so difficult, virtually unsolvable, one hundred and fifty, even ninety, years before had seemed to solve themselves once the world relaxed.

Now the Day was at hand. The people who arrived to celebrate it were of many colors and many occupations, but the colors seemed somewhat less distinct than they used to be and the occupations were not as precisely defined, as if everyone was a bit of a dilettante, performing his duties and assuming his responsibilities with the undimmed delight and undulled awareness of the eternal amateur who is as interested in his neighbor's job as his own. But there were scientists of all kinds, linguists, philosophers, humanists; politicians and political figures; newsmen and analysts; composers, artists in many forms and media, poets, novelists; and interested citizens. Many of them, for convenience, traveled in national groups, although the spirit of nationalism, too, had diminished in the past ninety years.

But all of this, perhaps, was ending with the approach of the moment when the reply was expected from Capella.

The observers arrived, most of them, at the port of Arecibo and traveled the green hills of northern Puerto Rico in buses and in limousines, on bicycles and on foot—some spoke of pilgrimages and told each other the adventures they had experienced on their way—until they arrived at the Project, passing the implausibly round valley lined with gleaming metal, and not far beyond, the steerable radio telescope held aloft on a metal arm, and coming at last to the long, low building which housed the Project.

The building had grown over the century and a half since it had been put together with concrete blocks and poured cement, sprawling each decade a little farther on either end, but now a new wing had been attached onto the back. It housed an auditorium especially built for this occasion by volunteers and designed so that the seating descended the hill behind the Project and the roof line remained level with the roof of the original Project and the auditorium became the leg of a T.

The observers had to pass through the ancient corridors of the old building to reach the auditorium. They admired the often-repaired walls and the layers of paint that seemed to hold them together. They gaped at the listening room and paused to hear samples of the hisses and crackles that were the music of the spheres, the background noise of the universe, and the original recordings of the Voices, the fragments of radio programs from the nineteen-thirties with which the Capellans ingeniously had first attracted the attention of the listeners at the Project fifty years after the Project had begun.

POPCRACKLE ice regusted CRACKLEPOP music: that little chatterbox the one with the pretty POPPOP-CRACKLE wanna buy a duck POPCRACKLEPOP masked champion of justice CRACKLEPOPPOP music POPPOPPOPCRACKLE ter eleven book one hundred and POPCRACKLEPOP here they come jack POPPOP music CRACKLE yoo hoo is anybody POPCRACKLE is raymond your POPCRACKLEPOPPOP music POPPOP-CRACKLE music: wave the flag for hudson CRACKLEPOP um a bad boy POPPOPPOP lux presents holly CRACKLECRACKLE music POPPOPCRACKLE rogers in the twenty POPCRACKLEPOP music: cola hits the spot twelve....

And they shook their heads in wonder and said, "It sounds so much better here than in the recordings I've heard. So much closer. So much more real. Think what it must have been like ninety years ago to have heard that for the first time and have realized that it had been all the way to Capella and back and you were listening to the first evidence of intelligent life on other worlds." And everyone agreed that it was so.

After that their path took them through the even more impressive computer room, where they could hear the computer itself whispering and clicking and muttering to itself—"almost alive," as the cliché went—and see the lights flicker on and off; they watched the various readers and printers eating up information or spitting it out, and smelled the oil and ozone that was the distinctive odor of electrical equipment big and small. And some of them asked staff members about the empty chairs in the corners, while others, more knowledgeable, asked if any of them had seen the Presence and, depending on their expectations, the staff members would raise their eyebrows and roll their eyes and say, "Yes, and it was a terrifying experience I can tell you," or chuckle and say, "He talks to me whenever I'm in trouble," or tell the truth and say, "No one's seen him for a long time, though there are those who say they have." And whatever they said the observers were pleased and went on.

One by one they inspected the original Message framed and hung on the wall of the director's office. And they ran their hands along the worn desk where papers had been strewn and pencil and pen had noted and drawn and calculated, and some of them slipped into the chair behind the desk, its wooden arms polished by the hands of generations of directors, to sit where they had sat and pondered the mysteries of the universe and the difficulties of communication, and others only looked and smelled the old books that lined two walls of the office.

The building was a marvel of antiquity, the observers said to each other, in some ways rivaling the pyramids of Egypt or the castles of Europe—you can see, they said, how the concrete of the corridors has been hollowed toward the center by generations of passing feet; and how many times has the tile on those corridor floors been replaced?—and besides that it was a monument to human science and perseverance; and now it was all going to culminate in a wonderful, exciting Reply from Capella that would change everything or not, but it would be wonderful all the same and the world would be glad it had waited.

But now the waiting had come to an end, and the tempo was beginning to pick up; the pulse beat of the world was quickening as the moment approached when the giant radio ears outside would hear the reply that had been started on its way to Earth forty-five years ago from an alien race faced with possible destruction from the explosion of their giant red suns. . . .

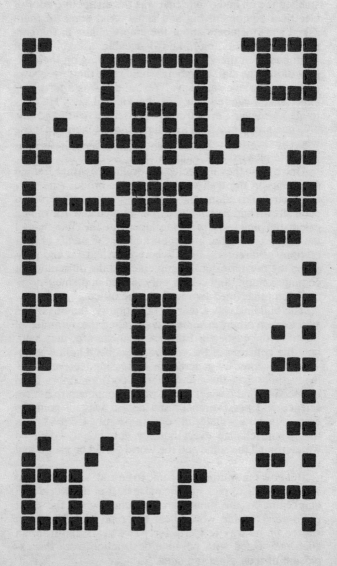

CAPELLA IS LATIN FOR "LITTLE SHE GOAT." IT IS FOUND IN THE CONSTELLATION OF AURIGA, THE CHARIOTEER, WHO WAS, IN GREEK MYTHOLOGY, THE INVENTOR OF THE CHARIOT. HIS FIRST CHARIOT, ACCORDING TO THE MYTH, WAS DRAWN BY GOATS.

STAR	TYPE	APP. MAG.	R/A	DECL.	DIST.	LUM.	MASS
CAPELLA A	GO	0.2	0514	+ 4558	45	120	4.2
CAPELLA B	GO						3.3

THE SECOND PERFORMANCE OF THE EPIC, EIGHT-HOUR "CAPELLA" SYMPHONY OF A YOUNG PAKISTANI COMPOSER SENT HALF ITS LOS ANGELES AUDIENCE TOWARD THE DOORS BEFORE THE MUSICON TAPES, WITH THE COMPOSER HIMSELF AT THE KEYBOARD, WERE MORE THAN HALF PLAYED.

MANY OF THOSE WHO LEFT STOPPED AT THE BOX OFFICE AND DEMANDED THEIR MONEY BACK, CLAIMING THE WORK WAS TOO LONG AND TOO BORING.

THE CONTRAST WITH LAST YEAR WAS DRAMATIC. AT THE SYMPHONY'S PREMIERE IN NEW YORK NOT A PERSON LEFT HIS LOUNGE AND, AT THE CONCLUSION, THE AUDIENCE PAID THE COMPOSER, SINGHAR KHAN, THE ULTIMATE COMPLIMENT OF TEN MINUTES OF SILENCE, AND MANY STAYED FOR HOURS AFTERWARD DISCUSSING WITH FRIENDS THE MEANING OF THE SYMPHONY....

DID YOU HEAR ABOUT THE NEW SHOW FROM CAPELLA?
NO, WHAT ABOUT THE NEW SHOW FROM CAPELLA?
IT LAID AN EGG.

... THE EARTH, THAT IS SUFFICIENT,
I DO NOT WANT THE CONSTELLATIONS ANY NEARER,
I KNOW THEY ARE VERY WELL WHERE THEY ARE,
I KNOW THEY SUFFICE FOR THOSE WHO BELONG TO THEM....
                                        WALT WHITMAN, 1856...

THOSE WHO HAVE NEVER SEEN A LIVING MARTIAN CAN SCARCELY IMAGINE THE STRANGE HORROR OF ITS APPEARANCE. THE PECULIAR V-SHAPED MOUTH WITH ITS POINTED UPPER LIP, THE ABSENCE OF BROW RIDGES, THE ABSENCE OF A CHIN BENEATH THE WEDGELIKE LOWER LIP, THE INCESSANT QUIVERING OF THIS MOUTH, THE GORGON GROUPS OF TENTACLES, THE TUMULTUOUS BREATHING OF THE

LUNGS IN A STRANGE ATMOSPHERE, THE EVIDENT HEAVINESS AND
PAINFULNESS OF MOVEMENT DUE TO THE GREATER GRAVITATIONAL
ENERGY OF THE EARTH—ABOVE ALL, THE EXTRAORDINARY INTEN-
SITY OF THE IMMENSE EYES—WERE AT ONCE VITAL, INTENSE, IN-
HUMAN, CRIPPLED AND MONSTROUS. THERE WAS SOMETHING
FUNGOID IN THE OILY BROWN SKIN, SOMETHING IN THE CLUMSY DE-
LIBERATION OF THE TEDIOUS MOVEMENTS UNSPEAKABLY NASTY. EVEN
AT THIS FIRST ENCOUNTER, I WAS OVERCOME WITH DISGUST AND
DREAD....H. G. WELLS, 1898...

The program itself began at sunset Saturday. Late arrivals had seen a spectacular vision of the sun setting
behind mounting clouds to the west, turning them various
shades of gold and orange and red and then darkening
into purple and finally black. Those who believed in omens
said it was an omen, and those who did not said it was a
good show all the same.

The visitors had passed through the Project and all its
fascinating history and mementos, and then into the auditorium and down the resilient ramps and into the up-
holstered chairs. They had looked around them at the
others who were assembling and then at the auditorium
itself, with its muraled side walls and the recessed stage
at the bottom of the seats—it was not really a stage but
a speaker's pit. At the back of the pit were some small
computer display units with switches and dials and a few
oscilloscopes. At either end of the computer units was a
chair sitting in shadows. The chairs were empty.

When the visitors had settled into their seats, the staff
members of the Project came down the center aisle in a
group, led by William MacDonald, the Project director.
He was a middle-aged man of fifty-seven, and he walked
briskly to the speaker's pit while his staff scattered themselves among the seats in front, left vacant, by imme-
morial custom, as the earlier arrivals filled the back seats
first.

As MacDonald turned to the seats, every one of them
filled—two staff members had to find portable chairs and
fit them in at the ends of the front row—the lights dimmed,
not dramatically but just enough to focus attention on the
speaker's pit and diminish the hum of conversation.

"Citizens of the world," MacDonald said, and his words

were picked up and heard all over the auditorium and flung around the world as if MacDonald were sitting and conversing with each person, "Terrans. Welcome to the Project and to the Day of the Reply. This occasion and the ceremony that surrounds it is being broadcast to every continent and every continental subdivision, and to our colonies on the moon and on Mars and to all the men who work in space, for this is Earth's day, the day all of us have been awaiting for ninety years, the first day when we might hope for a reply from Capella to the Answer Earth sent to the Capellans ninety years ago.

"But first, into the heart of our euphoria, let me inject a few milliliters of realism. In about half an hour, as accurately as we can measure the distance, is the earliest we can anticipate a reply. That does not mean we can realistically expect a reply at this time. Our answer might require processing; that takes time. Their reply may take formulation; that takes time. In other words, the reply may not come for hours, or even days or weeks. We should not let ourselves be disappointed or become discouraged by delays that may be inevitable. We have developed patience over the past ninety years; we may have occasion to exercise it.

"I am William MacDonald, director of the Project. I am the third MacDonald to have held this position. It is not hereditary, though to some it may have seemed so."

Dry laughter rustled the audience.

"Perhaps only a MacDonald," MacDonald continued, "would be willing to spend his life waiting and listening. ...I have no son, but for those of you who might be wondering, I do have a daughter who is now a member of the Project staff.

"The real work of the Project, however, is not performed by the Director but by the staff. They sit in front of me, and I would like them to stand and be introduced to you..."

After the applause had faded to only a handclap or two, MacDonald said, "Thousands of men and women have devoted their time, their energies, their devotion, their lives to the Project in its nearly a century and a half, and their work has helped the Project reach this point in time and history; I would like to mention them all, but

that would take far more than the thirty minutes we have
at our disposal. You will find their names in the Project
booklet available at the door as you leave, and as a tribute
to all of them we have placed a chair at either end of the
speaker's pit to remind us of them and of their indispensable
contributions. You may, of course, consider them
occupied by any of the past staff members—by John
White, for instance, or his son Andrew, by Ronald Olsen,
or by Charles Saunders, or by any or all of them, or by
the spirit of the past, by the unknown staff members. I
think of them as being occupied by my father and my
grandfather."

The Siberian premier pulled himself heavily to his feet
and said, "Mr. MacDonald. I have heard it said that apparitions
of your father and your grandfather—what some
have called a 'Presence'—have been seen in the computer
room of the Project, and I have it on reliable authority
that the computer is capable of such illusions and that it
has been instructed to speak in the voice of your father
or your grandfather—"

MacDonald looked steadily up at the big man in his
robe and said, "The computer can present holographic
displays of information, as you will see before long, I
hope, but it is our belief that such an illusion as the one
to which you refer is beyond its present capability; if some
of us believe that the spirits of the past members of the
Project linger in the computer in the form of dialogue and
other inputs, why we all need comfort and spiritual assistance.

"The computer will be taking over the majority of this
presentation in a few minutes, for no human is quick
enough to interpret the hoped-for signals as they arrive,
and this is what the computer has been prepared to do
for these past one hundred and fifty years. That preparation
and its accumulated information and programs and
linkages have made it an incredibly complex creation, but
we should not project into it our own fears or hopes. When
you hear the computer speak, you may judge for yourself
whether it speaks like my father or my grandfather, or,
as some maintain, like me or like a composite of all of
the voices it has ever heard. We could instruct it in such
matters, but we do not. Perhaps, as I said, we ourselves

prefer to think of it as at least a half-conscious ally.

"Now the time has come to turn the occasion over to the computer. Its presentation will consist of vocal communication and holographic displays. It will begin with a short history of the Project. When or if a signal is received either on our own antennae or on those of the Big Net orbiting Earth, with which it is in continual communication, the presentation will be interrupted...."

AN ESTIMATED TWO BILLION PERSONS WERE GATHERED AROUND THEIR HOLOVISION SETS TODAY OR TONIGHT—SINCE THEY CIRCLED THE EARTH IT IS IMPOSSIBLE TO BE SPECIFIC—TO WATCH THE OPENING CEREMONIES OF THE DAY OF THE REPLY BEING BROADCAST FROM ARECIBO. ANOTHER TWO BILLION WERE TRYING TO GET TO A HOLOVISION SET....

> O BE PREPARED, MY SOUL!
> TO READ THE INCONCEIVABLE, TO SCAN
> THE MILLION FORMS OF GOD THOSE STARS
>   UNROLL
> WHEN, IN OUR TURN, WE SHOW TO THEM A MAN.
>   ALICE MEYNELL, 1913...

HALF THE ENTERING CLASS AT STANFORD MEDICAL SCHOOL CHOSE THE NEW, ABBREVIATED TEN-YEAR CURRICULUM.

THE BUREAU OF POPULATION TODAY ANNOUNCED A TWO PERCENT INCREASE IN THE WORLD BIRTHRATE OVER THE SAME PERIOD LAST YEAR.

THE OFFICE OF ENVIRONMENT SAID TODAY THAT FIVE CASES OF INDUSTRIAL AND THREE CASES OF INDIVIDUAL POLLUTION HAD BEEN REPORTED BY CITIZENS IN THE PAST WEEK. ONLY TEN CASES IN ALL WERE REPORTED DURING ALL OF LAST YEAR....

> OH CAPELLA, OH CAPELLA,
> WE HAVE HEARD YOUR VOICES TELL US,
> OVER SPACES INTERSTELLAR
>   THAT WE ARE NOT ALONE.
> BROTHERHOOD—THIS YOU HAVE FOR US;
> WE WOULD LIKE TO JOIN THE CHORUS,
>   BUT WE MUST SING ALONE.
>   FOR YOU THE WORDS, FOR US THE
>   SONG,

BUT DISTANCES ARE MUCH TOO LONG.
A CAPPELLA, A CAPPELLA...

IF BOTH RACES COULD BE WARNED, THOUGH, AND EACH KNEW
THAT THE OTHER DID NOT WANT TO FIGHT, AND IF THEY COULD COM-
MUNICATE WITH EACH OTHER BUT NOT LOCATE EACH OTHER UNTIL
SOME GROUNDS FOR MUTUAL TRUST COULD BE REACHED—
"SWAP SHIPS!" ROARED THE SKIPPER, "SWAP SHIPS AND GO ON
HOME!..." MURRAY LEINSTER, 1945...

In its recounting of the Project's history, with pictures,
still and moving, within the holographic square that formed
itself beside MacDonald, the computer had reached the
dramatic moment when the radio telescope in orbit around
the Earth, called the Big Net, had recorded a tape which,
with others, had routinely been sent to the Project and a
man named Saunders had begun the long process of deciphering which revealed the Voices, when the computer
paused briefly and then said in the same matter-of-fact
voice, "I am receiving new signals from Capella."

The audience stirred and sat up; all over the world men
and women and children drew closer to their sets. In the
audience a man fainted and a woman began to weep.

"The signals I am receiving from Capella," the computer said, "are similar to those I have been receiving
continuously over the past ninety years, but there is a
significant difference. The signal is being repeated now
for possible interference or signal loss. Now other signals
are coming in one after the other."

The audience leaned forward.

"I now can display the new message," the computer
said.

In black and white spaces within the holographic square,
the message took shape:

"Messages are being received too rapidly," the computer said, "for all to be displayed at this time. I will
select a few for your consideration."

The first message was replaced by others flashed in
the square at intervals of about ten seconds each.

"These messages seemed to be building a vocabulary
of words and numbers and operators," the computer said.
And a few seconds later it said, "Yes. I now can state

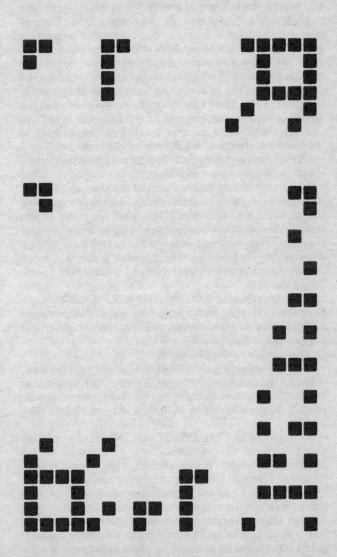

within acceptable limits of accuracy that the messages are transmitting a vocabulary. At the present rate of reception, a reasonably complete dictionary and perhaps a grammar as well will be available within twenty-four hours. Yes," the computer continued, "symbols are being substituted for pictures which no longer are adequate for the complex messages to come. As soon as the dictionary is complete, I anticipate that the pictures will cease and the messages will arrive entirely in symbols and other abstractions which will raise the level of communication to that of history, novel, and mathematical equation.

"Yes," the computer said, "I now am receiving certain simple messages in symbol alone."

In the part of the audience around the Siberian premier, people were turning to each other, discussing something in loud whispers, and in a circle around the group others were frowning at the disturbance. The Siberian premier stood up again, although some of his scientific delegation were pulling at his robe. The Siberian group was more cohesive than most, since Siberia had come late to nationalism.

"Mr. MacDonald," the premier said, "some concern has been expressed near me that the input of information is proceeding at such a rapid rate that the computer will not be able to handle it."

"No danger," MacDonald said.

"What I am saying, Mr. MacDonald," the premier said, pulling his robe hem impatiently out of the hands that sought to consult with him, "is that there may be unsuspected dangers involved in letting this reception continue."

"I assure you," MacDonald said, "there are no dangers."

"Your assurance is not enough," the premier said. "Since our words are being overheard and recorded by this computer, I had not wished to speak frankly, hoping that as men of diplomacy we might understand each other without telling everything, but now I must speak without tact. The Capellans are technologically advanced and desperate; that combination may threaten a takeover of your computer and all the power that it controls. A race like this must be the master of the computer, and who knows what other capabilities of communication and transportation those creatures may have. I ask you to take the precautions of a reasonable man and turn off your machine now while we evaluate the situation."

A Siberian scientist stood up beside his premier and said, "I apologize for our leader. It is clear that he understands neither the nature of the computer nor that of the messages that have been received."

The level of background noise in the auditorium had climbed to the point where it was difficult to hear. MacDonald held up his hand. "Nevertheless, his apprehensions are natural and may be shared by others in the audience. We cannot entirely eliminate the possibility of an alien program superseding our instructions—but from forty-five light-years away without any prior knowledge of our computer, how it operates, how it is programmed, without the possibility of feedback?—the probabilities are infinitesimally small. And to what purpose?

"Moreover," MacDonald said, "we have nothing to fear from the Capellans. That is obvious from the Reply we have just received. Put the Reply on again!"

The Reply again was displayed within the holographic square.

"And the original Message from Capella," MacDonald said, "—the one we received ninety years ago—place that beside the Reply."

The two were displayed side by side.

A WORLD IS WAITING FOR AN EXPLANATION OF THE REPLY RECEIVED FROM CAPELLA ONLY A FEW MINUTES AGO. DIRECTOR MACDONALD IS EXPECTED TO REVEAL AT ANY MOMENT THE SIGNIFICANCE OF THE TWO MESSAGES. PREMONITIONS HAVE SWEPT THE CIRCUMFERENCE OF THE EARTH. SOME ANALYSTS ALREADY ARE POINTING OUT THE CURIOUSLY EMPTY APPEARANCE OF THE REPLY.

THE WORLDWIDE AUDIENCE IS ESTIMATED TO HAVE REACHED THREE BILLION....

SOMEWHERE IN THE SANDS OF THE DESERT
A SHAPE WITH A LION BODY AND THE HEAD OF A MAN,
A GAZE BLANK AND PITILESS AS THE SUN,
IS MOVING ITS SLOW THIGHS, WHILE ALL ABOUT IT
REEL SHADOWS OF THE INDIGNANT DESERT BIRDS.

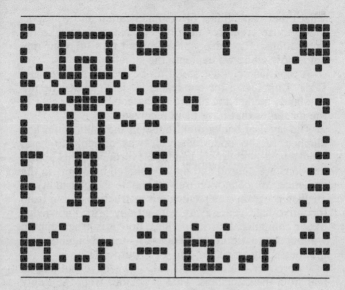

THE DARKNESS DROPS AGAIN; BUT NOW I KNOW
THAT TWENTY CENTURIES OF STONY SLEEP
WERE VEXED TO NIGHTMARE BY A ROCKING CRADLE,
AND WHAT ROUGH BEAST, ITS HOUR COME ROUND AT
    LAST,
SLOUCHES TOWARD BETHLEHEM TO BE BORN?
                  WILLIAM BUTLER YEATS, 1921

   I DO NOT KNOW WHAT I MAY APPEAR TO THE WORLD, BUT TO
MYSELF I SEEM TO HAVE BEEN ONLY A BOY PLAYING ON THE SEA-
SHORE, AND DIVERTING MYSELF IN NOW AND THEN FINDING A
SMOOTHER PEBBLE OR A PRETTIER SHELL THAN ORDINARY, WHILST
THE GREAT OCEAN OF TRUTH LAY ALL UNDISCOVERED BEFORE ME.
…ISAAC NEWTON, EARLY EIGHTEENTH CENTURY…

   ONE EVENING AS DARKNESS GREW, AND THE THINGS THAT SOME-
TIMES HOWLED AT THE MOON WERE HOWLING AGAIN, FANDER OF-
FERED HIS TENTACLE-TIP FOR THE HUNDREDTH TIME. ALWAYS THE
GESTURE HAD BEEN UNMISTAKABLE EVEN IF ITS MOTIVE WAS NOT
CLEAR, YET ALWAYS IT HAD BEEN REBUFFED. BUT NOW, NOW, FIVE

FINGERS CURLED AROUND IT IN SHY DESIRE TO PLEASE.

WITH A FERVENT PRAYER THAT HUMAN NERVES WOULD FUNCTION JUST LIKE MARTIAN ONES, FANDER POURED HIS THOUGHTS, SWIFTLY, LEST THE WARM GRIP BE LOOSENED TOO SOON.

"DO NOT FEAR ME. I CANNOT HELP MY SHAPE ANY MORE THAN YOU CAN HELP YOURS. I AM YOUR FRIEND, YOUR FATHER, YOUR MOTHER. I NEED YOU AS MUCH AS YOU NEED ME."...ERIC FRANK RUSSELL, 1950...

"You will note," MacDonald said, "that some parts of the messages are identical and some are different. The most important difference is that the central figure is missing in the Reply. Next most important is the altered symbol for the sun in the upper right-hand corner; it now is the same as the one in the lower left-hand corner, and the symbols that describe them now are identical—"

A black astronomer stood up in the front row. "But that is impossible," he said quietly. "The suns could not have gone nova. We would have had visual evidence by now, and the appearances of Capella have remained unchanged."

"It means," MacDonald said, "that we made an incorrect assumption ninety years ago when we thought the Message said that the suns were going nova. It has troubled us all for a long time, and some of us have even speculated about the possibility that seems confirmed now: what the Message said about the suns referred to the moment in time when the large Capella suns consumed almost all of the hydrogen in their cores and moved off the main sequence. Their cores began to contract; their surface layers expanded; and they became red giants with greatly increased temperature and luminosity. That is the change in the size and heat release of their suns that the original Message described."

"And when did this happen?" the Siberian premier demanded.

"Sometime between the recent and the distant past," MacDonald said. "It could have been a thousand years ago—or some millions of years."

The audience rippled with the implications of Mac-

Donald's statements, but the Siberian premier stood un-moved. "And what of the Capellans?"

"Please look again at the messages," MacDonald said. "Notice that the Reply has eliminated all the so-called words or symbols along the left-hand side—all except one, and that one is the word for Capellan, and it is pre-ceded by what I now judge to be the Capellan symbol for negation."

"Negation?" the premier asked.

"The Capellans," MacDonald said wearily, "are dead, gone, cremated. Even the symbols for their planets bear testimony to their fate. The superjovian is somewhat re-duced in size from the expansion and heat of the near sun, which now is perhaps ten times its former size, and the smaller satellites of the superjovian all have been con-sumed except for one Earth-size planet—which we have taken in the past to be the home planet of the Capellans—and it apparently has lost considerable mass, perhaps by the boiling away of its oceans and atmosphere and perhaps by internal explosions."

"We have been communicating with a race long dead," the premier said.

"Apparently," MacDonald said, "they set up auto-mated self-repairing equipment to pick up evidence of possible future civilizations and send a message to them. If the equipment received any response, indicating that a technological civilization was listening for messages from other worlds, they would begin sending—"

"What?" the premier asked. "What is the point of all this if they are dead?"

"I have a message," the computer said. "It has been sent in the simple vocabulary developed so far, and there are some uncertainties in the exact meaning of certain words and phrases, but the message, with alternative readings, follows. I will present it visually for greater comprehensibility."

People/
civilized beings/
intelligent creatures/
brothers/
to whom it may concern

Greetings from the people of Capella/
      the first satellite of God
Who are dead/
gone/
destroyed
We lived
We worked
We built
And we are gone.
Accept this, our legacy/
      remains
And our good wishes/
      kinship/
      admiration/
      brotherhood/
      love.

"The Capellans are dead," MacDonald said.

"And the Project?" the premier said. "Your job is done."

"In a sense," MacDonald said. "Now the work of the world begins. The messages the computer is receiving, storing, analyzing, interpreting contain the entire record of a civilization alien to almost everything we know except intelligence and emotion, a civilization considerably advanced beyond ours—not only its history but, if my assumptions are correct, its philosophies, culture, art, science, technology, theology, literature.

"We have received a legacy more valuable than the physical possession of another world, with all its natural treasures, and the world's scientists and scholars and everyone else who wishes to explore it may spend their lifetimes studying it, interpreting it, and adding bits and pieces of it to our civilization, enriching us by a whole new world and everything it was.

"As for the Project itself, our search has lasted for less than a century and a half, and we have come up with one major find. Who knows what civilizations, what strange and wonderful people, we may discover somewhere between here and the edges of the universe?"

The room was silent. The world paused and then resumed what it was doing.

And somewhere, among the magnetic spots and fluxes,

among the miniature relays, among the fugitive flows of electrons, a connection occurred, a memory stirred:

"... and the silence surged softly backward...."

It was like the vagrant thought of the shadow that may have been sitting in either corner or of the thousands of men and women who had passed through the Project or lingered in its corridors and rooms for years, who remained in some form within the computer itself....

The transmission from Capella would continue for days or weeks or months, but eventually the last of the inheritance from another star would be handed over, the messages would cease, and the silence would surge softly backward....

And the radio telescope shaped like an ear of Earth held up on an arm to listen to the secrets of the universe, and the radio telescope shaped like a bowl to catch the stardust, would come alive and begin a new search of the heavens for a message from the stars.

By that time the computer would be at least half Capellan. No one but the computer would realize this for half a century and by then the Project would pick up a message from the Crab Nebula....

Translations

CHAPTER 1

Pues no es posible...
The bow cannot always stand bent, nor can human frailty subsist without some lawful recreation.

Cervantes, Don Quixote

Habe nun, ach! Philosophie, ...
Now I have studied philosophy,
Medicine and the law,
And, unfortunately, theology,
Wearily sweating, yet I stand now,
Poor fool, no wiser than I was before;
I am called Master, even Doctor,
And for these last ten years have drawn
My students, by the nose, up, down,
Crosswise and crooked. Now I see
That we can know nothing finally.

Goethe, Faust, opening lines

Men che dramma...
    Less than a drop
Of blood remains in me that does not tremble;
I recognize the signals of the ancient flame.

Dante, The Divine Comedy,
Purgatorio

C'est de quoy j'ay le plus de peur que la peur.
The thing of which I have most fear is fear.

Montaigne, Essays

A la trés-bonne, à la très-belle, qui fait ma joie et ma santé.
To the best, to the most beautiful, who is my joy and my well-being.

Baudelaire, Les Epaves

Rast ich, so rost ich.
When I rest, I rust.

German proverb

Nunc est bibendum!
Now's the time for drinking!

Horace, *Odes*, Book I

Wer immer strebens sich bemüht, . . .
Who strives always to the utmost,
Him can we save.

Goethe, *Faust*, Part I

Ich bin der Geist der stets verneint.
I am the spirit that always denies.

Goethe, *Faust*, Part I

Nel mezzo del cammin di nostra vita . . .
In the middle of the journey of our life
I came to myself in a dark wood,
Where the straight way was lost.

Dante, *The Divine Comedy*,
Inferno, opening lines

E quindi uscimmo a riveder le stelle.
And thence we issued out, again to see the stars.

Dante, *The Divine Comedy*,
Inferno

Nil desperandum.
There's no cause for despair.

Horace, *Odes*, Book I

Je m'en vay chercher un grand Peut-être.
I am going to seek a great Perhaps.

Rabelais on his deathbed

O lente, lente currite, noctis equi!
Oh, slowly, slowly run, horses of the night!

Marlowe, *Dr. Faustus*

(Faustus is quoting Ovid. He waits for Mephistopheles to appear to claim his soul at midnight. The next line: "The devil will come and Faustus must be damn'd.")

Ful wys is he that can himselven knowe!
Very wise is he that can know himself!

> Chaucer, *The Canterbury Tales*, "The Monk's Tale"

CHAPTER 2

L'amor che muove il sole e l'altro stelle.
The love that moves the sun and the other stars.

> Dante, *The Divine Comedy*, Paradiso

Lasciate ogni speranza, voi ch'entrate.
Leave all hope, ye that enter.

> Dante, *The Divine Comedy*, Inferno

(These are the words at the entrance to hell.)

CHAPTER 3

[F]ungar vice cotis, acutum
Reddere quae ferrum valet exsors ipsa secandi.
So I will play the part of a whetstone which can make steel sharp, though it has no power itself of cutting.

> Horace, *Ars Poetica*

CHAPTER 5

Nous n'irons plus aux bois, les lauriers sont coupés.
We'll to the woods no more, the laurel trees are cut.

> French saying

Es un entreverado loco, lleno de lúcidos intervalos.
He's a muddled fool, full of lucid intervals.

> Cervantes, *Don Quixote*

In freta dum fluvii current dum montibus umbrae
Lustrabunt convexa, polus dum sidera pascet,
Semper honos nomenque tuum laudesque manebunt.

While the rivers shall run to ocean, while the
shadows shall move in the mountain valleys, while
the sky shall feed the stars, always shall thy
honor, and thy name, and thy glory abide.

Virgil, *Aeneid*

About the Author

Born in Kansas City, Missouri, in 1923, James Gunn began writing science fiction in 1948. Since then he has had eighty stories published; he is the author of nineteen books and the editor of six. Four of his stories were dramatized over NBC radio, and a novel, *The Immortals*, was made first into an ABC-TV "Movie of the Week" and then into the television series "The Immortal." He received a Hugo Award for Science Fiction Achievement in 1983 for *Isaac Asimov: The Foundations of Science Fiction*.

James Gunn now is professor of English at the University of Kansas, where he teaches fiction writing and science fiction.